A Month of Sundays

John Owens

Published under license from Andrews UK

For Ivonne

Week One

Monday

If John O'Driscoll had been asked whether there was any way in which a week that had begun with him vomiting into a nun's handbag could finish on an even more disastrous note, he would have laughed the idea off as ludicrous. He would, however, have been wrong, and the fact that his failure to predict the future would come as less of a surprise to those who knew him than it did to him said much for the esteem in which O'Driscoll's abilities were generally held. For John O'Driscoll was often wrong: in fact, there were those who said that he had made it his life's work to be wrong about pretty much everything.

To begin at the beginning though, the accident involving Sister Bernadette's bag and his own bodily fluids happened at the end of an evening that had begun with Duffy's suggestion of a "quiet pint," and on that basis alone, O'Driscoll should have known it would end in tears. "Come on, just a quickie," Duffy had insisted, deaf to his friend's plea that he had already agreed to spend the evening helping organize a social evening for the old people of the parish. Against all better judgment, O'Driscoll had agreed and in no time the two young men were established comfortably in the back bar of The North Star on Ealing

Broadway with several hours of a warm Spring evening at their disposal. When O'Driscoll looked up and saw his friend returning from the bar holding tumblers of whiskey, a series of tiny alarm bells began to ring in his head and had he heeded their warning chimes, the evening might have turned out very differently. But in the conviviality of the moment, the protest he made was but a token one and his doom was sealed.

"Jesus Christ, are you trying to ruin me altogether?" he said when he saw the glasses arriving.

"Yes," replied Duffy simply. "Anyway, you might thank me for it tomorrow if it finally helps you pluck up the courage to speak to Karen Black. Tell you what, I'll come with you and help you set up, and I'll have a little chat with her for you."

"No you bloody well won't," said O'Driscoll, for even though beguiling images of Miss Black filled his every waking moment, the thought of a drink-inflamed Duffy being let loose anywhere near her was a prospect too awful to contemplate.

And so it was that several whiskeys and several chasers later, the two arrived at the church hall of Saint Catherine's in time to help make preparations for the dance, which was due to start at nine o'clock. An evening spent with a roomful of amorous octogenarians was not the entertainment that O'Driscoll would normally have sought out on a Monday night but, not for the first time, he had failed to take evasive action when the call for volunteers had gone out. There was also the little matter of his teaching contract being up for renewal and he was hopeful that an unassuming yet poised performance at tonight's event would stand him in good stead when the school's governing body met in a few weeks' time to decide the following year's staffing.

At the gates to the church, O'Driscoll stopped to take stock of the situation and consider the range of strategies that he had devised, over the course of his twenty-nine years, to foster the illusion of sobriety. That these devices rarely extended beyond the expedient of putting a half pack of mints sideways into his mouth, and that, although he himself fondly imagined them to be worldly and subtle, they invariably fooled no one was neither here nor there, for the sense of being master of one's own destiny implicit in such acts helped O'Driscoll feel sober and that was the important thing. Now he straightened his tie, cleared his throat, burped softly and then spluttered as an unexpected jet of carbonated air raced through his nostrils. He felt in his pocket for a packet of Extra Strong Mints, broke it in two and offered one half to his friend, secure in the knowledge that through this cunning act of deception, their drunkenness would shortly be enveloped in a menthol infused cloak of invisibility.

At the bottom of the steps that led into the dank and forbidding church grounds, there was a small stream and they crossed it with the feeling of unease that ancient travelers might have experienced passing over the River Styx. Nodding a greeting to the ancient Irishman with the Pioneer badge who guarded the entrance like a gnarled and toothless Cerberus, they passed into the warmth of the church hall attached to the school where they both taught. As they did so a familiar aroma, sweet and redolent of hops, wafted across from the far corner of the room.

"Bloody hell, they've got a bar!" exclaimed Duffy and it was the existence of this makeshift arrangement in the corner that was to prove O'Driscoll's undoing two hours and twenty minutes later. As they processed this new information, O'Driscoll suddenly caught sight of Karen Black heading towards the cloakroom and his stomach gave a familiar lurch. Miss Black, as she was known by her Year Four pupils, had joined the school at the start of the year and had immediately mesmerized O'Driscoll to the point where, in her presence, his brain refused to function beyond sending primitive signals to his eyes, imploring them not to stare longingly at her legs, breasts or parts in-between.

By each picking up a stack of chairs and carrying them across the room, O'Driscoll and Duffy contrived to arrive at the makeshift bar seemingly by chance.

"As we're here, we'll have a couple of whatever you've got," announced Duffy to a large shape that could be dimly apprehended searching the shelves under the bar.

"Ye will, will ye!" came a well-known growl as the figure unwound and revealed itself to be none other than Father Kennedy, parish priest, school governor, and a man whose sudden terrifying appearance was in danger of reducing O'Driscoll's bowels, already made watery by the presence of Miss Black, to a state of even greater liquidity. The priest had, over the years, established a fearsome reputation among the Catholic population of West London. He ruled his parish using a system of terror that Robespierre or Stalin would have envied, and on dark nights the mere invocation of his name was said to reduce misbehaving children to quivering acquiescence and send small animals scurrying for cover. And if he was "old school," as some said, it was only in the sense of having crawled from the primordial slime of some ancient Borstal, carrying with him the value system of that sinister Dark Age.

Kennedy looked at them menacingly from under thick, bushy eyebrows, his great craggy face topped by an unruly white thatch. From flaring nostrils protruded great clumps of nasal hair whose oscillations O'Driscoll watched transfixed, for the movement of these tendrils was said to be an infallible barometer of the priest's state of mind, and it was common knowledge that when he was angry, they danced wildly.

"Good evening, Father," said Duffy, for with O'Driscoll examining his spiritual leader's nose with the intentness of a medieval scholar reading a set of bulbous and hairy runes, it was clear the responsibility for opening verbal proceedings lay with him. "Lovely evening," he went on with the insouciance which had, over the years, wreaked havoc among the fairer sex of West London. "We've come to help you prepare for the social evening. Such good work you and your team do - made us feel guilty so we've rearranged our squash match and here we are. Pretty parched though, after our training run, so we thought we'd grab a quick drink of something before getting to work." As usual, Duffy's charm had a disarming effect and within a couple of minutes, the two found themselves in the possession of cans of lager handed across by a Father Kennedy who, apart from giving vent to a muttered "Gypsies!", remained silent.

Not for the first time, O'Driscoll contrasted Duffy's easy charm with his own tongue-tied awkwardness, especially when dealing with the turbulent priest who was Chair of Governors at the school where both young men worked. His mind drifted back a few months to the church fete of Christmas 1994 and the *faux pas* which had blighted his first term and from which he was still trying to recover. In an effort to ingratiate himself with the powers that be, the newly-appointed teacher had volunteered to have a large poster printed which could be pasted onto the church noticeboard ahead of the event. Hoping to demonstrate appropriate levels of Catholic piety, but having typically left himself too little time to do the job properly, O'Driscoll had frantically searched the pages of *Hymns Ancient and Modern* for a suitable inscription. Hastily scanning the titles – *Here I Am, Lord, Here at Your Table, Lord, Here I Am to Worship, How Great Is Our God*, he had eventually chosen the shortest title, scribbled the artwork himself, rushed it off the printer and pasted up the returned poster with but minutes to spare before the opening ceremony.

And so it was that Father Kennedy had stood in the grounds of St Catherine's before the great and good of West Ealing, directly in front of a large white poster emblazoned with the legend:

"HERE I AM, LARD."

As the priest began to speak, few had noticed the words or connected them with him, indeed the outline of his great paunch actually cast a section of the notice board into shadow, although unfortunately for O'Driscoll, not the part that contained the inscription. But before long, a frisson of laughter had started to ripple across the crowd and when Kennedy had turned and read the words his face had assumed an apoplectic hue and he had hurried through the remaining words of his welcome before storming off into the presbytery, flanked on either side by a small scurrying nun.

While this was going on, O'Driscoll had been happily engaged in a daydream involving the rescue of Karen Black from a madman with a machete who had entered the church grounds and was terrorizing stallholders and visitors alike. In the fantasy, he had drawn the lunatic away from the crowd by striding into his field of vision and announcing firmly, "I'm the one you want!" The madman's eyes had fixed on him hungrily, allowing O'Driscoll to coax him into a quiet area of the playground and wrestle him to the floor and disarm him. He had achieved the whole thing with no damage to himself other than a small but satisfyingly bloody cut on his arm, and Karen had been approaching him with moist eyes and a trembling lip, offering to use her blouse to staunch the flow.

His unhurried contemplation of this rather fetching image had been abruptly terminated by the arrival of Mrs. Goodwin, admin officer from the school office. "You're the new chap who did the poster, aren't you?" she announced breathlessly, her nose twitching with excitement. "Oh, dear, I'm afraid you've put the cat well and truly among the pigeons. Didn't you have the proof checked before you sent it to the printers? No? Really! Oh, dear, that *was* a mistake!" Shaking her head she continued, "I wouldn't like to be in your shoes when Father Kennedy finds out it was you. In all the years I've worked at St. Catherine's, I've *never* seen him so angry." She had patted O'Driscoll's arm consolingly, allowed her nose one final excited quiver and then followed it away with the set air of one who has bad news to impart and is weighing up how best it can be shared with as wide a circle as possible.

As the full horror of the catastrophe had dawned on O'Driscoll, his first instinct had been to throw himself on the priest's mercy - surely Kennedy would respond favourably to an apology, frank and manly in tone, which accepted responsibility for what was an honest mistake but also hinted at a superhuman work ethic that thought nothing of working long into the night to help the parish. It was even possible, if one allowed one's flight of fancy to soar to the giddiest heights, to envisage Kennedy, who was after all, only human, seeing the funny side of it.

O'Driscoll tried to summon a picture of a smiling priest chuckling and shaking his head as he said, "Ach, it was only one letter, I suppose, my son," but it was no use. The O'Driscoll

13

imagination was a hardy organ and routinely processed data that lesser imaginations might have baulked at, but even it had its limits and the power surge that was generated as it tried to create an image of Father Kennedy chuckling, caused it to overload and crash with the loss of all functions.

Nevertheless determined to face the music, O'Driscoll approached the presbytery door and raised his fist to knock. Drifting through the oak of the door, he could hear disjointed words and phrases, faint in tone but unmistakably the issue of Father Kennedy.

"Did ye read that sign? ...... What fecking gypsy.....?"

There was a pause in which could be heard a soothing murmur, female and obviously issuing from one of the nuns, before the Kennedy bellow rose once more to a muffled crescendo.

"O'Driscoll!"...... laughing stock! ...... useless fecking tinker! ...."

O'Driscoll's hand had dropped from the door and he had hurried from the premises, pausing only to revisit the scene of his crime and make a frantic but unsuccessful attempt to unglue the notice.

Dragging his thoughts back to the present and the ongoing church social, O'Driscoll focused his now bleary eyes on the bustle around him. A succession of old people was passing before him and the air held that elusive whiff – part talcum powder, part urine – that he always associated with large assemblies of the elderly. His stomach gave another lurch as he caught a glimpse of Karen bending over a wheelchair, her shapely bottom outlined pertly against the cloth of a pair of black cotton shorts and in desperation, he grabbed another lager from the bar – anything to ward off the erection that previous experience had taught him would inevitably follow. He downed three-quarters of the beer in one go and scanned the room in search of an activity that would keep his mind occupied with pure and chaste thoughts.

His gaze fell on Sister Bernadette, the austere figure who was Mother Superior of the convent attached to St Catherine's and Deputy Head of the school. Tall and forbidding, she dressed in the same uniform of grey woolen robes whatever the weather or season, while on her head she wore a wimple whose formidable dimensions set her apart from the rank and file of the Order in the way an officer's pips distinguishes him from the enlisted men. Thus attired, she moved around the school smoothly and with no visible evidence of propulsion, and her upright figure was a familiar sight as it sailed along the corridors. She was no less active at night when her wraith-like form could be observed gliding silently around the convent, its silhouette casting sinister shadows among the cloisters. The unusual headgear and her distinctive carriage, together with a faint but discernible wheeze resulting from childhood exposure to bronchitis, had been noted among the student body and had earned Sister Bernadette the soubriquet "Darth Vader".

"Anything I can do, Sister?" asked O'Driscoll, again catching a delicious glimpse of Karen in his peripheral vision as he approached.

"Yes, thank you John. You could dance with Mrs O'Higgins," said the nun, and before he knew it, O'Driscoll was being whirled around the room in the arms of stout, moon-faced widow from Kerry. The evening passed in a blur as dance followed dance and O'Driscoll found himself passed among a succession of elderly matrons as they performed increasingly more complex variations on a dance to which he had been exposed as a child among the Irish clubs that dotted West London. It involved vast numbers of people taking up stations in a kind of giant grid on the dancefloor with others being whirled from one point to the other in a complex but indecipherable series of manoeuvres. By the time he had passed through twenty minutes of this, his head and stomach were whirling and it was only the application of three more lagers from the makeshift bar that restored his equanimity. The rest of the evening became a blurry confusion involving light and movement, and the syncopated rustle of dozens of pairs of plastic drawers as the geriatric crowd buzzed around the floor in a giant incontinent swarm.

The final unraveling of the evening came when, as they began to clear up, Duffy found a half- bottle of Bells behind the makeshift bar. He quickly poured two huge measures into plastic cups and with a "Get this down your neck, son" to his friend, he made as good as his word. O'Driscoll heaved his drink back in one go and within seconds, he knew he had made a terrible mistake. He remembered watching a film where a deranged scientist had dropped a single tincture of one liquid into a huge vat of a totally incompatible one and now as the whiskey lay sourly on top of the bubbling pool of lager, his stomach began to seethe and churn and a deadly chain reaction began.

O'Driscoll swallowed several times and took a series of deep breaths as he fought to exert his authority over the vomit that was seething upwards, but it quickly became clear that the vomit had its own ideas about which one of them was in charge. Looking desperately around him, he sought a route that would extricate him from the impending disaster. The room was half-empty and staff and helpers were engaged in stacking chairs and clearing tables. Blundering towards a door, his route carried him close by the delectable Karen and as he crossed her path, she smiled at him. In normal circumstances that smile would have made all the travails of the day worthwhile but O'Driscoll knew that she could not be allowed to witness what was about to unfold. She would not be smiling for long if he puked on her. The facial contortion he bestowed on her as he passed, although intended as a smile, caused her to jump hastily back.

Just as he got to the door, he heard a voice in his ear. "Ah, John, I was looking for you." It was Mister Li, the elderly Science master. "You have booked the overhead projector for tomorrow morning. Will you be using it?" Shaking his head wildly, O'Driscoll passed through the door into a short corridor. He made a conscious effort to take long, slow breaths to calm the volcanic mass that was bubbling in his stomach, but all his past experience told him he was fighting a losing battle as the sour, heaving soup began to rise through his esophagus. He had literally seconds to spare when he saw the large canvas hold all resting against the wall. It was filled with exercise books and papers and it was recognizably the property of Sister Bernadette.

O'Driscoll looked wildly around, his hand in front of his mouth as his body convulsed, but apart from Sister Bernadette's hold all, the corridor was bare, so he took one step, bent over and directed a stream of vomit neatly into the bag. Without breaking step, he reached for the door that led into the courtyard and propelled himself in one movement in the direction of the shrubbery. His momentum carried him into the cover of the bushes where he evacuated the remainder of his stomach, unseen.

Inevitably, he bumped into Duffy ten minutes later as he was attempting to creep away from the scene of his crime. Duffy as always contrived to maintain an air of grace and ease no matter how much alcohol he had consumed. He greeted his friend with practiced bonhomie and before he knew it, O'Driscoll was having the first of a series of "steadiers" suggested by Duffy as the perfect antidote to the earlier accident. The remainder of the night became an incoherent procession through a succession of bars and clubs until he finally staggered back to his small flat in Southall at three o'clock in the morning.

Tuesday

It was not birdsong or the rays of the sun that woke John
O'Driscoll the next morning but a chorus of hawking and
spitting as the cash and carry that lay below his flat on Southall
Broadway opened for business. As he lay in that delicious
vacuum that precedes the return of memory, his mind began to
untangle the events of the previous evening and drifting at
random and in no particular order into his consciousness came a
kaleidoscope of images; Karen Black's delectable bottom....
Father Kennedy's undelectable nostril hair.... the mole on Mrs.
O'Higgins's chin.... Sister Bernadette's bag. With a start,
O'Driscoll sat bolt upright as the image of Sister Bernadette's
hold all filled to the brim with his vomit appeared in his mind's
eye and as the details of the preceding evening slowly returned
to him and incrementally increased his sense of unease, his hand
made an unconscious southward journey and began to scratch
his scrotum in search of solace.

He was hopeful that he had been unobserved as he
evacuated the contents of his stomach, but in the state he had
been in, it was hard to be sure. Casting his net wider for
evidence of further crimes, he didn't think his insobriety had

been so obvious as to make him stand out in the crowd and he was fairly sure he hadn't made inappropriate comments to any of the matrons of the parish. He had kept so far out of Father Kennedy's way that it was unlikely that he had blotted his copy book further there, and most important of all he was certain that his interactions with Karen Black had been so fleeting that he could not have said or done anything to blacken his reputation.

As he scratched around in his scrotal area, his face contorted itself into a succession of strange shapes and a whoosh of air rushed silently from his mouth. He was aware that a range of disturbing mannerisms had begun to manifest themselves when he was in a state of anxiety and although he believed he had the grimaces under control, he could not say the same for the sudden exhalations of breath that escaped from him, sometimes in a silent whoosh but more often in an audible form that can best be rendered into print as "OOST!"

The whole situation was causing O'Driscoll some disquiet for he was not a stupid man and was aware that ejaculating the word "OOST!" at random moments was not a practice calculated to impress the school leadership or improve his prospects of gaining that vital contract extension. And it was unlikely to reduce Karen Black to the sort of quivering pliancy that she occupied in his wilder imaginings. But O'Driscoll was uncomfortably aware that since the last interview he had had with the school leadership on the subject of his future, the noises had begun to appear with greater frequency and, more worryingly, they seemed to be increasingly audible to those around him.

Only the day before, a lady on the 207 bus had received a shock when the otherwise innocuous-looking young man sitting beside her had enunciated suddenly and with great clarity the word "OOST!" Aware of the unease that he was causing among his fellow passengers, O'Driscoll's anxiety levels had begun to rise and he was about to give voice to another "OOST!" when, realizing the vicious circle he was in danger of entering into, he desisted abruptly. A moment later, he coughed loudly and extravagantly, hoping to cloud at least one of the "OOSTs" in uncertainty, but the damage was done and the lady next to him spent the rest of the journey sitting as close to the corner of her seat as she could without actually falling off it.

He dragged himself wearily back into the here and now and a scant hour later found himself hemmed in a corner of the staff room, listening to morning briefing with a hand over his mouth, desperately trying to divert his beery breath downwards and away from his colleagues.

"A big thank you to everyone who helped with the dance last night," said Mr. Barnet, the Head. "Just a note to be careful if you are taking the children across to the church hall. Sister

Bernadette thinks there might be a vomiting bug going around among the old people...." at this point he heard a violent exhalation of air from somewhere to his right "....so if any pupils start developing symptoms, get them straight home. Now, moving on to the Year Six mass next Sunday - Miss Gillespie, could you continue to work with the choir; Mr. Li, would you mind doing the programme; John, can you arrange to get the hymn books re-covered, they're looking tattered? Oh, and Karen could you do the flowers again?" O'Driscoll considered this directive as he made his way to his classroom to teach Geography to 5R. He was surprised that, after the fiasco with the poster, he had been considered for a task that involved printing but, on reflection, it wasn't too bad a job, and would involve him in the minimum of fuss on the day of the Year Six mass, one of the major events of the Spring term.

Later in the staffroom, sipping tea that had come from the communal pot and that was so strong and dark it left rows of little tidemarks on the china of the cup, he listened idly to the gossip that was going on around him. Mrs. Goodwin, the woman who had gleefully informed O'Driscoll of his *faux pas* with the poster, was holding court and the topic being debated, a recent court case where a homosexual couple had been refused accommodation by the owner of a bed and breakfast, was one that she considered herself well-qualified to discuss on the basis of she and her husband having run such an establishment a generation ago.

"Now don't get me wrong, we're very tolerant, me and my Reg," she was saying. "*Very* tolerant, and at the end of the day, there's a lot worse going on in the world, isn't there? We always knew the ones of that persuasion who came to stay at The Willows, although of course they were a lot less flagrant about it than they are these days. I like that, I mean I can have a perfectly nice conversation with someone without having to think about what he's got and where he's going to stick it as soon as I've left the room. Take that nice quantity surveyor from Greenwich, he was at it hammer and tongs with whichever young man he'd brought with him, but you'd never have known it to talk to him."

There was a palpable air of unease in the room. "Who's doing assembly this week?" asked someone, trying to change the subject, but Mrs. Goodwin was not to be deterred. "Yes, we would have been happy to have that sort at The Willows all the time. Very quiet and well-behaved they were as a rule, no drunkenness to speak of and, according to Reg, surprisingly clean. He said it was like a Turkish bath in some of their rooms the way they were always showering and titivating themselves." She paused to take a drink and her face took on a thoughtful expression. "Reg said they washed themselves to absolutely abnormal levels, it was as if … you know … they were trying to scrub off more than the dirt. He said there was probably some psychiatric reason behind it all, there usually is, isn't there? No, the only thing Reg said you'd have had to look out for was their bedlinen, you'd have had to keep that separate and wash it under a hotter cycle, because of the different stains."

The silence which greeted these words was finally broken by a timorous voice saying, "Different stains?"

"Yes," said Mrs. Goodwin "Reg says it stands to reason there'd be different stains with the kind of things …"

"Who's for a game of darts!" came a cry from the Science teacher and there was a sudden movement of bodies away from the soft chairs.

"Yes, Reg says you can tell a lot about people from their bedding," went on Mrs. Goodwin, sipping her drink reflectively as she surveyed her much-diminished audience. "He reckons if there was a T.V. programme - you know like that *Through the Keyhole* - only you had to guess who the famous person was from their soiled bedlinen, he'd make a fortune." She paused to take another sip from her coffee and gently nibbled the corner of a custard cream. "You know what my Reg says?" she continued, fixing a birdlike eye on the teenage work experience girl who was sitting, transfixed, opposite her. '*A fitted sheet tells no lies!*' that's what he says."

Later, passing the Cozy Kleen Launderette, O'Driscoll recalled Reg's syllogism and wondered whether the leadership of the church had thought of incorporating it into Catholic dogma. Perhaps some conclave of portly Italian theologians might even now be applying it retrospectively to the Shroud of Turin. His train of thought was, fortunately, terminated by his arrival at The North Star, where he had arranged to meet Duffy and Micky Quinn for a pint and by the time he joined them, the other two were already seated, Duffy's neat, well-groomed appearance a contrast to the lumpy dishevelment of Quinn.

To say that Michael Aloysius Quinn left a lasting impression on those meeting him for the first time would be to make something of an understatement. It was as if an ancient Gaelic warrior had been forced out of his animal skins and into a suit of modern clothes and then been hurled unceremoniously and with no respect for his dignity or his enormous girth into the 1990s. A belligerent freckled face sat atop the incongruously-suited body and above rested a dense carpet of matted red hair which had over the years resisted all attempts at cultivation and from which, or so his friends claimed, movements of a suspicious nature sometimes emanated. Below, Quinn's great paunch fought a running battle with his waistband while the habit he had of hitching his trousers up when deep in thought meant that wedges of stray shirt were forever struggling to escape the confines of his belt.

The three had known each other since childhood, having attended one of those London Catholic schools where red hair and freckles were the norm rather than the exception and where morning registration plodded through the alphabet in a desultory fashion until with the arrival of the letter "O" it suddenly swept into a gallop of O'Boyles, O'Carrolls, O'Connors, and O'Donnells. Each class contained a makeweight quantity of English children and there would be the odd Pole, and an exotic smattering of De Souza's and Fernandez's whose precise lineage was unclear, but the bulk of the population was comprised of children of Irish descent.

Although these hybrid creatures adopted the glottal tones of London and used the present perfect tense when speaking of their fights and their trips to watch Arsenal and Chelsea, they knew they were different, a breed apart, and many of them began to identify with the country of their ancestors, especially as they grew older and more aware of the troubled history between the two nations. That they were not Anglo-Saxon they knew, but on visits to the mother country, the reaction to their accents, ranging from "Plastic Paddy" at the friendlier end of the spectrum, to "English Wanker" at the other, left them in no doubt that they were not truly Irish either.

Over the first pint, Duffy and O'Driscoll filled Micky in on the events of the previous evening. "Jesus," said Quinn when he heard about the surprise package that had ended up in Sister Bernadette's bag. "I wonder if she noticed when she picked it up or did she end up carrying it all the way back to the convent?"

"Surely she'd have noticed," said Duffy. "I mean, it would've been lapping over the sides."

"On the other hand it might've dried," mused Micky, "which would've made things a bit more complicated when the poor woman got home and got the books out to mark them. They'd have looked like they were written in Braille."

"Anyway, enough of all that," said Duffy, dismissing Sister Bernadette and her troubles from his mind. "What was that big dance the old biddies were doing last night?"

"It sounds like one of those celidh things," answered Quinn, who had spent his childhood among the clubs of Kilburn and Cricklewood. "I heard my old dear talking about it, there's like this great big square with hundreds of old grannies moving around like ants. I can't remember what it's called, The Siege of something." As he spoke, his brow furrowed in thought and his hand worked away at some disarrangement inside his trousers, causing his left knee to gyrate alarmingly. A moment later, his face cleared and he banged the table, causing beer to slop from the glasses. "Venice! That's it. The Siege of Venice."

"Where?" asked Duffy.

"Venice."

"Venice? It's not The Siege of *Venice* you eejit, it's *Ennis*."

"Ennis?"

"Yes, Ennis. It's in County Clare!"

"Are you sure? I'd swear it was Venice."

"You ignorant great tub of lard" said Duffy. "What on earth would the old biddies who do that dance have to do with Venice?" He went into a shrill falsetto. *"Morning, Mrs. Maguire, I'm just off down into Venice to buy a bag of potatoes, there's a grand little Spar in the Piazza San Marco.* Jesus Christ," he went on, reverting to his normal voice, "I'm surrounded by idiots."

Micky hitched up his trousers defensively. "I was sure it was Venice."

"It's *Ennis*," said Duffy, who was now warming to his theme. "I spent a fortnight there every summer when I was a kid. What a place!"

Quinn shrugged. "Anyway, Ennis, Venice, what's the difference?"

"I'll tell you what the difference is," said Duffy, whose holiday experience clearly still rankled. "Most of Venice is underwater and most of Ennis bloody well should be!"

His friends exchanged glances and Quinn replied, "Thank you, Judith Chalmers. I'm surprised the Irish Tourist Board hasn't snapped you up. You're a walking advertisement for the old country. Anyway, apart from the Siege of…. wherever it was, did anything else happen last night?"

"Well, I'm afraid our friend here missed another opportunity," said Duffy. "Instead of laying siege to Karen Black, he spent the whole night swooning in the arms of Mrs. O'Higgins."

"Jesus Christ, O'Driscoll, are you a man or a mouse?" asked Quinn. "It's obvious you fancy the arse off her so when are you going to get your act together and ask her out?"

In truth, O'Driscoll's infatuation was so debilitating that in Karen's presence, he became speechless. He was aware that to most people she was no more than conventionally pretty, but to him the sum of her parts was overwhelming. She was small and graceful and dark and dimpled, her eyes were huge, her lips cherubic, her voice low and pleasant. She appeared to be without conceit of any kind, she listened with interest to whoever was talking, even Mrs. Goodwin, and when she smiled she revealed a set of perfect teeth. O'Driscoll loved her to distraction but was aware that the strength of his feelings was an impediment to developing things further. If he literally couldn't speak when she was in the same room, engaging in the kind of witty, sexy banter likely to make her notice him wasn't really an option, and it was only in his daydreams that he was able to function with the charm and style that was so lacking in his real-life interactions.

"If you don't get a shift on, John, she's going to fall for me," said Duffy. "A girl can only fight so hard."

O'Driscoll ruefully conceded the truth in this for Duffy accomplished his conquests with the kind of grace and charm that he could only dream about. He had few illusions, therefore, that in the normal course of events, Karen would sooner or later fall prey to Duffy's charms and although the prospect was terrifying, he could see no way of avoiding it unless some kind of miracle occurred. His only hope lay in meeting Karen in a social situation where his alcohol intake had reached the stage of easy uninhibited wit, but not the point where it had begun the descent into incoherence, but as piss artists the world over know well, this is a finely calibrated line and one that can be all too easily crossed.

"She'd have more sense than to go anywhere near a big ugly fuck like you, Duffy," he said. "She's a woman of taste and sophistication."

"She certainly is," said Duffy." I heard someone say the other day that she's really into literature. You could tell her about that nativity play you produced last year, John, you know the one where the shepherds ended up fighting the sheep and the three wise men didn't have the brains to find their way onto the stage? That might impress her."

Later, half-asleep and three-quarters drunk as the bus trundled homewards along the Uxbridge Road, O'Driscoll recalled the remark and the interior of the 207 gradually morphed into a 1950s version of the Orient Express, belching a cloud of smoke into the night sky as it moved slowly eastwards into the mysterious Balkans. Ian O'Driscoll, the famous writer of spy novels, sat deep in thought in one of the train's sleeper compartments and as he considered the new scene in his latest book, he knew that it was essential he got it just right because beautiful, delectable *femme fatale* Karen Black would be reading it and if she liked it, the seduction that he had had in mind for some time might move a step closer.

He was describing the first meeting between the master spy and the exotic leading lady, Fanny O'Plenty, but as the scene took shape, he was conscious that his mind was playing tricks with him and that the figures of Fanny and Karen were intermingling so that sometimes he seemed to be describing one and sometimes the other. He was aware therefore that the person he was describing and the person he was trying to impress with the quality of that description were one and the same but as is the way of things in dreamland, there seemed nothing remotely illogical about this. Pausing for a moment, he lit one of his specially blended Turkish cigarettes and sucked the cool, fragrant smoke into his lungs.

For a few minutes, the ticking of the compartment clock marked the leisurely passage of time until, with a decisive movement of his Conway Stewart fountain pen, he wrote,

As she emerged from the sea, dripping with water, her scanty clothing could not conceal the contours of her lithe body and the proud jut of her ripe young breasts...

He stopped and drew on his cigarette, a faraway look in his eyes, before abruptly crossing out the final words and substituting,

...the firm swell of her proud young breasts...

A moment later, his pen raced across the page once more, producing,

...the thrusting jut of her firm young breasts...

Finally, putting all his eggs, as it were, in one basket, he wrote,

...the firm, proud jut of her thrusting, ripe young breasts...

He stopped, temporarily exhausted, looked through the haze of cigarette smoke at the words on the page and sighed wearily. Suddenly, he straightened, picked up his pen and with that quickening of the pulse which all artists will recognize, wrote,

As she emerged from the sea, dripping with water and moved with feline grace onto the beach, her scanty clothing could not conceal the contours of her firm, lithe young body. Yet she was more than just a graceful savage, for as she moved across the sand, the keen, darting glances she threw around her suggested that beneath the animal beauty there lurked a shrewd, native intelligence. As she moved forward, her ripe young breasts jutted proudly against the cloth of the skimpy garment that covered her form, the taut fabric straining against the thrust of those splendid orbs.

Fleming/O'Driscoll sat back, satisfied that the passage had given readers a sufficiently nuanced introduction to the multi-layered character that Fanny would turn out to be, and it only remained to turn on the electric ceiling fan and call for another dry martini. When the master spy did pull languidly on the bell rope, however, it brought forth not the deferential, tuxedoed waiter he had expected but a belligerent be-turbaned bus conductor, at which point John O'Driscoll awoke abruptly and scuttled off the bus, realizing after he alighted that he had actually disembarked two stops early.

Wednesday

The following morning found O'Driscoll approaching the presbytery with a lagging step and with the watery bowels that always seemed to precede an interview with Father Kennedy. It was the final planning meeting ahead of the Year Six mass that was held every year to celebrate the achievements of the eleven year-olds who would soon be leaving the school. In truth, the term "planning" was something of a misnomer, for in reality the meeting, like all the others, would simply ratify whatever it was Father Kennedy had already decided and because Kennedy was a man welded so rigidly to his dogma as to make that of the North Korean politburo seem subtle and nuanced by comparison, there were usually few surprises.

Sister Bernadette, Mr. Li, who taught science, Miss Gillespie the music teacher and Karen Black were also attending the meeting and upon entering the room, O'Driscoll's heart skipped a beat as he noticed the only seat free was the one next to Karen. His attempt to slide into it in one graceful movement caused the table to move suddenly, almost upsetting a glass of water onto Father Kennedy's lap and the priest stared balefully at O'Driscoll, the hairs in his nostrils danced crazily, but aware that he was in mixed company, he confined himself to grunting something unintelligible and turned back to continue his conversation with Sister Bernadette.

"Hi John," said Karen, and he felt a tantalizing scent of perfume. "I meant to ask whether you were all right at the end of the do the other night, you looked a bit under the weather."

O'Driscoll was caught between conflicting impulses. He could milk the "under the weather" query in the hope of getting some sympathy from Karen; on the other hand, Sister Bernadette was sitting only feet away and it was known up and down the school as a shrewd old cat. If she got wind of him not having been well, and put two and two together she might come up with four, which was, in pints, almost exactly the volume of vomit that had ended up in her bag on the night in question.

Opting for a middle course, he croaked out a greeting from lips that had suddenly become as dry as sand. "Hi Karen," he said. "No, I was OK," and immediately kicked himself for the banality of his words. Here he was, sitting next to the most beautiful girl in the world, with the language of Shakespeare, Donne and Dryden at his disposal, and all he could come up with was "No, I was OK." What a wanker, he thought to himself bitterly as he plumbed the depths of his being for something to say and finally, conscious of the growing silence, blurted out the words, "I see West Ham lost again." Once more he cursed himself for a fool but to his surprise, Karen smiled and replied, "They'll never get anywhere with that defence."

"You a football fan?" he asked, surprised.

"Well, you have to use the term loosely if you support West Ham," she replied.

"West Ham," interjected Mr. Li suddenly, and with his careful oriental diction, the words sounded like "Wester Harm." He shook his head, "Never recovered from the loss of John Lyall."

Not for the first time, O'Driscoll marveled at the way that the game of football could bridge the most unlikely gaps. Here was a petite English rose on one side, and an elderly Chinaman on the other, the three brought together by a shared understanding of the treacherous waters that swirled around in the lower reaches of the Premiership. Mr. Li had taught at the school for several years and was one of that generation of Chinese whose English is self-taught and the result of painstaking labour over battered and tattered textbooks. Like many such students, Mr. Li's English had an unusual rhythm to it, with formal, linguistically accurate sentences that nevertheless sounded odd to the ears of native speakers.

He had picked up most of his conversational English from old editions of *The Gem* and *The Magnet* which had somehow made the journey to his hometown in Hubei province and which depicted a mythical pre-war world inhabited by characters like Billy Bunter and Harry Wharton. It was a world where the sound of rising bell summoned ruddy-faced boys to Greek and Latin prep and the start of Michaelmas term was signaled by grumbling porters decanting trunks onto a quadrangle that echoed to the sound of cricket practice on Top Side. Through much study, Mr. Li had absorbed the speech patterns of these battered tomes and the consequence was that his speech could, at any moment, lapse with disconcerting suddenness into the vernacular of a fantasy world from half a century ago.

O'Driscoll was about to launch into an analysis of the London football scene when he realized Father Kennedy had called the meeting to order. "Thank ye all for coming," said the priest, "I think preparations are well in order for Sunday." He turned to Sister Bernadette and his face assumed a benign expression. "Did you want to say anything, Sister?"

"Just that the choir sounded beautiful when I heard them this morning," said the nun and Miss Gillespie inclined her head graciously at the implied tribute to her teaching. The music teacher had selected the dozen most angelic Year Six girls to line up behind her in the section of the church reserved for the choir, and was to stand in front of them leading the singing. Miss Gillespie was a prim, erect woman of uncertain but advanced years whose interactions with colleagues were formal and reserved and who lived alone and emanated a frigid disapproval when any talk of romance came up in the staff room. She was, in fact, the personification of the sort of spinsterish old maid popularized in fiction, and the subject of much staff banter, "poor sexless creature" being one of the kinder epithets employed by Mrs. Goodwin to describe her.

"How are the programmes coming along, Mr. Li," asked Sister Bernadette. "Vurr well," came the answer, "the final proofs have been submitted to Father Kennedy." At the mention of proofs, the priest snorted and Sister Bernadette gave O'Driscoll a look of sadness and quiet reproof combined in equal measure before saying, "Yes, it is so important that *every* piece of printing, no matter how small, goes through the proofreading process."

O'Driscoll had hoped the printing error might have been forgotten, but clearly it loomed large in the minds of the powers that be, and with teaching contracts up for renewal, it was not a happy thought. O'Driscoll was in his second year at the school, but in the newly deregulated world of education, his contract of employment remained a temporary one, with its renewal at the end of each academic year at the school's discretion. There were a number of others in the same predicament and the shrewder of them had already done the maths which suggested that with next year's shifting pupil demographic, unless there was a resignation from within the ranks of the permanent staff, one of the four teachers currently on a temporary contract would have to go. The prospect of being that teacher filled O'Driscoll with such dread he was barely able to contemplate it, for it would mean he would never again be able to spend large periods of his life gazing longingly at Karen Black from afar without summoning up the courage to actually do something about it.

But it wasn't only this that made the prospect of losing his teaching post an unwelcome one, it was also the fact that being employed at Saint Catherine's laid to rest the thorny issue of what he was to do with the rest of his life. Like many before him, O'Driscoll had drifted into teaching because he hadn't known what career he wanted to pursue and because he couldn't be bothered to go to the trouble of researching the jobs market and thinking up what lies to put in the "hobbies and interests" section of his applications. Now that he was in teaching, it seemed to offer him a stable base from which to pursue his true vocation in life, which was spending as much time as he could in the pub with his mates.

He was also aware, in the inconsequential way that the young consider their parents' feelings if they consider them at all, that his mother and father were rather proud of the ascent their son had made to the rarified heights that the teaching profession still represented to their generation. *"My son the teacher"* while still not having the social cache of *"my son the doctor"* or *"my son the lawyer"* was still a massive improvement on *"my son on the lump with McAlpines,"* while the catty references made towards one poor soul and her son *"on the dole but doing a little illegal drug dealing, wouldn't you know,"* showed how seriously these factors weighed in the world his parents inhabited.

So, it was essential that O'Driscoll try to keep himself on the right side of the school leadership, particularly as staffing decisions for the next academic year would be made by the Easter holidays, only a few weeks away. He hoped his mishap with the poster might have receded from the collective memory but the fact that it was still registering on the ecclesiastical radar was not a promising omen.

"You, what's your name?" growled Kennedy, and with reluctance, O'Driscoll dragged himself back into the here and now and waited with trepidation for what was to come. "We're hoping the job we've given you will not be beyond your powers," the priest continued with elaborate sarcasm.

"How is the rebinding of the hymn books coming along, John?" asked Sister Bernadette more kindly, and O'Driscoll pretended to clear his throat to disguise the "OOST!" that had been triggered by the priest's words. He explained that thirteen of the Ancient and Modern series of hymn books - one for each of the choir, plus Miss Gillespie - had been rebound in red kidron with the title picked out in gold leaf and that the books would be delivered to the church on the morning of the mass. "That sounds lovely," said Sister Bernadette and there was a murmur of approval around the table. O'Driscoll resolved to guard against the possibility of another mistake but consoled himself with the knowledge that having been once bitten, he would now be twice, if not thrice shy. After all, with such a simple task, what could possibly go wrong?

The conversation meandered on in a similar vein with staff reporting back on their areas of responsibility and, as he listened idly, O'Driscoll became aware that the physical proximity of the lovely Karen was having a disturbing effect on him. At one point, she stirred slightly and he felt a tantalizing waft of scent. Acutely conscious of the fact that her thigh rested but inches from his own, he found to his horror that he was developing an erection. Desperately looking for an image to reverse the convulsion taking place in his trousers, he focused every fibre of his being on the figure of Sister Bernadette as she sat across the room.

At first, this strategy appeared to be having the desired effect, but gradually the thin, angular figure opposite began to blur and a terrible shape-shifting seemed to commence. The face inside the wimple began to change, the cloth of the nun's habit became deliciously contoured as it filled with the delectable shape of his beloved, and the outfit appeared to have developed an oriental-style slit at the side, through which a tantalizing sliver of thigh could be glimpsed. The figure seemed to envelop him, its slender fingers extended, as from moistened lips a soft voice whispered, "Mother Superior says we're not supposed to do this, but...."

There was consternation around the table as with a strangled yelp, John O'Driscoll suddenly leapt to his feet and left the room in a hunched, crablike scuttle, knocking against the table again and sending a dollop of water onto Father Kennedy's notes. "Ah, feck," growled the priest before hastily clearing his throat and bestowing an apologetic leer on the females present.

It was a good five minutes before the door reopened and John O'Driscoll shuffled awkwardly to his place with the muttered words, "Sorry, cramp." It had taken that long to restore himself to a state of physiological equanimity, and he had managed the feat by focusing his imagination on the least alluring person he could think of and when that didn't work, refining the image to make it even more repulsive. That he figure conjured up turned out to be Margaret Thatcher in a black chiffon negligee took him aback somewhat, but having, as it were, no better material to work with, he decided to give it his best shot. And so it was that Mrs. O'Reilly, Father Kennedy's elderly housekeeper cum cleaner came upon a lanky young man who appeared to be undergoing some kind of religious experience for he was kneeling in a corner of the corridor with his face to the wall chanting, "The Blessed Margaret... The Blessed Margaret...!" He then made a noise which she was unable to identify but later compared to the sound of air rushing out of a vacuum cleaner.

Around the table, the few remaining items were dealt with and Father Kennedy finished the meeting with what he evidently considered to be a pep talk. "Thank ye all again for taking the time to come over. I don't need to tell ye how important this mass will be for the school and the parish. Bishop McCarthy himself will be there, and I'm sure ye'll all do ye're best to make sure there are no hitches," with a pointed look in O'Driscoll's direction, adding, "and the service is one that we can all be proud of."

As people began to gather their possessions, Karen placed her hand lightly on O'Driscoll's arm. He could feel the soft pressure of her fingers and, still reeling from the events of the last few minutes, fought to concentrate on the words she was saying. "By the way, John," she said, "I heard that you were interested in the theatre."

"Yeah, I go occasionally," he replied, wondering what was coming.

"Well," she said, and he had never been more conscious of her physical proximity, "it's just that I've got these two tickets for *Antony and Cleopatra* at The National and I was wondering…"

For a moment the room swam around him as O'Driscoll digested the implication of her words. "I'd love to come…" he began, his heart thumping in his chest. "Shakespeare's one of my…" he stopped, as he saw an expression close to panic appearing on her face.

"No, no," she said quickly, "It's just that…" the words tumbled over one another in their hurry to get out, "you see, there's been a change of plans and I … we… won't be able to go, so I was wondering if you'd like them?"

The expression *"his blood ran cold"* was one O'Driscoll had heard many times but until that moment he had never realized how accurately it described the sensation he was experiencing. Desperate to say anything to remove the panic-stricken look from Karen's face, he gabbled, "Oh, of course. Saturday night. Great! I'd love to take it… take them…. the two of them. I can take my… I mean, I can take one of my… brilliant. Thanks." He swallowed an "OOST" that had begun to form in his diaphragm and finished lamely, "I'll get them tomorrow."

As he scanned the room to work out the quickest way of extricating himself from the situation, he realized the eyes of the others were on them and that the whole excruciating exchange must have been witnessed by them all. With a hurried farewell, Karen headed towards the door and as the rest of the group gathered their possessions prior to departing, O'Driscoll became aware that Father Kennedy's little piggy eyes were resting on him with an amused gleam in them. "Well, Mister O'Driscoll," said the priest with the self-satisfied air of a porker who has yet again successfully avoided the market van, "you seem to bring as much success to your personal life as you do your professional one."

O'Driscoll trawled his consciousness for a suitably withering put down, but having considered, "Fuck off, you ignorant old twat," and, "Shove it up your great fat hairy arse," he rejected both and chose instead to contort his face into its most fearsome configuration and fire the resulting grimace off in the direction of his tormentor's departing back. With this action safely executed, he made good his own escape, wondering not for the first time why it is the crushing rejoinder never seems to emerge when we need it most.

Thursday

The beer and the conversation in The North Star flowed easily and within a couple of hours had moved on to the Conservative government that had ruled the country for as long as anyone could remember, and which was hanging tenaciously on to power, despite a series of sex scandals that had ravaged its ranks.

"We'll never get the bastards out!" said Duffy, who was apt to become pessimistic when drink had worked its way into his system

"I dunno," said O'Driscoll. "Ever since John Major started his back to basics campaign, every Tory MP in the country seems to have gone sex mad. They've been rogering anything that moves - constituency agents, diary secretaries, research assistants - you name it, they've shagged it. Things have got so out of control that some of them are even sleeping with their own wives."

"Sleaze or no sleaze, the people of this country are too thick to vote the Tories out," proclaimed Duffy with mournful satisfaction.

Duffy's girlfriend Faith had brought her friend Maureen along and the girl leaned across and ruffled Duffy's hair. "Don't be so pessimistic," she said. "You never know what might happen once those new guys Blair and Brown get on the case."

"I'll drink to that," said Duffy. "In fact, does anyone fancy a tequila slammer to toast the end of Tory misrule?" The idea met with general approval and before long, the table was awash with glasses, segments of squeezed lemon, and granules of salt. Micky, attempting to throw salt over his shoulder for good luck, landed a handful in Maureen's face and she screamed in mock horror. Chaos replaced order as the tequila disappeared, and by 9.30 a chorus of "The Red Flag" was competing loudly with a series of verses telling the story of how four and twenty young ladies from Inverness in Scotland attended a gathering where they all underwent a life-changing experience. The landlord looked on lugubriously, consoling himself with the thought that the group, although loud and drunk, were never obnoxious or aggressive to other customers and that his bulging till was all the evidence he needed of what their presence would do to his takings on a quiet Wednesday night.

Realizing he was out of money, O'Driscoll slipped out to visit the cash point machine located a couple of minutes away. He was in the euphoric condition attained when significant quantities of hard alcohol have been imbibed in a short period of time and it was in this happy state, a couple of minutes later, that Sister Bernadette, Miss Gillespie and Karen Black happened upon him as they hurried through the precinct.

"John O'Driscoll!" exclaimed Sister Bernadette. "By the grace of God, it's a miracle! Can you give us just half an hour of your time to help the school. Father Kennedy has arranged a public meeting to showcase the good community work that the church and school does in the parish. We're holding it in one of the town hall meeting rooms, and lots of groups are attending – the old people for whom we did the social evening the other week, for example – and there's a reporter there from the Ealing Gazette, and one from The Catholic Herald too. We've asked some staff to come along and take part in the question and answer session – Karen and Miss Gillespie here – and we were to have had Geoff Turnbull, but he called an hour ago to say that his daughter has been taken ill. Father Kennedy was anxious that we have a representative from the male staff to show how everyone is behind the community work the school does. You know how people get these stereotypical images of how primary schools are all run by do-gooding middle-aged women. We were nipping round to see if Mr. Barnet was available, as he lives up towards Ealing Common, but if you could give us a half an hour, we'd be so grateful. It would just mean sitting at the front with us and answering questions about the work the school does." She stopped to draw breath after what, for her, had been a long and impassioned speech, quite different from the measured tones she usually adopted. "It would be very helpful to the school," she continued, lowering her voice slightly, "and I'm sure Father Kennedy would be so pleased that it would be a personal feather in the cap for you."

Sister Bernadette stopped speaking again and the three figures, representing as they did womanhood in all its diversity, stood looking at O'Driscoll expectantly. John O'Driscoll was not a complete fool, and in the normal course of events, realizing he had just spent upwards of three hours in the pub, he would have run a hundred miles rather than get involved with a scheme that was filled with the potential for drunken indiscretion. But the condition O'Driscoll was in at that moment was a truly dangerous one. He had taken on board industrial quantities of hard liquor, but only in the recent past, and was in a state of heady optimism and euphoric goodwill towards all humankind. He looked at the three faces in front of him, Sister Bernadette wearing a look that was almost imploring, Miss Gillespie wearing a look that was almost human, and Karen gazing at him with a diffident, appealing look that turned into a smile.

It was the smile that did it, melting O'Driscoll's heart completely, and a few minutes later, he found himself sitting on a raised dais at the front of a half-full meeting room in the town hall. The chairs were arranged in a semi-circle facing the audience, with Father Kennedy in the middle, flanked on either side by Sister Bernadette and Miss Gillespie, with O'Driscoll and Karen occupying the seats at either end. O'Driscoll had crammed a wedge of extra strong mints into his mouth on the way across the road, and with that precaution safely observed, sat gazing benevolently out at his audience.

"Thank you to Father Kennedy for outlining so cogently the range of activities carried out by the church and school," said Sister Bernadette. "And now it's over to you, the audience. We have asked a cross-section of staff to be available to answer any questions you may have, so feel free to ask them anything you'd like." She briefly introduced the teachers and then made a gesture suggestive of opening the floor for questions. There was an uneasy pause, before an elderly man asked whether the school had plans for a pilgrimage to Lourdes next year. Father Kennedy answered in the affirmative, saying funds had been made available from the diocese to subsidize the trip, and following his gaze, O'Driscoll noticed a figure clad in ecclesiastical purple who he took to be Bishop McCarthy sitting in the second row, wearing an unworldly smile.

Here was an opportunity to put right any damage that he may have unwittingly done following the unfortunate incident with the poster and he resolved to make sure he showed by his answers what a special place St. Catherine's was. In fact at that moment, as waves of tequila coursed through his veins, O'Driscoll was filled with an overwhelming love for the school, for the church and for the whole of humanity in all its myriad forms. The next question was from a pious-looking elderly lady in tweeds who asked whether the knowledge that God was always with them was a help in the good work that was being done in the community. Father Kennedy answered that naturally God's love was a tremendous solace, underpinning as it did every good deed that was done in the parish.

"We would expect no other answer from those called to Holy Orders," said a supercilious-looking young man with a notebook who was obviously one of the reporters, "but I wonder, could we have a comment from one of the lay members of staff?"

This was O'Driscoll's opportunity and he wasn't going to miss it. "I absolutely agree with what Father Kennedy just said," he began, "and those of us seeking to do God's work from, shall I say, a *civilian* perspective, (there was a gratifying murmur of laughter at this) are conscious of how much we depend on the love of God to help us." Emboldened by this start, he went on, "Of course, there are many competing kinds of love in the world, as I am sure you are all aware. There is the love of a parent for its child, and…" here he paused and favoured the audience with an indulgent smile, "… there is, of course, the love of a child for its parent."

This public speaking was straightforward, he thought to himself and his voice took on a louder, more confident tone as he gazed benevolently out at his audience. "There is also the love of a woman for a man," he continued, risking a look across the line of chairs to where Karen was sitting, and noticing her eyes were cast down in a way that appeared to be at once demure and at the same time distinctly arousing. He really must take her to one side after the show and declare his love for her, he decided, the liquor reaching the core of his being and inducing an overwhelming feeling of goodwill to all of mankind. He paused for a moment, where was he, mustn't lose his thread?

"As I was saying, there is the love of a woman for a man and…" he stole another covert glance at his beloved, "there is the love of a man for a woman." He wondered whether this would be a good time to illustrate to the audience how powerful this love could be by sharing with them his feelings for Karen, but decided it wouldn't be appropriate just yet.

"But," he continued, endeavoring to demonstrate by his words the strength of his support for the school, "it is the love of God that underpins everything we do at St Catherine's. It is evident in the way Sister Bernadette prepares the confirmation class with such attention to detail and," he searched for another example, "it is there in Father Kennedy's address to the infant class who are preparing for their first communion. When he describes the infinite pain of hellfire and the unspeakable horror of eternal damnation as he prepares the little ones for the trials ahead, one has only to look at the expressions on their little faces to know that it is a moment they will remember all their lives."

O'Driscoll concluded and sat back, satisfied with his efforts on behalf of the school. He really did seem to have a gift for public speaking, he reflected with an inward smile. Returning his attention to the meeting, he realized that Sister Bernadette just finished answering a question about the R.E. curriculum.

"I absolutely agree with Sister Bernadette," he said in the same measured tones he had used earlier, nodding his head emphatically. "R.E. is a subject with an extremely high profile at St. Catherine's, thanks to Sister Bernadette, and we must not forget the beautiful... the ... er ... excellent assistance given to her by Miss Black here, on my left." As he indicated Karen's presence with a languid wave of the hand, he glanced once more in her direction, but as before her gaze appeared to be fixed resolutely on the floor in front of her.

She looked incredibly desirable in a demure, Jane Austen-ish way as she sat there with downcast eyes and hands clasped in front of her, and as anyone familiar with Miss Austen's work knew, that modest aspect was but a mask that concealed the passionate nature that lay beneath. O'Driscoll felt a wave of sympathy coursing through him at the thought of all those heroines forced to sit at the breakfast table making polite conversation about the price of linen or lace when in reality they were aching to be taken out to the stables and given a good Darcying. His feeling of oneness with the rest of humanity was now so strong that he wanted to sing at the top of his voice and whirl Karen from her seat and dance her around the floor, but realizing that this might interfere with the smooth running of the Q and A session, he confined himself to agreeing vocally and emphatically with the next five answers that were given by other members of the panel.

When it came time for closing remarks, he agreed "emphatically" with Sister Bernadette on the benefits of good school/parent relations, he agreed "absolutely and totally" with Miss Gillespie on the importance of good music teaching in the curriculum, and he agreed "absolutely, totally and fundamentally, if I may say so," with Father Kennedy's views on fully engaging parishioners in the work of the church. As the meeting meandered peacefully towards a conclusion, he contented himself with the satisfying thought that he had done good and altruistic work for the school while also earning himself some useful credits with the powers that be.

Relaxing now that proceedings were almost over, he saw a final opportunity to end the meeting with exactly the right note of informality. Bishop McCarthy had been called to make a final summing up and, after praising the work of the staff and governors of the school, had finished with the words, "….and, we are all members of God's family."

"If I could echo the bishop's words," O'Driscoll said, forestalling with an airy wave of the hand Father Kennedy's efforts to intervene, "and speaking as a member of the staff at Saint Catherine's, I can say that is *exactly* how we see ourselves (he would enter just the right note of levity to bring things to a satisfactorily light hearted conclusion). "We *are* a family at Saint Catherine's, a bit of a dysfunctional family to be truthful, the kind of family with skeletons in the cupboard, and secrets to hide." That got their attention, he thought with satisfaction, and indeed there was a perceptible stirring in the audience. He even thought he saw one of the blokes with notebooks scribble something. "But, if I may say so…" and here he thought an indulgent smile would be appropriate, "like all dysfunctional families, we keep our dark secrets hidden away and present a united front to the rest of the world." He leaned back in his chair and noted with satisfaction that his final remarks had produced a ripple of appreciative laughter and even a smattering of applause.

"Thank you, Mr. O'Driscoll!" said Father Kennedy with what seemed a little more emphasis than was strictly necessary and O'Driscoll reflected that the priest was possibly feeling a little outshone by his young co-panelist. He must remember in future to allow others the opportunity to share in the limelight and win some plaudits for themselves, or as many as they could get without having his natural talent.

The overwhelming feeling of satisfaction that proceeds from a successful public performance had now reached the core of his being and he made a point of shaking hands with his fellow panelists and assuring them what a success the evening had been, after all he didn't want them to feel overshadowed just because he had stolen the show. He had just finished shaking the bishop's hand for the third time and was casting around for another arm to begin pumping when he realized the progress of the group had taken it out of the meeting room and they were outside in the street. Father Kennedy and the bishop were heading towards the church, Karen was in the process of getting into the car of the elderly woman with tweeds who was obviously dropping her home, and only Sister Bernadette and Miss Gillespie remained.

"Well, John," said the nun, "we didn't realize we must have taken you away from your friends when we met you. You'll want to get back to them, I expect."

Glancing at his watch, O'Driscoll realized it was only ten o'clock and that the interlude in the town hall had occupied a bare half-hour. Resisting a sudden urge to give Sister Bernadette a kiss - the Jedi Council would probably take a view on such a breach of protocol - he shook her hand warmly, and that of Miss Gillespie, and made his way to The North Star, where events were unfolding even more raucously than when he had left. He reckoned that he was about four tequilas behind everyone else and, as another chorus of "Georgie Graham's red and white army" echoed around the bar, he wasted no time in making up the deficit. The rest of the evening passed in a blur and he could not have said what time it was that he tumbled at last exhausted into bed.

Friday

It was just after five a.m. by the luminous dial on John O'Driscoll's watch when he raised a tousled head and allowed the memories of the preceding evening to coalesce into something approaching chronological order. What he remembered was a good night in the pub, in the middle of which he had performed with surprising grace and confidence during the session at the town hall. Perhaps he had dominated things a tiny bit but, well, fortune favoured the brave, and he remembered some very demure, butter-wouldn't-melt images of Karen that he couldn't help feeling boded well for the future. With that, he lapsed back into unconsciousness.

It was just after six a.m. when O'Driscoll next cast a bleary eye at his watch and turned over, reflecting as he did that his mouth was feeling exceptionally dry. That would be the tequila, he thought, and hadn't he done well to perform so well at the meeting, considering how much of the stuff he had taken on board. There was, however, a nagging doubt in his mind about the town hall session. Had he talked too much, he wondered? He had certainly interrupted Father Kennedy on one occasion, something he would never normally do. On the other hand, there was the applause that greeted his final intervention, which had to be a good sign, and on that positive note sleep again overtook him.

The hands on John O'Driscoll's watch stood at seven o'clock when he awoke suddenly, instantly aware of a troubling knot in the pit of his stomach as his mind began to replay scenes from the town hall Q and A. The applause which only an hour ago he had attributed to his easy wit could just have easily been a mocking response to his ineptness, while what he had imagined to be admiring laughter now seemed more likely to have been titters of derision. The more he thought about the evening, the more he shrank from the memory of his performance and waves of anxiety began to course through his system.

By eight a.m., O'Driscoll was showered, dressed and in the grip of an attack of galloping paranoia. The last traces of the tequila that had been such a source of sustenance the night before were now exiting his system, leaving his internal mechanism at the mercy of random, jumbled images and thoughts. The looks that he had the night before judged to be admiring ones, could just as easily have been an embarrassed reaction to the sight of someone making a colossal fool of themselves. How could he have seen Karen's downcast expression and refusal to meet his eyes, as some kind of demure,

18th century come on, when it was clear to any fool that she was merely embarrassed by the actions of an idiot whose drunken antics had dragged the good name of the school into the mire?

By nine o'clock, John O'Driscoll was prowling the corridors of the school looking for someone who had been at the town hall the night before so he could gauge how criminal his misbehaviour had actually been. He remembered a phrase that had stayed with him after last year's staff trip to see *Macbeth*, *"O full of scorpions is my mind,"* and he wondered bitterly whether whatever it was the Scottish nobleman had taken on board matched the paranoia generated by the after-effects of a dozen tequila slammers. He spied Sister Bernadette in the distance but as he moved towards her, she swept into an adjacent corridor, leaving him to conclude that she had seen him coming and been so horrified by his behaviour of the night before that she had been unable to face him.

In the distance he saw Karen, walking down the corridor towards him. "Morning, Karen," he said, trying to make his voice sound as casual as possible while waiting for the aversion of eyes and embarrassed body language that would signal his disgrace.

"Oh, hi John," she answered, "how are you feeling today?"

He immediately concluded that she was referring to his condition of the night before, but trying to keep his voice even,

answered, "Not bad, thanks. A bit knackered, to be honest."
There was a slight pause before he screwed up the courage to
ask the question whose answer might determine his whole future
at St Catherine's. "How did you feel it went last night?"

"Fine," she replied, "but can I ask you something?"

"Of course."

"I just wondered, were you on medication or anything?"
she asked.

His heart dropped into his boots but he tried to keep his
voice light as he answered, "Actually, I did accidentally double
the dose of my red pills, and I think they may have reacted with
the blue ones that I'm only supposed to take when I get
psychotic. Was it that obvious?"

"No," she laughed as she replied, "not to anyone who
doesn't know you well, but you did seem a little…odd now and
again, very opinionated and, well, you interrupted Father
Kennedy a couple of times." She laughed again. "He looked
quite cross the second time."

This was beginning to sound like it hadn't been the
unmitigated disaster that he had feared. Karen had noticed that
he had been a little different from normal, but she did not give
the impression of someone who had found his conduct

reprehensible. In fact, she was talking to him in terms that were interestingly relaxed and friendly.

"You don't think Father Kennedy was too pissed off?" he ventured.

"Not at all," she replied, "I heard the bishop complimenting him on the quality of his young staff as they were leaving."

O'Driscoll felt his knees go weak with relief and he resisted with difficulty the urge to grab Karen and shower her on the spot with kisses of gratitude as she continued with a smile, "So those happy pills didn't do you any harm after all."

"Actually," he confessed after a moment, "it's interesting what you said earlier because I was on a kind of medication last night."

She looked at him enquiringly and he went on, "Well, we were in The North Star and... things got a bit out of hand ... it was Duffy's fault, really ... and... well, before I knew it I'd had ten tequila slammers."

Karen put a hand over her mouth and her eyes widened as she said slowly, "You'd had ten tequila slammers?"

"Actually it might have been twelve," replied O'Driscoll in the interests of honest disclosure, "and of course there were the few pints we'd had at the start of the evening."

He filled her in on the sequence of events that had ended with him addressing a town hall meeting with enough alcohol in his system to incapacitate a rhino. "Actually," he concluded, "when I woke up this morning, I had no idea whether I had insulted Sister Bernadette, importuned Miss Gillespie, or offered to elope with Father Kennedy. You will confirm that I didn't do any of those things?"

"No, but you were giving the bishop some decidedly ambiguous looks," said Karen and she joined in his laughter. "Bloody hell," she repeated in awe. "Ten tequilas before going to a public meeting with Father Kennedy! You do lead a charmed life, John."

"I read somewhere that Churchill used to have a whiskey and water before giving a speech," he replied. "It's really only an updated version of that."

She smiled and the acuteness of her proximity and the warmth of their shared laughter made him abandon all his inhibitions. "Karen," he blurted out, "there's something I've been meaning to ask you..." but even as he spoke, he remembered the expression on her face when he had misunderstood the offer of the Shakespeare tickets and his nerve failed. His mouth began to open and close like a fish but all that emerged was a strangled "OOST!" and although he attempted to disguise the "OOST!" by breaking into a prolonged fit of coughing, he could see from her face that it hadn't worked.

Now he had another problem: Karen's proximity was beginning to produce disturbing stirrings in his trousers, and it was only by conjuring up an image of Mrs. Thatcher at the dispatch box in a basque that he was able to reverse the process. At that moment, one of Karen's pupils rushed up to say the class was waiting for her to unlock the door and she headed down the corridor wearing an expression he was unable to read. Looking around, he realized that Miss Gillespie and Mr. Li had materialized next to him and for the want of something better to say, he asked the elderly music teacher if she was prepared for Sunday's Year Six mass.

"My girls will be ready to do the school credit, I hope," she said with a wintry smile. "The hymn books will be ready for use, I presume, Mr. O'Driscoll?" He hastened to assure her they had been delivered the day before and had been placed, still in their packaging, at the entrance to the pew where the choir would be seated.

"I'll help you unpack them, Miss Gillespie," he finished, "if I get there before the start of the mass, but I've got a family commitment and it might be touch and go." The "family commitment" consisted of the extra couple of hours he hoped to spend sleeping off Saturday night's drinking session, but she was not to know this, and O'Driscoll was reluctant to give up any more of the weekend than he absolutely had to. With a frosty nod, Miss Gillespie moved off, leaving O'Driscoll and the elderly Chinaman together.

"Have the preparations for Sunday's mass gone as planned, John?" asked Mr. Li.

"As far as I know," replied O'Driscoll.

"It'll hopefully pass off without incident," said Li with a twinkle.

O'Driscoll knew he was referring to the cock-up with the poster but he did not begrudge his colleague the reference. Rather, he felt there was a fellow feeling between them because of an incident that had occurred a couple of days after the fete, during the end of term carol service. Mr. Li had been acting as master of ceremonies and things had been progressing uneventfully until he had stood up to announce the penultimate carol, that perennial favourite, 'Away in a Manger.' He made the announcement with his usual clarity of speech, but unfortunately pronounced the final word to rhyme with "banger" and this had been the cause of an immediate and sustained outburst of hilarity among the student body. The laughter had rippled up and down the pews and teachers leapt to their feet and stared threateningly along the lines of pupils, but the laughter had now gained a momentum of its own and it had taken the arrival of Sister Bernadette, sweeping into the room like an avenging Jedi, to quell the disturbance.

The mirth had not been confined to the student body and parents and members of staff could be seen wearing carefully suppressed smiles, but Father Kennedy, when informed of the *faux pas*, by Mrs. Goodwin had not been amused. Wasn't it bad enough, he was alleged to have thundered, that he was surrounded by 'tinkers and gypsies', without having to cope with 'heathens' as well!? Mrs. Goodwin's own take on the whole thing had been the rather cryptic observation that while you could take the man out of the Orient, you couldn't take the Orient out of the man, an aphorism apparently inspired by that noted anthropologist, her husband, Reg.

The incident left O'Driscoll with a kindred feeling for the elderly Chinaman, if for no other reason that they shared in the opprobrium of the cantankerous cleric. He smiled at Li's enquiry about the mass and said, "If anything goes wrong on Sunday, I wouldn't like to be in my shoes." His tone was playful but an image of Father Kennedy's nasal hairs performing a wild but synchronized fandango flashed across his mind and he resolved to put his mind at rest by checking the missals one final time before the service started.

Saturday

It was midnight in a night club on the Uxbridge Road whose name O'Driscoll couldn't remember, and the place was heaving with talent. Duffy could pull without trying and often did. He claimed sometimes he only went through with the subsequent act out of politeness, but O'Driscoll had to concede that, Duffy apart, the lads were not a company designed to set the hearts of the ladies beating. He himself was tall, gangly and uncoordinated with, in the words of an ex-girlfriend, "the face that launched a thousand shits," while Micky Quinn was all curly red hair and freckles, his lumpy shape bulging and expanding into whatever space his ill-fitting clothes would allow. The other two lads were no oil paintings either but what they all shared was that grey-white Irish skin colouring that resembled semi-digested porridge and which no exposure to the sun could darken or make attractive.

With the last slow dance trailing away to silence, O'Driscoll watched as Quinn, after much resolute trouser hitching and several false starts, finally approached a girl he had been eyeing up, the whole performance calling to mind a bull which has spied a particularly fetching heifer in an adjoining field and is pawing the ground preparatory to having a run at her. The girl had watched his display of wheeling and curveting with a stony countenance and met his opening remarks when he finally did arrive with a reply so brief and terse that its import could not be mistaken. While all this was going on, Duffy's figure could be seen in the distance exiting the premises with something blonde and svelte in suede attached to its arm. O'Driscoll wondered anew how Duffy did it – he could and often did spend the whole evening apparently propping up the bar with the lads only to disappear right at the end with some stunner. The remainder of the party gathered in the foyer, their failure on the romantic front not weighing too heavily on their shoulders, and it remained to be decided what to do with the fag end of the evening.

"Do you still have that bottle of Jack Daniels at your flat?" asked Rocky.

"I do indeed," said O'Driscoll, brightening, "and what's more, we have the perfect number for a friendly game of poker!"

*****

It was five a.m. in O'Driscoll's flat and the card school was over. Quinn was asleep in the flat's only armchair, great trumpeting snores echoing around the room as his chest rose and fell. Sweeney had gone home and Rocky was crashed out on the bed next door. O'Driscoll sat in a chair at the table and as he poured himself a final drink, he reflected on the evening behind them and how single-sex education in Catholic schools could produce such comically maladjusted adults. Growing up without any meaningful contact with girls of their own age meant that as teenagers, the boys had no coping strategies when they did finally have cause to interact with the opposite sex. It wasn't a problem for the good-looking lads, they simply got pulled whether they liked it or not, but for the unlovely, the tongue-tied and the socially awkward, into all of which categories O'Driscoll placed himself firmly, it could be years before they were able to form meaningful adult relationships. At this moment, and as if to reinforce this point, Quinn stirred in his sleep and delivered a fart that seemed to shake the room to its foundations.

Floating in that half-world that precedes sleep, O'Driscoll smiled to himself as he recalled the "Venice/Ennis" misunderstanding and the comic misconceptions that can result from young ears mishearing the words of adult talk. His mind went back a decade to his teenage years and to The Girl. She had come across from Ireland by boat and train to spend a week with his sister's friend Sinead and she had a fragile, elfin beauty that knotted his stomach and made the breath catch in his throat. He had watched from a distance – six-feet two inches of tongue-tied, adolescent gawkiness – until one summer day the girls

71

came calling and she floated down his garden path, the late-afternoon sun turning the soft down on her arms into strands of iridescent gold. She had that dreamy, ethereal quality that exceptionally beautiful people sometimes have and his whole being was consumed by a yearning to be with her, talk to her, hold her, kiss her, but he had no idea how any of these miracles might be achieved when she wasn't even aware of his existence.

It was known that she came from a family of staunch republicans and that she wore that badge with a pride as fierce as any *Cumann na mBan* warrioress and he instinctively felt if he could only show her the same republican fire burned in him, she might turn those cornflower blue eyes on him with something more than mild curiosity. But in truth, his knowledge of the history and culture of his native land was derived almost entirely from listening to the eight LPs, six by *The Clancy Brothers and Tommy Makem* and two by *The Dubliners*, whose scratchy rhythms crackled from the back room of the family home every Saturday night in a relentless, lonely loop.

The girls had reached the pond at the bottom of the garden and he knew if he didn't do something soon, it would be too late and they would be gone. And then he Gods smiled on him for as the girl bent down to examine a lily, her hand slipped into the pond and came up covered in a thick, black ooze and he remembered the Blackened Hands, the ruthless gang of cutthroats who had terrorized Ireland and whose crimes were alluded to in sombre tones whenever the elders of his family gathered.

"The Blackened Hands - a name steeped in blood and treachery."

"And the whole thing the work of those creatures Churchill and Lloyd George, may God forgive them."

"A ring of Crossley Tenders around Cork while the city centre burned."

"And the arrogant so and so's standing there as bold as brass stopping the firemen from putting out the flames."

"Ah, but they reckoned without Tom Barry and his brave boys."

"Down into the mire they went to fight for Ireland's freedom."

"A flying column lay waiting on the road at Kilmichael."

"And a few minutes later, those same brave articles were smiling on the other side of their faces!"

In the young O'Driscoll's mind, the chronology of events was uncertain, and he suspected it was equally so among the adults relating the tale, for sometimes the burning of Cork would precede the ambush at Kilmichael, while at other times the sequence of events was reversed. But what never changed were the sepulchral tones employed and the gloomy relish with which the story was told. The narrative left a deep impression on him and he had often pondered on the origin of the murderous gang's name. Had it derived from a secret mark, like the black spot in *Treasure Island*, or was the title merely symbolic of the dark acts carried out in the name of the crown? As he looked at the girl's arm covered in mud up to the elbow, he saw his opportunity and blurted out, "You'd better wash that off or we'll think you're one of the Blackened Hands."

"Wha'?" she replied, for although she had the delicate beauty of a fairytale princess, she spoke with the guttural vowels of Dublin's north side.

"You know… the Blackened Hands," he repeated, "the ones who came over from England during the troubles."

She looked at him evenly for a moment and then speaking slowly and deliberately and enunciating each word carefully, said, "It's not the *Blackened Hands*, you gobshite, it's the *Black and Tans.*"

She finally turned those cornflower blue eyes on him and as he squirmed under her gaze, he saw an expression of mild distaste appear on her face, the sort of look that someone examining a vaguely interesting but physically repellant insect might wear. Even though a decade and a half had passed, he still cringed at the memory of that look and he allowed himself a wry smile as he reflected on the power that some images have to transcend time and space. On that note, and with the rumble of Quinn's snore providing a suitably martial commentary on his thoughts, O'Driscoll drifted into sleep and into the coming day.

Sunday

The next morning, leaving Quinn sleeping on the sofa and snoring fit to wake the dead, O'Driscoll jumped into his battered Ford Cortina and made his way to St Catherine's, only to find the church deserted. Realizing his bleary eyes had misread the time on his watch and that he had, in fact, arrived an hour early, he thought he would try to turn the situation to his advantage and in the process, create the impression of someone whose religious faith is so strong that it literally propels him out of bed on a Sunday morning by knocking on the sacristy door and announcing himself.

As he arrived at the well-remembered door, he quailed momentarily but, hearing muffled voices coming from inside and realizing that the door had been left slightly ajar, he entered. O'Driscoll's nostrils were immediately assailed by an aroma comprising in roughly equal parts of bacon and beeswax, for Mrs. O'Reilly, Father Kennedy's elderly and irascible housekeeper, had traditional views on matters domestic and coated every surface with the waxing product during her daily cleaning routine. O'Driscoll could still hear muffled voices but they were clearer now and appeared to be coming from the half-open door to the living room. He was debating whether he should signal his presence by coughing tentatively or take the bull by the horns and move authoritatively into the room when he realized that he was being observed from across the hallway by Parnell, Father Kennedy's cat. Named in honour of Irish nationalism's great 19th century champion by Mrs. O'Reilly's husband, Parnell had been recruited several years before to deal with some church mice that had been unwise enough to stray into Father Kennedy's domain. Having dispatched the unfortunate rodents forthwith, Parnell had turned his attention to the feline population of the parish and set about them with an alacrity that his famous namesake might have envied, and soon no property in the parish was to be found without one of his progeny sunning itself in the garden. Parnell regarded O'Driscoll inscrutably for a few moments, licked a paw fastidiously and then wandered off in the direction of the bins.

"Will you be having another rasher, Father?" From the half-open presbytery door came a female voice which O'Driscoll recognized as belonging to Mrs. O'Reilly, but it was a softer, gentler version of the harsh tones she usually adopted. There was a short silence and then, somewhere between a murmur and a grunt, an answering, "I will."

Mrs. O'Reilly continued in a soft breathless voice quite unlike her usual one, "And I'm sure you could make room for another couple of pieces of white pudding. It's Galtee – your favourite – got specially from the market, and you do need to keep your strength up, what with three masses to say and the sick to visit as well."

O'Driscoll had not until that moment imagined that the priest's duties included calling on the infirm and couldn't help feeling that the prospect of a visit from Father Kennedy would be enough to induce a complete recovery in any invalid with an ounce of sense. Perhaps Lazarus himself had been anticipating a visit from some biblical version of Kennedy – it would certainly account for the alacrity with which history's most notorious malingerer had restored himself to health and vitality.

"I'll just be having a couple of pieces of the white pudding," came Kennedy's voice, adding, "I wouldn't want to be getting a corporation, now," and through the half-opened door, O'Driscoll saw a large ecclesiastical hand patting a large ecclesiastical stomach.

"Not a bit of it," crooned Mrs. O'Reilly. "Sure, a man has a much greater air of dignity when he is carrying a little condition, not like those skinny articles you see around these days. Now Father, there's the last sausage there," she continued, pushing it onto his plate, "t'would be a shame for it to go to waste."

"Ah Mrs. O'Reilly, you'll feed me to death if I'm not careful."

"Go on with you! Now Father, will you have another cup of tea – the pot's still warm?"

Still debating whether to move authoritatively into the room and declare himself, or to creep back down the hall and escape, O'Driscoll looked around and noticed that Parnell had returned and was once more regarding him with studied insolence from across the corridor. Under the cat's unnerving stare, his nerve failed completely and he beat a hasty retreat, entering the church, which was now open, a few moments later.

John O'Driscoll was not normally a young man who sought out the limelight but, aware of what was at stake and unable to contemplate the thought of what life would be like if his tenure at the school came to an end, he steeled himself and swept around the church on a number of spurious pretexts. He made an unnecessary journey to the pew where Miss Gillespie and the girls were sitting, and ostentatiously went through the motions of checking the hymn books, looking surreptitiously across at Father Kennedy to see if his presence was being noted. The priest returned his look and muttered, "O'Driscoll," by way of a greeting, but as Bishop McCarthy was at that moment standing right alongside him, he then had no option but to introduce the bishop to O'Driscoll, which he did with a short description of the role that the young teacher was to play.

"Rebinding the hymn books, splendid, splendid!" said the bishop in the cultured tones of the Irish east coast. "One finds that events such as this are so much more successful when the burden of preparation is a shared one." Rubbing his hands enthusiastically, he went on, "I am reminded of the passage from *Matthew* where Our Lord first spoke to the Pharisees on the subject of...." But it was no use, O'Driscoll had left him in body and spirit. He had just seen Karen on the other side of the church looking ravishing in black, and with a muttered apology, he retired to a pew at the back where, unnoticed by the congregation, he would be able to indulge in a solitary daydream.

There was a perceptible increase in the bustle and movement around the church as the service time grew near. Altar boys scurried up and down the nave and teachers checked for the umpteenth time that their pupils were sitting, well-behaved and quiescent in their places. In a radical new departure for Saint Catherine's, a video camera had been purchased, which would film the events of the service, and by some strange alchemy, project the moving images onto a huge screen which had been erected at the back of the altar. It was cutting-edge technology for 1995, and Father Kennedy was proud of the minute detail with which it would record the sacred proceedings ahead.

As the mass began and Kennedy's nostril hairs, each three feet high and whirling furiously, were projected in all their glory onto the screen, O'Driscoll drifted into a delicious reverie. Fanatical separatists from an obscure central Asian territory had overrun the church and within minutes were set to detonate the industrial quantities of explosive strapped to their bodies, causing massive devastation and loss of life. John O'Driscoll had volunteered to undertake the task of opening negotiations with them and Karen was trying desperately to prevent him going into the church.

"But John," she said, her bosom heaving (*Heaving! - that was one that O'Driscoll/Fleming hadn't thought of!*), "you can't. It'll be certain death." She took a deep, shuddering breath and said in halting tones, "And what about... us... I'd thought that we ..."

O'Driscoll was never to know what was to follow that "we...," because at that moment he was jerked out of his reverie by a commotion at the front of the church. Mildly annoyed at having his fantasy so rudely interrupted, he looked ahead to see what the cause of the disturbance was, secure in the knowledge that, whatever had gone wrong this time, at least they couldn't pin it on him. It took him a couple of seconds to make sense of what was happening and then the blood froze in his veins and the ground seemed to shift beneath his feet. An "OOST" began to form in his diaphragm, but died unborn and unlamented around his larynx, for the most emphatic "OOST" ever uttered would not have conveyed a fraction of the horror he was feeling at the images unspooling before his disbelieving eyes. At some point, the cameraman must have changed position because a picture of the choir was now being projected in enormous detail onto the screen behind the altar. Elderly spinsterish Miss Gillespie was standing in front with the twelve girls, all chosen for their radiance and innocence, in a line behind her. Each was holding a large red missal, upon which could be clearly seen, huge and picked out in gold leaf, the inscription:

HYMENS

ANCIENT AND MODERN

As the realization of what had happened hit him, O'Driscoll's brain went numb, his mind refusing to work other than to wonder inconsequentially whether it was the Ancient Greeks or Romans who had coined the phrase about the Gods making merry in their mischief. He couldn't remember, other than to reflect that the group of deities entrusted with his care must be possessed of particularly capricious senses of humour, for with cruel symmetry they had once again chosen to change the meaning of a message completely by altering just one letter. For O'Driscoll, the outcome in either case was the same, immediate disgrace and ignominy, followed by banishment to the edge of the ecclesiastical universe, and any hopes he might have held for a future at St. Catherine's would surely be consigned to the same outer darkness.

There was a buzz of noise around the church and Father Kennedy could be seen looking behind him, eyes squinting as he tried to make out the inscription projected on the huge screen. O'Driscoll watched in horror as the realization of what had happened slowly dawned on Kennedy and the piggy eyes that he knew so well began to relentlessly quarter the area, scanning each pew as they narrowed their field of search. Meanwhile, the object of his search stood transfixed, like a rabbit caught in headlights, until finally, after what seemed like an age, the priest's eyes alighted on him. Kennedy's nostril hairs began to dance a demented hornpipe whilst one of his hands made a gesture towards O'Driscoll that was assuredly not a sign of the cross. As the priest's mouth worked in a manic but silent pantomime, O'Driscoll saw rather than heard his name being invoked in a wrathful ecclesiastical bellow and his body began to experience a familiar sensation - the frantic fizzing and churning in his bowels as they began the process of turning to liquid.

Week Two

Monday

The instant John O'Driscoll woke, he knew that something awful, something truly awful had occurred and as the full weight of what he had allowed to happen bore down on him, he mouthed silent imprecations and scratched his scrotum in misery. It was nearly twenty-four hours since the Year Six mass, but O'Driscoll still felt the pall of disgrace hanging over him. Actually, the disaster could have been worse, had it not been for the quick thinking of the cameraman, who cut power to the camera and thus blotted out the unholy image on the screen. Perhaps three-quarters of the congregation had no idea anything was amiss, but there had been enough who had seen what was on the screen to ensure O'Driscoll's disgrace.

By a supreme collective effort of will, the service proceeded in a more or less normal manner. The camera was found to be working again and Miss Gillespie and the girls remembered to keep their missals resting firmly on the pew in front of them as they sang, but it did not need the presence of a camera for the rage on Father Kennedy's countenance to be apparent. He strove to maintain an air of composure but his inner turmoil was evident in the manic flaring of his nostrils and the frantic cavorting of the hairs that lay within them. At the end of the service, O'Driscoll had rushed forward and, in a frantic attempt at damage limitation, picked up a missal and looked around in an elaborate pantomime intended to suggest that somehow a malign substitution had taken place.

Bishop McCarthy, who had been oblivious to the disturbance at the start of proceedings, strolled over to the choir area and, before anyone had the chance to stop him, picked up one of the missals. After examining the front cover, he turned to O'Driscoll, who had been hovering nervously nearby, and said, "An unusual spelling, Mr. O'Driscoll." Growing up as one of seven boys on a farm outside Clonmel, Bishop McCarthy had entered the local seminary at twelve and thereafter moved in an entirely male-oriented world where knowledge of female anatomy was extremely limited. The word on the missal, therefore, meant nothing to him other than perhaps some variation on the noun "hymn", such as "hymnal". Dimly apprehending this in the midst of the turmoil, O'Driscoll gabbled frantically, "Yes, Bishop, it's a new spelling that the... er... the ecumenical commission recommended, but... er... on reflection, we feel we'll probably stick with the traditional one."

"I think you have chosen wisely, my son," said the bishop. "I feel that in our headlong rush for change, we forget to respect the traditional terminology that has stood us in good stead for so many years." Inclining his head gravely but not unkindly in O'Driscoll's direction, he returned the missal to the pile and moved towards the main body of the church.

The fact that the catastrophe had passed completely above the head of the bishop had not, however, helped O'Driscoll when the inevitable inquisition had taken place in Sister Bernadette's office after mass. By some miracle, Father Kennedy had been called away on parish business, and without his terrible presence, the atmosphere was less charged, but in some ways this made O'Driscoll feel even more guilty. Sister Bernadette gently but firmly established that the missals in question had remained in their packaging until minutes before the start of mass, and therefore the printing could not have been checked. Her final words had been not unkind. "You have much potential, John, but you need to realize that achievement can only be assured by rigorous attention to detail."

What the implications were on his future, O'Driscoll hadn't dared to ask and he could only hope when the school leadership did finally meet to decide the following year's staffing, the incident might have been forgotten. Groaning anew at his remembered shame, he dragged himself out of bed, breakfasted on half a cup of coffee, and an hour later, found himself in the staff room listening to morning briefing.

After an uneventful day, the hour of eight o'clock found O'Driscoll sitting in the audience at the National Theatre, waiting for *Antony and Cleopatra* to begin. He had effected the transfer of tickets from Karen without further embarrassment to either party by arranging for her to leave them in his pigeonhole, and was then faced with the tricky decision as to whether he should go ahead and attend the performance, and if so, whom to take with him. He would have preferred word to have got back to Karen that he had cut a conspicuous figure as he entered the National Theatre in the company of a shapely blonde, but if truth be told, he would have settled for a companion with lines built more for comfort than for speed. To be brutally honest, if a fat bird with mousy hair and boils had been available, he would have accepted her presence with gratitude. But the fly in the ointment was that none of these creatures existed in the O'Driscoll firmament, which was why as his gaze moved around the theatre and came to rest on the seat next to him, it alighted on the recumbent form of Michael Quinn, his great carcass spreading out to fill the available space and his boots resting on the back of the seat in front of him.

Quinn had considered the theatre invitation on Saturday lunchtime when the two had gone for a pint in the Hamborough Tavern on Southall Broadway. "Does anyone get their kit off?" had been his first question.

"It's Shakespeare, Mick," O'Driscoll replied wearily. "No one gets their kit off, or flashes their tits or does a dance with tassels. In fact in the old days, the female parts were played by young boys."

Micky considered this information as he took a leisurely draught from his pint. "Jesus," he said eventually, "there must have been a lot of paedoph…. paeda…. how's your father in the theatre in those days."

"I think you'll find things are pretty much the same today," said Tania the barmaid tartly. She was an aspiring actress and had clearly been finding the impresarios on the West End audition circuit a difficult group to impress.

"Anyway, are you coming or not?" asked O'Driscoll, whose patience had been worn thin by his friend's prevarication.

"Well, on the plus side, I've got nothing else on," said Quinn, taking another long pull from his pint. "But against that, there's the prospect of spending the evening with a crowd of pretentious arseholes." He stopped again to take a third swig from his rapidly diminishing pint before adding, "Present company excepted, of course," and Tania smiled. For once, O'Driscoll had to agree with Micky's sentiment - he liked Shakespeare but too often the audiences were full of people for whom an evening at the theatre was a chance to show how clever they were and how much they knew about the play in question.

The next few drinks had lifted Micky's mood to a point where he was able to contemplate the evening with equanimity, which was how the two came to be sitting side-by-side and relatively sober in the stalls of the National Theatre. Scanning the audience idly, O'Driscoll's eyes suddenly alighted on the moustachioed figure of the Head, Mr. Barnet, who was sitting a few seats along in the same row. Next to him was Mrs. Goodwin, and further along Mr. Li, Miss Gillespie and several other members of Saint Catherine's staff. He realized that Karen's tickets must have been part of a group booking and his heart sank at the prospect of spending an evening making small talk with people whom he had little in common. Mr. Barnet saw him at the same moment and nodded a greeting to him. The Head was a stout, middle-aged man with a florid complexion and a large moustache. His father had been a fighter ace who had become a minor celebrity during the war and no one entering Mr. Barnet's office could fail to be aware of this, for RAF memorabilia was dotted around the room and there was a framed photo on the wall showing a young man in a leather jacket leaning negligently on the wing of a fighter aircraft. In another frame was an obituary from *The Daily Telegraph* which began:

Group Captain Charles Barnet D.S.O., known to his many friends as "Boko", saw action in several theatres of war in the last conflict, notably during the defensive action which came to be known as "the Battle of Britain". He also served with distinction in the North African campaign, where....

O'Driscoll had never got any further than that, but was aware, like everyone else, how Mr. Barnet revered the memory of his father, and how he lived and breathed in a world of fliers in general and the RAF in particular. As well as sporting the luxurious growth on his upper lip, the Head habitually dressed in a dark blue blazer and beige slacks, and often sported a cravat instead of a tie. He talked with the strangled vowels of a bygone age and when he made reference to the war, aeroplanes and flying, which he often did, his speech was peppered with examples of RAF jargon and terminology that struck an unusual note in the 1990s. With a sinking heart, O'Driscoll noted the intervening seating was empty so there was no impediment to conversation between the two parties.

"Evening, young O'Driscoll," said the Head. "Didn't know you were coming tonight."

"It was a late decision," answered John, and turned to introduce Micky. "This is my friend, Michael Quinn."

"Glad to meet you, young feller," said the head, extending a large hand. "Are you chaps looking forward to the show?"

"Rather!" replied Micky who, determined to play the part of a Shakespeare aficionado to the full, hitched his trousers up with a flourish so theatrical that Sir John Gielgud himself might have envied it.

"You chaps coming to the bistro after the show for tea and stickies," called out Mr. Barnet, adding, "my treat, of course." Hastily pleading a prior engagement, O'Driscoll and Quinn hurried back to their seats just as the lights went down.

It took no more than a couple of minutes for O'Driscoll to realize that Mr. Barnet was one of those annoying bastards whose sole purpose when visiting a theatre is to demonstrate his knowledge of the play being performed - the kind of bloke who, upon hearing an amusing piece of dialogue will laugh loudly and extravagantly, the laughter being itself a performance intended to showcase his familiarity with the text. Early in the performance, there is a scene where Cleopatra and her handmaidens discuss where they would like an extra inch on their man, and one of them says, "Not on his nose!" It was in truth a line that could have been delivered by Barbara Windsor or Kenneth Williams to a suggestive tuba accompaniment, and upon hearing it for the first time, O'Driscoll had wondered whether The Bard had had some premonition as to the prism through which future populations might view that particular play. It was nevertheless a line clearly intended to be funny, and as it approached, Mr. Barnet's shoulders began to shake and his belly to wobble as he prepared himself for the laugh he was about to deliver.

"Ah – ha – ha – ha – ha!" he enunciated at the precise moment the actress began to deliver the line.

"Ah – ha – ha –ha!" he continued, shaking his head and wiping his eyes with a large spotted handkerchief.

A couple of rows away, a loud "Oh – ho – ho – ho!" echoed across the auditorium and Mr. Barnett froze in his seat and then frowned. He scanned the room surreptitiously in search of his rival and there was a palpable sense of him squaring his metaphorical shoulders as he prepared to go into battle. For the remainder of the performance, O'Driscoll struggled to follow what was happening on the stage as he listened to the herculean struggle taking place between the two foes. A volley of Ah – ha – ha – ha's would be fired off from Mr. Barnet's seat, only to encounter in mid-air and travelling in the opposite direction, an artillery burst of Oh – ho – ho – ho's.

Mr. Barnet would sometimes vary his attack by firing off a salvo of snorts, but this would be immediately neutralized by the deployment of a defensive pattern of barks. Sometimes the "ha's" would seem to have it in the bag, but then back would come the "ho's," as increasingly powerful weaponry was deployed on both sides. Before long, O'Driscoll's head was spinning from its demented umpiring role and he was glad when the performance finished and they were able to move to the foyer, where Mr. Barnet continued to harrumph and chortle and shake his shoulders, the effect not unlike some great engine which continues to vibrate and clank long after its motor has been switched off.

"Did you enjoy the performance," O'Driscoll asked Mr. Li, for want of something to say.

"Absolutely ripping, I thought," answered Li. "A fellow could go a month of Sundays without seeing anything so top hole."

In truth, it had been a decent enough evening, reflected O'Driscoll. The only downside was if word got back to Karen that he had attended, word would equally get back that his companion, far from being a ravishing blonde, had in fact been a big fat, red-headed Irishman. Declining as gracefully as they could, Mr. Barnet's repeated invitation to join them for "tea and stickies," the two lads headed gratefully into the pub next door, where a few minutes later they were seated at a table attacking their second pints.

By this time, Micky was facing a losing battle to get to Euston for his last train to Watford, whereas O'Driscoll's flat was a simple journey on the N89 night bus. "You might as well crash at my place, Mick," he said. "You practically live there anyway, and with the smell you left last time, the rats will be disappointed not to reacquaint themselves with you."

And so it was that several hours later, the flat echoed again to the sound of Quinn's mellifluous snore, while O'Driscoll sat at the table in that twilight world between wakefulness and sleep. A video player lay under the small TV set that was perched uneasily on a small table in the corner and was playing one of the four videos that comprised O'Driscoll's collection. On this particular occasion, the words and images that echoed around the room were very familiar, for when Santino Corleone opened the package that had just arrived at a heavily guarded compound in upstate New York, it was in fact the twenty-second time that year that he had done so.

And when fat Clemenza told the puzzled mobster that the dead bloater yielded up by the parcel was an old Sicilian message suggesting that capo regime Luca Brazzi slept with the fishes, it was the twenty-second time that year that he had done so. And when Santino's brother Michael removed the telephone receiver he was holding from his ear and dropped it back into its cradle, it was the twenty-second time that year that he had done so. As the portentous Godfather theme music battled for supremacy with the even more portentous Quinn snore, John O'Driscoll drifted into sleep and into another day.

Tuesday

"Morning, chaps," said Mr. Barnet, giving his left moustache an exploratory twirl as he began briefing in the staff room. "I just wanted to remind you all about the exchange programme I mentioned last week. I'll be talking about it in more detail during assembly, but the long and short of it is that next week we'll be playing host to two Year Six pupils, one from France and the other from the U.S.A. Right, that's it chaps, up and at 'em! Oh, by the way, John, can I have a word with you in my office?"

O'Driscoll followed his leader down the corridor with lagging footsteps and a heavy heart. He could count on the fingers of one hand the number of times he had been invited into the Head's office and never before had he been called into the august presence alone. He steeled himself for what was to come – it was probably going to be another bollocking about the Year Six mass, or worse, a warning to prepare himself for bad news about next year. He had held onto the hope that, because Mr. Barnet hadn't been at the church, details of the blunder might not have gotten back to him, but obviously some twisted bastard

- Mrs. Goodwin sprang to mind - had taken the opportunity to put in a bad word.

Indulging himself in a brief fantasy where Mrs. Goodwin had been taken hostage by separatists wearing explosive belts and the entire school staff had a whip round to donate some detonators, O'Driscoll followed the Head into his office. He looked around as he sat on the proffered chair and saw the familiar collection of RAF inspired memorabilia, on the wall framed newspaper cuttings and photos and on the desk a couple of model aircraft and a paperweight that claimed to have been fashioned from the nacelle of a Bristol Beaufighter.

"Now then, young feller, need to ask you a favour," began Mr. Barnet, causing O'Driscoll to wonder anew at what was coming. The Head was not wearing the expression of someone about to dish out a bollocking, in fact if anything, he was looking slightly ill at ease.

"It's like this," continued the Head, giving his left moustache a tweak, "We're taking on a temporary teacher for the rest of the year to cover Doreen Clarke's maternity, and I was looking for someone to act as a kind of mentor to her. You have a good way with the youngsters, stimulating classroom environment etc. but no insubordination in the ranks, just the type to show a newly-qualified teacher how to navigate through those treacherous waters we all face when we're new to the profession. So how about it, will you take it on?"

O'Driscoll listened to this request with some surprise. Receiving plaudits from the school leadership was not something he was used to, especially after recent events, but it was true. He did have few problems managing behaviour in the classroom and it was pleasing to think that his good practice was being recognized. As to Mr. Barnet's question, one didn't turn down such a request from the Head and it simply remained to accept it in such a way as to bank as many brownie points as possible to set against future cock-ups.

O'Driscoll sat back in his chair and crossed his legs in a manner suggestive of deep contemplation. With equal gravity, he folded one arm across his chest and rested the thumb and forefinger of the other on his chin. The image he was hoping to project was one where the seriousness of the task was understood, but equally there was a cold-eyed confidence in his own ability to carry it through. Studying American politics for his degree, he had read with admiration of the goal-oriented yet pragmatic operating style of the Kennedy White House and it was as if this steely eyed, can-do realism was now suddenly parachuted into West London. O'Driscoll slowly uncrossed his legs and reversed the configuration of arms, hands and chin, while continuing to rest a steady eye on the waiting Mr. Barnet.

"Well sir, no man worth his salt turns down a mission.... er.... request from his chief," he said gravely.

"That's the kind of thing I like to hear," said Mr. Barnet, rubbing his hands. "Now, here's something else I need to gen you up on," he went on, transferring the tweaking action to his right moustache. "The temporary teacher in question is known to me on a personal basis, and that's why I want someone right from the top drawer to look after her. Fact is, she's the granddaughter of a good friend of my father's. You'll have heard of Binkie Pugh, of course?"

O'Driscoll hadn't but was reluctant to appear like the kind of White House staffer who hasn't read the latest briefing paper, so his head performed an indeterminate rotating movement intended to buy itself some time.

"Or rather to give him his proper moniker, D.H. Pugh, the distinguished Second World War flying ace," went on Mr. Barnet with a smile, and O'Driscoll made a sound intended to indicate that, of course, now the gentleman in question had been identified by his correct title, no possible confusion remained.

"Binkie and my guvnor served together in the R.A.F. during the last show, batted on some sticky wickets, don't you know, and got themselves into some damned dicey predicaments. Anyway, to cut a long story short, lifelong friendship ensued and as a result, self and Binkie's son Douglas brought up almost as brothers. Both my Pater and Binkie now flown life's final mission, sitting up there right now with a couple of celestial G and Ts in their hands, I shouldn't wonder, but, and here's the thing, before they went topside, made Douglas and self-promise that we'd look out for each other - thick and thin, and all that. Well, the young lady coming as a supply teacher is Douglas's daughter, so when the position came up and she was in the frame so to speak, couldn't let old Douglas down." Mr. Barnet paused for a moment and O'Driscoll filled the vacuum by nodding empathetically, as if the procurement of teaching positions for the offspring of dead air aces was a run of the mill experience for him.

"Thing is," went on the headmaster, lowering his voice confidentially, "might be better if it wasn't widely known that the young lady was a friend of the family. You know what it's like, no impropriety of course, but tongues wag in a place like this. I've told the young lady, Prudence is her name, by the way, to keep mum about myself and her father being chums, so that side of the show is all pukka."

With fingers now travelling in the direction of his left moustache, the Head continued, "So what do you say, young O'Driscoll, two paces forward if you're willing to have a crack at the thing. Quite understand if you'd rather not, but dammit, I think you're the man for the job."

Having finished with this rhetorical flourish, Mr. Barnet leaned back and waited for a reply. O'Driscoll sat forward in his chair and assumed an expression which he hoped conveyed an appreciation of the seriousness of the job, but also a clear-headed confidence in his ability to carry it out, the kind of expression that he imagined the daring young technocrats of the Kennedy administration had worn when instructed to create a range of exploding cigars that would bring the nascent regime of Fidel Castro to an inglorious end.

"Well, young feller?" said the head, this time with a slight note of impatience in his voice, and O'Driscoll realized that he had once more allowed his mind to wander. Putting all the vigour he could muster into his voice, he replied firmly, "It would be an honour, Mr. Presi.... Mr. Barnet. I'll be glad to help in any way I can."

"That's the spirit!" said the Head and was in the process of pumping his colleague's hand when Mrs. Goodwin entered with some papers in her hand.

"I've got the details of the exchange students, Mr. Barnet," she began, but as she took in the scene, her nose began to quiver and her eyes darted back and forth between the two figures.

"I hope I haven't interrupted anything... important," she said, the tip of her nose performing minute oscillations in search of enlightenment.

"Not at all, Mrs. Goodwin, just discussing some points of the.... er.... curriculum," replied the Head. "Ah, the exchange programme, let's have a look. Don't know whether you're genned up on the business, young John," he said expansively, "but we're swapping a couple of students with our sister schools in France and the U.S.A. for a couple of weeks. We'll be sending Margaret Marsh and Thomas Hughes," he said, referring to two Year Six pupils whose saintliness was guaranteed to show Saint Catherine's in a positive light, "and these are evidently details of the young shavers they're sending us in exchange. Let's have a look," he put on a pair of reading glasses. "Right..., the French chappie is apparently called Henri Rives, aged ten, bit of a philosopher by the looks of this... now let's have a look at our cousin from across the big pond... hmm... name of Brett Donnelly, eleven years-old, and a confident and outgoing young man, it says here. They're a solid-looking brace, Mrs. Goodwin, have we sorted out a decent billet for them?"

"Well, sir" said Mrs. Goodwin "I was going to suggest that, with me and my Reg having had experience of the hotel business, we might put them up in our own humble abode."

"Capital!" replied the Head. "A splendid idea, have 'em where we can keep an eye on 'em, eh? Please go ahead Mrs. Goodwin, and thank you for helping out – you are a treasure beyond rubies!" Mrs. Goodwin got up to leave, and O'Driscoll made to follow, but the Head called him back and waited until they were alone.

"One final point. Prudence is a delightful young lady, but she is... how can I put it... not very wise in the ways of the world, full of youthful idealism and all that sort of thing. Also, she doesn't have any classroom experience, apart from what she picked up during her teaching practice. To cut a long story short, she's going to need careful nurturing. Can I rely on you, old chap?" Stifling an impulse to salute, O'Driscoll indicated his willingness to take on the task and, having agreed with the Head a suitable time to meet Prudence, made good his escape.

It was pleasing to think his star might finally be in the ascendency, especially in view of the tough decisions that would shortly have to be made about teaching contracts, so O'Driscoll spent a happy lunch hour in the staff room drinking tea and listening in a desultory fashion to the conversation that was going on around him. Mrs. Goodwin was again holding forth and over the course of the lunchtime gave her opinion on the war in Bosnia (sad, but what else could you expect, really, from Bosnians), the sexual indiscretions of President Clinton (his poor wife, but you know what they say about ginger-haired men), the disloyalty to her in-laws of Princess Diana (if she was mine, I'd put her across my knee), and the rash of sleaze scandals in the Conservative Party (doesn't surprise me in the least, you wouldn't believe what we used to find in the rooms after they had their conferences). This last observation produced a stampede towards the door from those who remembered her previous comments about The Willows and its wash cycle requirements. Joining the exodus, O'Driscoll began the journey back to afternoon lessons, only to see ahead of him in the corridor a cluster of arguing boys surrounding the figure of Mr. Li.

"They stole my Kit Kat!" a fat boy was wailing.

"Did you purloin this boy's chocolate?" Mr. Li was saying severely to two well-known Year Six miscreants, Joseph Harty and Anthony Price.

"We found it, sir, found it on the floor, sir," answered Price, and Harty nodded his agreement.

"It appears this item of confectionary belongs to you," said Mr. Li to the fat boy who took the bar and hurried off.

Mr. Li looked gravely at the two remaining pupils. "This type of behaviour reflects badly on the school," he began, "especially when it involves Year Six fellows. We do not tolerate the abstracting of comestibles here at Saint Catherine's. Is that clear?"

The two boys exchanged bewildered looks but other than that, seemed at a loss for a reply.

"Do you understand," went on Mr. Li, trying a different tack, "how serious a matter it is to be accused of snooping another fellow's tuck?"

The two boys looked at each other again, wearing panic stricken expressions as Mr. Li, who was growing increasingly angry at their apparent retreat into dumb insolence, thundered, "For the final time, have you been snooping another fellow's tuck? Answer me!"

"Can't sir!" replied a visibly agitated Price.

"Why not?" shouted Li.

"Can't answer you, sir!" howled Price. "Don't know what you mean, sir!"

"It's quite simple…," shrieked Mr. Li, patience now completely expired. O'Driscoll judged this to be an opportune moment to intervene before the situation got completely out of control.

"Mr. Li is telling you that stealing food is a serious offence and one that could get you into trouble," he translated, to the relief of the two boys. Equanimity restored, Mr. Li decided to give the miscreants the benefit of the doubt. "I will overlook the matter this once," he said.

"Thank you, sir."

"Now outside, the pair of you. Chaps like you should be punting a footer around the quad on a beautiful day like today, not frowsting in their studies. *Mens sana in corpore sano,* what?"

The boys exchanged glassy-eyed looks but otherwise forbore to comment.

"Right, cut along then!"

Once more Li's words elicited no response and the two boys exchanged further panic-stricken glances.

"Didn't you hear me?" said the elderly Chinaman, his voice rising in anger. "Cut along, I tell you!"

"Back to class, lads," said O'Driscoll quietly and the boys scuttled gratefully off.

"Thank you for your assistance, John," said Mr. Li, when they were alone. "I do wonder whether the boys have difficulty understanding my English. Is it clear enough to you?" O'Driscoll wondered whether it was worth hinting it was not the clarity of his colleague's speech that was the problem, rather some of the vocabulary he employed, but decided against it on the basis that Mr. Li was such a nice man. "On the contrary," he said brightly, "your diction would put most native Londoners to shame," and that was at least true enough, he thought as Li smiled and they made their way companionably down the corridor and once more into battle.

O'Driscoll passed a routine afternoon teaching P.E., did some marking and then headed to Ealing Leisure Centre for a five-a-side game. An hour's football did wonders for his physical condition and the six pints he poured into his dehydrated body immediately afterwards had the same effect on his mental state, so he arrived home just after closing time pleasantly knackered. A couple of hours later, the flat lay silent but for the distinctive voice of Shane McGowan, which was emanating from a tiny cassette player in the corner. '*I could have been someone,*' lamented Shane for the thirty-second time that year as O'Driscoll lay among the detritus of a large doner kebab, a can of Stella Artois cradled in the crook of his elbow. '*Well so could anyone,*' answered Kirsty McColl in the scornful tones with which all females seemed to invest that particular lyric, and on that note, as the can of Stella toppled slowly forward and began to disgorge its contents into the crotch of his trousers, John O'Driscoll drifted into sleep and into another day.

Wednesday

There was an air of activity around the Kennedy White House as John O'Driscoll, Special Assistant to the President, moved authoritatively through the West Wing, nodding crisply here and there to those whose seniority entitled them to such a greeting. An authentic New Frontiersman from the top of his crew cut head to the soles of his wingtip shoes, in-between he wore the regulation Camelot uniform of dark suit, button down shirt, sober tie. Striding purposefully into the Operations Room, and nodding curtly to the secret serviceman on the door, he noticed the usual crowd - Bundy, McNamara, Rusk - gathered round a conference table, while Lyndon, as usual, sat away to one side nursing his grievances. Over on the other side of the room was the real centre of power, the President, sitting in his favorite rocking chair, with in attendance, brother Bobby, arms folded in that familiar hunched pose, and Kenny O'Donnell.

"You wanted to see me, Mr. President?" said O'Driscoll, getting straight to the point. The Kennedys were not ones to waste time with pointless small talk.

"John," said the President, looking up from his yellow legal pad. "Thanks for coming over, I've got a job for you". As he spoke, he took his glasses off with his left hand while his right index finger tapped a tooth in that inimitable way he had. "I want you to go out to California and sort out those squabbling bastards," his New England accent elongated the vowel sounds of the expletive, "ahead of that damned Primary next year. We need someone who'll kick ass and get things done. Kenny here says you're the man for the job and I agree with him. Think you can handle it, John?"

O'Driscoll looked evenly at Kennedy. "Mr. President, does a bear shit in the woods?" he said and there was a chuckle from the three men. You had to be in the inner, inner Kennedy circle to use profanity with the President.

"Good, and you get on a plane tonight?" asked JFK. "I'm sure there'll be some lovely girl who'll have her Saturday night ruined," he went on with a twinkle, "but I'm equally sure when you explain that it's a matter of national importance, she'll understand."

"That's OK, Mr. President, they'll understand" said O'Driscoll, putting a stress on the 'they', and generating a conspiratorial laugh from his leader.

"Then get to it, young man. I haven't got time to sit here chewing the fat with you gang of Irish Mafiosi," said the President, lowering his voice. "I've got to discuss affairs of State with that crowd over there, God help me!" He inclined his head towards the conference table and it was O'Driscoll's turn to laugh as he headed for the door.

"See Evelyn for your air tickets," called out O'Donnell , and O'Driscoll waved an arm in acknowledgement.

He headed straight into the office of the President's long-term secretary, who raised her face as he came in, revealing the features of.... Mrs. Goodwin? Nose twitching and eyes darting, she asked what she could do for him. Totally confused, Special Assistant O'Driscoll looked through the window to Mrs. Goodwin's left, where the White House swimming pool could be observed. Lounging around on sunbeds were several bikini-clad lovelies from the typing pool, waiting to service the President after his meeting, and the young staffer couldn't help noticing that one of the nubile figures bore a striking resemblance to Karen Black. In the corner of the pool area, old Joe Kennedy sat in the bath chair to which a stroke had confined him, and leaning over him apparently in the process of giving him the last rites, was the unmistakable figure of Father Kennedy.

Oh, God, thought agent O'Driscoll, it's a dream - of course it is, it's a bloody dream - and a moment later this intuition was proved correct as Vice-President Johnson pirouetted into the secretary's office wearing a pink satin tutu beneath his shirt and waistcoat. The images of Camelot began to recede and the distinctly more prosaic ones of Southall rushed in to fill the space, as O'Driscoll realized that he didn't work in the White House as a Special Assistant, or even a catering assistant, but was a primary school teacher from West London in danger of missing morning briefing if he didn't get his skates on. Showering in record time, he grabbed a coffee and made it to school with minutes to spare.

Briefing was noteworthy only for the announcement that the two exchange students would be arriving the next day, and as the meeting dissolved, Mr. Barnet beckoned O'Driscoll over and told him the new supply teacher was waiting in his office.

"I think we'll let her shadow you for the day so she can get to know the ropes and then I'll introduce her at briefing tomorrow," said the Head as they walked down the main corridor. "Does that meet with your approval, young man?"

O'Driscoll replied in the affirmative and as they walked into the office, Mr. Barnet made the introductions. The figure that rose to greet O'Driscoll had the dimensions of a pear, but it was a large and battered pear, a pear that has perhaps fallen off the harvester or been knocked about on its way to market. It wore dungarees of bright yellow, a jumper of bright red, and a scarf of bright green and underneath all this, its feet were encased in a pair of oxblood Doctor Martens. The whole kaleidoscopic ensemble called to mind one of those presenters of children's programmes for the very young, and as Mr. Barnett performed the introductions and Prudence spoke, her earnest, rather breathless voice reinforced the image.

"Thank you so much for agreeing to be my mentor," she said in a breathless gushing voice and as she spoke, she blinked several times. Behind the thick lenses of the glasses she wore, her eyes were transformed into enormous white spheres that vanished and reappeared with disconcerting suddenness. "Uncle Lionel... I mean Mr. Barnet said you were going to take me under your wing. I can't wait to meet the children and see their angelic little faces looking up in awe and wonder."

O'Driscoll regarded her a moment while he considered his response. He thought of 5R, who he would be teaching in a few minutes, but try as he might, could not conjure up an image of them in which the word "angelic" had any place, and as for "awe and wonder" it was more likely to be found on the faces of staff as their best-planned lessons were reduced to chaos and confusion.

His mind drifted back to his own first encounter with 5R, when as a callow new addition to the teaching staff of the school, he had been asked at short notice to cover a Geography lesson. The member of staff who had directed him towards the classroom wished him luck as she did so in tones that had seemed to O'Driscoll to have an ominous ring to them.

"Right, settle down," he had said with what he hoped was an air of calm authority. "Now, you've been looking at the geography of Russia, I'm told. So what," he asked, turning to write on the board as he spoke, "is the capital of Russia?"

"A pair of hairy bollocks," came a voice from behind him, and O'Driscoll realized too late that he had committed the cardinal error of turning his back on the enemy.

He turned and faced the class. "Don't think for a moment that I don't know who said that!" he said, looking sternly out at the sea of faces ranged in front of him. He was aware that his voice, far from emanating authority, sounded thin and reedy, but he carried on. "I know exactly who said that, and that person is in serious trouble, let me tell you!"

"Who did say it?" innocently inquired a carroty lad in the third row.

"Now you… you just…," said O'Driscoll pointing a quavery finger at the boy before gathering himself. "Any more of that kind of talk," he continued, "Joseph Cahill, isn't it? Any more of that talk from you, young man, and you'll be in as much trouble as… as... that other person I was talking about."

He had hoped that this display of authority would quell the mutiny but if truth be told, he barely survived the lesson and was aware that in the brutal world that is education, many aspiring teachers have had their credibility irreparably damaged by such a start. He had in the end hung on by the skin of his teeth but it was a sad reflection on the Darwinian nature of his profession that many didn't survive such an introduction. On this sobering note, O'Driscoll dragged himself back to the present, and asked Miss Pugh if she would like to accompany him to his classroom so they would be ready for the start of the teaching day.

"Right 5R, I'd like to introduce you to a new teacher who will be with us for the rest of the year," he said as he began the lesson. "Her name is Miss Pugh and she's going to be spending a couple of days seeing how we do things before working in the classroom on her own." This was the signal for Prudence to retire gracefully to the back of the class but instead she cleared her throat and moved forward to the front of the room where she took up position in front of O'Driscoll's desk.

"I'd just like you all to know how much I'm looking forward to working with you," she began, blinking twice and causing two girls in the front row to start violently. "As you get to know me, you will find that I am your friend and I expect we shall have some exciting adventures together." As she spoke, O'Driscoll noticed glances being exchanged among the more high-spirited members of the class.

"And children," continued Prudence, "I do not want you to think of me as Miss Pugh. If we are to be such friends, I want you to call me by my first name, which is Prudence." She looked at O'Driscoll. "I'm sure that won't be a problem."

As far as O'Driscoll was aware, the school policy was that members of staff should be addressed by their surnames, but he didn't want to dent Prudence's enthusiasm, so he confined himself to replying that they could check this out later by looking at the policies folder. But Prudence had already moved on. "And do you know what, children?" she said, having evidently come to a sudden decision, "my extra, extra special friends call me by a pet name I have had since I was a child. Would you like to know what it is?" The entire room waited transfixed during the short pause that followed this comment.

"They call me Bunny!" screamed Prudence triumphantly, jumping up and down several times and clapping her hands as she did so. At this point, O'Driscoll made a mental note not to check the policies folder, for whatever the school's view was on the use of first names, he could say with authority that there was no precedent for staff being addressed by the names of small, furry animals.

"Would you like to call me Bunny, children?" Prudence was now saying and O'Driscoll noticed another series of glances heliographing around the room. Assertiveness was not a quality one would immediately associate with John O'Driscoll, but he imposed himself quickly on the scene and directed Prudence with authority to the back of the room while he restored order. Amidst the bustle of the class getting ready for the lesson, Joe Cahill's hand went up.

"We were just wondering, sir, will be having any lessons with Miss Pugh on her own?" he asked with a gleam in his eye and the class waited with bated breath for their teacher to answer. O'Driscoll recalled seeing a wildlife programme on T.V. in which a piglet had been detached from its family group and attacked by a pack of hyenas, and there was something of that atmosphere in the classroom now. If the pupils were not exactly smacking their lips in advance of the anticipated ripping of flesh from bone, there was a febrile air in the room that boded extremely ill for the future, so giving as vague an answer as he could, he moved the discussion onto less contentious matters.

The lesson proceeded fairly uneventfully until right at the end, O'Driscoll asked the class if anyone could use their knowledge of physical geography to account for the formations of frost that appeared on windows after a cold night. Prudence's hand shot up and although at first O'Driscoll affected not to notice the short, bouncing figure at the back of the room, he was eventually forced to acknowledge her presence and nod for her to speak. With the same breathless delivery she had used earlier and with a series of little accompanying jumps to punctuate the words, Prudence informed the class that she had always been told they were little portraits left by the pixies as they flitted about on their mysterious night-time errands. In the breathless silence which greeted this explanation, another ominous exchange of looks could be observed passing among the pupils of 5R and O'Driscoll hastened to bring the lesson to an end and dismiss the class.

The door had barely closed behind the last of the small exiting figures when Prudence turned to O'Driscoll and, eyes shining and hands clasped excitedly in front of her, said, "Aren't they the darlingest little creatures?"

O'Driscoll looked at her for a moment while he considered his response. There was no doubt that Prudence was enthusiastic, and O'Driscoll had been in teaching long enough to know that in a profession filled with the burnt out, the cynical and the disillusioned, enthusiasm was a quality to be treasured. He searched for a form of words, therefore, that while painting a relatively realistic picture of the student body, would not be so negative as to shatter the illusions of the new teacher. "We do have many wonderful children here who are a joy to teach, but there are also some who can be a bit... lively, and it's just a case of making sure our strategies in the classroom cater for that."

Prudence smiled. "The only strategy that matters is for them to know that they are loved and cherished?"

"Yes…," he conceded, "but they need to know what behaviours are acceptable and what aren't."

Prudence smiled seraphically. "Children are incapable of actually being bad and the behaviours that some call "unacceptable" are only their little cries for help when they feel restricted by pointless adult rules."

"But don't you think some of them need a bit more… structure?"

"No," said Prudence firmly. "All they need is to feel our love and trust and once they know that's there, they blossom like flowers."

"Flowers?" repeated O'Driscoll.

"Yes, flowers," said Prudence, a note of impatience entering her voice. "Open your mind and try to think of them as budding flowers in a sunlit meadow."

O'Driscoll opened his mind and tried to think of them as budding flowers in a sunlit meadow but, with 5R in the frame, the only horticultural image that suggested itself was an outbreak of deadly nightshade festering dankly in the corner of a slum terrace.

"There you are," said Prudence, watching his convulsions with a benign smile. "I told you you'd see them as flowers. You do see them as flowers, don't you?"

"Er…. well, not all of them," he replied, trying to choose his words carefully. If Ms. Pugh saw the denizens 5R as little flowers, budding or otherwise, she was, in O'Driscoll's opinion, off her rocker and a suitable candidate for the nearest funny farm. However, Prudence was now in full flow, the words rolling off her tongue in a breathless rush. "They are little budding flowers crying out for the light that will allow them to bloom and blossom and we are the providers of that light and it is only by giving them the freedom to express themselves that we can open up their little minds." As the torrent of words subsided, she blinked again and her resemblance to an earnest but spirited owl struck O'Driscoll anew.

"Er, yes …" he said slowly, again seeking to find the right note. "We can discuss behaviour management strategies once you've had some time in the classroom. Your approach sounds very… interesting. How did it work during your teaching practice?" O'Driscoll was aware that every practitioner who attains qualified teacher status has to undertake blocks of teaching practice during which their lessons are observed and monitored by staff at the school where they are working, and also by tutors at the institution where they do their teaching qualification.

"Actually, I did my teaching practice at a small independent school run by a friend of Uncle Lionel... er... Mr. Barnet. The staff there was very kind to me and I mostly did shared teaching."

There was now a small, but growing niggle in O'Driscoll's gut that the project he had taken on so blithely might not be as straightforward as he had anticipated. Prudence Pugh, while undoubtedly enthusiastic and motivated, clearly had no reservoir of teaching experience on which to draw, not even by the sounds of it, a teaching practice in a mainstream State school, where many an idealistic young practitioner has had their first jolting experience of the realities of a typical classroom. It was, therefore, a thoughtful John O'Driscoll who finally got into his car at four o'clock and made his weary way home.

Thursday

Morning everyone," began Mr. Barnet as he began the ritual of morning briefing. "I have only two agenda points for today. The first is to introduce Miss Prudence Pugh, who will be joining us on supply to cover Mrs. Clarke's maternity. She's spending a couple of days shadowing John before we let her loose on the children and I'm sure that she's going to be an asset to the school." This comment elicited a rapid fire series of blinks from Prudence's great orbs that in the dimly-lit staffroom created an effect not unlike the strobe lighting that used to feature in discos before it was linked with seizures. "The next item concerns the arrival of the two exchange students, who will be starting at school today. Mrs. Goodwin has kindly agreed to look after the boys while they're in the UK, so I'm going to hand you over to Mrs. Goodwin who will brief you on the two lads and give you her first impressions of them."

Mrs. Goodwin moved with dignity to the front of the room. "Good morning everyone," she said, inclining her head in the manner of a minor aristocrat opening a village fete. "As you know, we will be looking after two exchange students, Brett Donnelly from the USA and Henri Rives, (she pronounced it

Henry Reeves) from France. I can say they were both happy with the standard of accommodation. I'd have been surprised if they'd said anything else, to be honest, with our background in the hotel business."

Mrs. Goodwin paused and visibly preened as she came to the next part of the announcement. "The French boy was so impressed when he found out that Reg and I actually have, chez Goodwin, a fully-functioning bidet. I don't suppose there's one English residence in a hundred that has one. We only had it installed last year because of Reg's health. He's had this nasty fungal infection since he did his National Service in Malaya and it keeps flaring up, you know… down there. You should see it when the weather's damp, all weepy and dribbling with a sort of purple rash all over.…"

"And the American boy," interjected Mr. Barnet with some haste, "was he equally happy with the accommodation?"

"Oh, yes," came the reply. "He was just as impressed, although he did try to make a few comments about the garden. You wouldn't believe it, he seemed to think we should have a basketball hoop on the wall. Well, my Reg told him straight, we don't play that game in this country, at least the girls play something a bit like it, but definitely not boys and he'd better put that idea right out of his head, if he didn't want the rest of the lads thinking he was ginger. After that, both boys had a good night's sleep, and they're in the school office now waiting to start the day."

"Thank you, Mrs. Goodwin," said the Head hastily. "Well, chocks away everyone and let's get out there and give 'em a … er, let's make sure the children have a good day."

O'Driscoll's leisurely progress down the main corridor was abruptly terminated by the arrival of a small, blinking figure in multicoloured dungarees who approached with the speed of a psychedelic express train and screeched to a halt inches away from him.

"John, I've got a wonderful idea for tutor time. Look," she said, waving a large book in front of his face, "they've got these face masks from the Peter Rabbit stories that you can cut out. Why don't we put them on our faces and pretend to be the characters in the stories and the children can interview us. What do you think? Do say you think it's a good idea!" She jumped up and down and made excited squeaking noises.

O'Driscoll looked at the cavorting figure in front of him and his heart sank. "Shall we have a talk about it when we look at next week's planning," he said and led her wearily in the direction of their classroom.

After an uneventful day, Father Kennedy convened a brief staff meeting to talk about the service to be held in the church the following Sunday. It would be a kind of rehearsal for the first communicants, who were due to receive the sacrament in a month or so. The service would be an opportunity for the pupils to experience the rituals and routines that surrounded the act of confession, because in advance of making their first communion, all the youngsters would need to make their first confession. Hoping his attendance at the event would stand him in good stead when teaching contracts came up for discussion, O'Driscoll had agreed to support the service even though he had not himself received Holy Communion nor made an act of confession for at least a dozen years.

As he sat at the meeting table, he watched Kennedy's expression closely but as the priest's eyes rested on him, they did so with no more than the normal baleful expression of an ill-tempered porker. Kennedy began the meeting and it was evident that he was in a benevolent mood, for the aura of calm that surrounded his bulbous red nose was disturbed only by the gentle rising and falling of the great nostril hairs as they slumbered peacefully. As he half-listened to the priest droning on, O'Driscoll found his eyes returning again and again to contemplate the soft murmuring of that great olfactory organ. It was as if some fearsome creature of mythology had retired to its lair and fallen into a deep sleep.

Kennedy explained that several priests would take up position in the confessional boxes and that staff would sit among the pupils offering support before going in to make their own confessions. At this point, O'Driscoll realized that he would have to make an act of confession and that, with the transgressions of a dozen or so years to sift through, it would need to be a kind of edited highlights version, with a lot of the minor midfield stuff left out and only the serious penalty area criminality included. He would give that some thought on the day, he said to himself as the meeting meandered towards a close and staff started to gather their things together. I wonder what Karen's doing now, he thought, and at that precise moment, the door opened and she entered the room, looking around her with a diffident smile that melted his heart completely.

"Ah, Miss Black" said Kennedy, giving her a leer that was evidently intended to put her at her ease. "Thank you for agreeing to take on the role of staff liaison for Sunday's service." He turned to the others. "Sister Bernadette and I decided it would be a good idea to have someone from the lay staff to coordinate the events and see that everything goes smoothly." Karen smiled again and there was a murmur of approval from the group.

"Will that involve liaising with parents?" asked Geoff Turnbull.

"Not really," answered the priest. "The role is to make sure that everything functions smoothly on the day and that there are no little…. hiccoughs." O'Driscoll could feel the priest's eyes boring into him like gimlets as he said the last word. Assuming an expression of deep concentration, he began an elaborate search of the sleeve of his jacket for pieces of stray fluff and, having disposed in this way of three imaginary cotton threads and a hypothetical hair, placed his elbow on the table and cupped his chin in it with the air of a man perfectly at ease with the world. As he gazed benevolently around him, however, his elbow slipped and he lurched forward, jarring his jaw against the side of his hand. Sitting up as unobtrusively as he could and rubbing his chin, he realized that Karen had begun to speak. "Sorry to impose on everyone," she said, "and I know it's Friday tomorrow, but I was wondering if we could have a quick meeting after school, just to make sure we're up to speed with everything?"

O'Driscoll made the same vague assenting noises as everyone else, but inside his heart was racing. Here, surely, was an opportunity to show he could work diligently and harmoniously as a member of Karen's team while allowing her to witness occasional flashes of individual brilliance that would mark him out as special. He was aware that these situations could throw up moments of unexpected intimacy and he imagined them leaning forward together to look at the order of service and her hair falling forward and brushing against his cheek. With this in mind, he made a mental note to pay extra attention to his grooming and personal care the next day and then, his head buzzing with anticipation, hurried towards The North Star where he had arranged to meet Duffy.

Oh, it's you two," said the landlord whose lugubrious expression was worn mainly for effect and actually concealed a rather tolerant nature. "Would it be asking too much for you to refrain from starting the singing until a reasonable hour tonight?" he asked. "We had a party of pensioners in last week and it got so bad, they had to turn their hearing aids off."

"It's all right, guv," said Duffy. "We're only in for a quickie - promise. Now could we have two pints to be going on with…. oh, and twelve tequila slammers, please."

The landlord allowed himself the faintest of smiles. "I wouldn't put it past the pair of you," he said as he poured their pints and they retired in good humour to the corner.

"Is Micky coming?" asked O'Driscoll.

"It's funny you should ask," replied Duffy. "He said he was yesterday, but I think he may have copped off with Faith's mate, Maureen. They were exploring each other's tonsils in a most thorough manner in The North Star last week."

A moment later, the figure of Micky Quinn hove into view and when suitable refreshments had been obtained and they had returned to their seats, Duffy opened the inquisition on the events of the previous week.

"Did you cop off with Maureen then?" he asked Micky. "I phoned Faith earlier and she was most mysterious. I think the girls have been in conference."

Micky hitched his trousers up, not an easy feat to accomplish while sitting down, and confirmed that he had indeed taken Maureen out the previous evening and then accompanied her back to her flat in Greenford.

"Did you creep away once you'd done the deed?" asked Duffy.

"No, I stayed the night," said Quinn, "and I tell you what, she did a cracking breakfast in the morning; two eggs, three sausages and," with a pause for effect, "black *and* white pudding."

"Are you going to see her again?"

"She seemed pretty keen."

"And what about you?" asked O'Driscoll.

Micky paused for a minute and seemed to be considering the matter for the first time. "Well…" he finally announced, "she seems friendly enough." He took a swig from his pint and his brow furrowed in thought. "And I suppose a shag is a shag, isn't it?"

His friends hastened to assure him of the wisdom of this assertion, a shag was definitely and indisputably a shag, but Quinn was still lost in thought and didn't appear to hear them. "Black *and* white pudding," he mused softly, a faraway look in his eyes, "you could put up with a lot for black *and* white pudding." At that moment, his face cleared and he banged the table. "Yes, I think all things considered, I will be giving the young lady in question the opportunity to extend her acquaintance with the Mighty Quinn." He slapped the table again, sending beer slopping from his friends' glasses. "Now, whose round is it, and who would like join me in a little whiskey to help this beer go down a bit easier?"

By the way, how the hell did you pull that blonde piece on Saturday night, Duffy?" he went on incredulously, when the spirits had been safely procured and delivered. "You didn't leave the bar for more than a couple of minutes the whole night long."

"By the judicious use of eye contact, Michael," replied Duffy. "The eye contact was reciprocated, and the rest is history." O'Driscoll reflected ruefully on the fact that the only one of the lads who had a steady girlfriend, was also the one for whom casual conquests came the most easily. Duffy had a long-suffering companion, Faith, and by dint of the fact that he was currently living at home with his parents, was able to keep his extracurricular activities a secret. For O'Driscoll himself, who had his own flat, liaisons of a romantic nature were few and far between, and it was more likely that his flat would vibrate to the sound of Micky Quinn's stentorian snore than anything of a more intimate nature. He cast his mind back several months to his own last such interaction, a hurried coupling with a girl he knew slightly in the garden of her parents' house after a party. The furtive rutting had, he supposed, satisfied a basic need, but they had both been so pissed that he, at any rate, had felt no desire to renew the acquaintance.

"Who's that new supply teacher?" asked Duffy, and O'Driscoll groaned as he described the nursemaiding role that had been assigned to him. "The trouble is," he concluded, "she's got this bee in her bonnet about dressing up and pretending to be characters out of Beatrix Potter."

"Beatrix Potter?"

"I think so ... or it might be *The Wind in the Willows*."

"Sounds like she's one of those creative types," said Duffy. "Just leave her with 5R for a couple of days and she'll either turn into the big bad wolf or have a nervous breakdown and resign."

"Trouble is I told old Barnett I'd try and keep her out of trouble," said O'Driscoll. "Anyway, enough of all that, are we still going to Cheltenham on Saturday?"

Prudence Pugh was instantly forgotten as arrangements were made for the trip to the races. Having a weekend bet on the horses was a vice generations of O'Driscolls had indulged in and few of John's childhood trips to town had been complete without a wizened Irishman sidling up to his father and muttering "I've got one at Haydock!" out of the corner of his mouth. Although O'Driscoll had inherited from his father no acumen in making his interest in racing a profitable one – indeed as he got older, he wondered whether there was congenitally defective gambling chromosome lurking in the family DNA - the experience had left him with the ability to talk in a mildly informed way about equine matters, especially in crowded bars full of other fools like himself. As the arrangements for Cheltenham were agreed and Duffy called another round in, O'Driscoll looked at his watch and reflected that if he had just one more pint, he could still be home by nine-thirty, well ten at the latest, with a quiet and alcohol-free evening ahead of him.

The next time his eyes focused on the hands of his watch, they stood at ten past four. As he surveyed the scene around him, he realized he was back in his flat and that he had just woken up. The detritus of an Indian takeaway lay scattered around and its aroma combined in a most interesting way with that of Michael Quinn's feet, which were resting on the table only a few inches away from his own. The remainder of Quinn's bulk was stretched inelegantly out on an armchair that was struggling with the unequal task it had been set, and Duffy was asleep in the only other chair the room possessed.

As O'Driscoll's eyes moved across the room, they came to rest on a group of swarthy men sitting around a restaurant table and he realized that the film, *Goodfellas*, which they had sat down to watch a couple of hours ago must be playing in a loop because the scene being enacted was one they had watched earlier. For the fourteenth time that year and the second time that night, Joe Pesci's high-pitched, psychotic tones could be heard requesting clarification from Ray Liotta as to whether and in what particular way he (Joe Pesci), was a source of amusement to him (Ray Liotta). As the camera focused on the darting, nervous eyes of Liotta and as Pesci's chilling words, "Funny? Funny how?" echoed malevolently around the room a tray of saag aloo slid unnoticed down the arm of the sofa and began to disgorge its contents slowly into John O'Driscoll's lap and on that note, he drifted into sleep and into another day.

Friday

O'Driscoll's first waking thought was that the Shakespearean scorpions of the previous week had been superseded by a gang of spiders because his mind was full of elusive half-thoughts that scratched uneasily around on the edge of his consciousness and then scuttled away like malevolent arachnids when he tried to catch hold of them. He shook his head in an attempt to disperse the unwelcome visitors and, remembering the meeting with Karen arranged for later in the day and the need make a special effort with his appearance, dragged himself out of bed and opened his wardrobe.

Apart from his "going out" clothes, there was little to choose from, but his gaze eventually fell on a pair of beige chinos which, if worn in combination with the brown linen shirt that sat next to them, might bestow on the wearer the sort of rumpled elegance that Colin Firth had achieved when he played the teacher in the film, *Fever Pitch*. O'Driscoll brightened at this thought, for wasn't the Colin Firth character, like himself, an Arsenal fan, and taking that as a good omen, he tried out the lop-sided smile Firth had worn to such good effect while doing up his tie in front of the mirror. He muttered the names of the

1971 double team, "Wison, Rice, McNab…." in what he hoped were authentically laconic tones before jumping into his elderly Cortina and making it to briefing in the nick of time.

Mr. Barnett stilled the buzz of conversation in the staffroom by clearing his throat and then handed over to Mrs. Goodwin for the latest bulletin on the exchange students. The school secretary appeared to be taking her role seriously for as she sat beside the Head, she wore the look of a chief constable about to commence an important press conference. "I can report that the boys spent a comfortable evening at the Goodwin residence," she announced, acknowledging Mr. Barnett's introduction with a sober inclination of the head. "The French lad is very quiet, spends the whole time with his head in a book, didn't even want to play *Family Fortunes* when Reg suggested it. Did I tell you that Reg has got *Family Fortunes* on one of those disc thingies that you play through the T.V? You wouldn't believe it, but no matter how many times you put it on, it still comes up with different questions. How do they do that? Anyway, I think Henri sees himself as a bit of an intellectual. The other lad, Brett, well, intellectual is one word you wouldn't use to describe him."

"Will the boys be staying at your house for the whole time they're here?" asked someone from the back. Mrs. Goodwin was known to be unwilling to give up a role which gained her such prominence, and she and the Head could be seen exchanging looks. "I'm sorry but I'm not in a predicament to answer that question at the moment," she said smoothly, before handing the audience back to Mr. Barnet. He announced that the two boys would be introduced to the rest of the pupils at school assembly that morning, and that the climax of their stay would be the visit of the governing body of Brett's school to Saint Catherine's at the end of the following week. "The chair of governors is actually Brett's father," went on Mr. Barnet, "so I'm sure we'll all do our best to ensure that Brett's experience is a positive one. There is talk of the exchange programme being expanded next year if this pilot is a success, which would give some of you an opportunity to visit the school in America. Mr. Donnelly is also chair of the foundation that would fund such a trip," he finished with a twinkle of the eye and a tweak of the handlebar, "so I'm sure I don't need to say any more."

It was only as O'Driscoll headed off to his tutor room that he began to realize how bad his hangover was, and he promised himself that for one Friday night at least, he would resist the lure of the pub if only the fates would repay him beforehand by granting him an easy, trouble-free day. At that moment, as if in mocking answer, he heard his name being called in an excited voice and a moment later, Prudence bounced along the corridor and fell into step alongside him. "Good morning!" she said brightly. "And how are you today? I can't wait for lessons to start so I can see those gorgeous children again. Shall I go straight to your classroom and wait for you there or would you like to talk about what we're going to do right away?"

Without waiting for a reply and in the same breathless voice, she went on to say that she had been thinking about how a range of National Curriculum subjects could be addressed by focusing on a single topic and she wondered if he had considered the possibility of doing this through the Beatrix Potter stories which were so wonderful, weren't they, and although she now agreed that wearing animal masks in class before introducing the furry creatures to the children might be a little premature, she felt sure once they had been exposed to the wonderful stories, they would be queuing up to ask questions and get in role themselves and was he familiar with the Beatrix Potter stories, well of course, everyone was because they were a kind of national institution and really the possibilities for using them to deliver a range of National Curriculum subjects were endless, weren't they, there were the wanderings of Peter Rabbit and Benjamin Bunny that had obvious links to the Geography curriculum and there was the Tale of Samuel Whiskers which was clearly an allegory for good and evil that would fit into the R.E. syllabus and, of course, the story of the bushy long-haired gentleman who turned out to be a wolf was a perfect way to address stranger danger and meet the needs of the P.S.E. curriculum.

O'Driscoll felt like King Canute as he struggled in vain to repel the tsunami of small, furry creatures that was washing over him in wave after wave. Prudence stopped for a moment to take in air and he opened his mouth to speak but it was too late and an instant later she was off again as another torrent of words began to cascade from her mouth. She said she would be happy to take on any number of the roles but her favourite was Jemima Puddleduck who was such a lovely character, wasn't she, and had he thought about which animal he would like to play, because in her opinion, he would be perfectly cast in the role of Johnny Town Mouse, not just because of his name but because she could tell from his complexion that he didn't get enough fresh air and she'd be prepared to bet that if she asked him when the last time was he'd walked in a field and smelt the primroses, he wouldn't be able to say and did he think they would be able to start the project right away or wait till the end of tutor time and had he noticed there was a funny garlicky petrol smell in the air and she hadn't wanted to say anything but she had noticed it when they'd met and it seemed to be following them down the corridor.

Resisting the temptation to disembowel her on the spot, O'Driscoll reminded her as patiently as he could that her brief would remain a watching one until the following week, when she was to begin her own teaching, and that they could discuss her… interesting project at another time. He comforted himself with the thought that a lot could happen in a week – she might get a cold, she might be called away by a family matter, she might be murdered by a mad axe man! Realizing that his nerves were in danger of becoming completely shredded by a combination of last night's alcohol and this morning's exposure to Prudence, he took a deep breath, grimaced, swallowed an "OOST!" and contrived to get the class through the first couple of lessons without undue incident.

It was after morning break that the school assembled in the hall for the regular Friday assembly. Proceedings invariably started with prayers, led by Sister Bernadette, or if he was available, Father Kennedy. On this occasion, the priest was otherwise engaged so the tenor of the prayers focused more on the universal love of the almighty than on the searing pain of eternal damnation, which was a relief to all concerned, except perhaps, Miss Gillespie, who was one of those Catholics for whom the teaching that life was a vale of tears filled with suffering offered a kind of mournful satisfaction.

After prayers, Mr. Barnet took the floor to introduce the two exchange students. The imminent arrival of two such exotic flowers had aroused considerable interest among the student body and as the head began talking, necks craned along the rows as children sought a glimpse of the new arrivals.

"I'm sure you will all give a warm Saint Catherine's welcome to our two exchange students," he began as the two boys were ushered onto the stage. Henri was thin and bony with a pronounced Adam's Apple and protruding ears. He wore the lugubrious expression of someone who expects the worst from life and has long ago resigned himself to his fate. The American boy, by contrast, gazed out across the hall with that air of ease that his countrymen seemed able to assume wherever they were. It was a look that suggested that anyone who wanted to mix it up with Brett T. Donnelly would be taking on more than they bargained for.

Making a mental note to keep his wits about him when it was his turn to teach the boys, O'Driscoll headed off to class to practise his lop-sided Colin Firth smile. By the end of the morning, it was making him drool slightly from one side of his mouth and when he tried it out on one of the dinner ladies at lunchtime, she jumped in the air, took two steps back and watched him suspiciously until he completed his purchases and left the line. Managing to keep Prudence at arm's length for the remainder of the day, a feat which he achieved by sending her on repeated journeys to far-flung corners of the school to gather imaginary resources for nonexistent lessons, he duly presented himself in the staff room, only to be told that Karen had been delayed. She had apparently left a message postponing the meeting until five-thirty, adding that she would understand if any of her colleagues had prior commitments and wouldn't be able to make it.

It was inevitable that Duffy should arrive at that moment and suggest a "swift half" as a pleasant way of whiling away the intervening time, and consequently, John O'Driscoll arrived back at school two hours later with half a gallon of lager sloshing about inside him and a fatuous smile plastered over his face. Having made a detour to the staff toilets and evacuated his bladder, he hurried towards the staffroom, glancing down at the front of his beige chinos as he reached the door. What he saw made him stop abruptly in his tracks, for so wayward must his post-urinary shaking have been that the crotch of his trousers was now crisscrossed with a latticework of wandering piss trails.

O'Driscoll was far from being the first person who would curse the unfortunate association of beer and beige chinos but even he knew that this early in the day, the results would not pass the most rudimentary inspection. Acting purely on instinct, he dropped into a crouch, entered the staffroom like a turbo-charged Groucho Marx and hurled himself across the room into the soft seating area on the other side of the meeting table. Landing in a heap on one of the sofas and aware of the puzzled looks that his entrance had provoked, he sat up, crossed one piss-stained leg over the other and gazed across at his colleagues, wearing a smile so lop-sided that more than one of them wondered whether he had suffered a mild stroke.

"Hi John, thanks for coming," said Karen with a bewitching smile and resumed her conversation with the group. "Father Kennedy has asked me to make sure everyone knows what they're doing so I just wanted to run through the schedule. He did ask me to make sure that you.... that .... er.... everyone was aware how important it was that everything went smoothly this time." The fact that it was impossible to tell from her manner whether or not she was aware of last Sunday's cock-up and his part in it, made O'Driscoll love her even more and he resolved there and then that he would move heaven and earth to ensure that nothing should happen do disturb the harmony of this week's service.

His mind drifted into a delicious reverie: a small but fanatical group of Red Brigade terrorists had taken Karen and her colleagues on the organizing committee hostage, and were holding the screaming crowd of parents and staff in a corner of the church, waving their guns and shouting incoherently. O'Driscoll had volunteered to take Karen's place as a hostage and as the transfer was taking place and they crossed in the doorway, her tearful eyes met his and she stammered, "John, I can't thank you enough..." A crooked smile playing about his lips, John O'Driscoll silenced her protests by placing a finger gently on her lips and strolled with languid grace and without a backward glance into the maelstrom and into the jaws of certain death.

They might even make a film out of it, and he brightened at the thought as he pictured the last scene with the O'Driscoll character, played by Colin Firth, expiring in the arms of the girl he loved, the final shot being a close-up of his hand as it unfolded to reveal a row of safely defused detonators. Reluctantly tearing himself away from this apocalyptic but rather pleasing image, he realized Karen was speaking and listened as she made a pretty speech thanking them all for coming and calling the meeting to a close.

With his bladder once again sending out urgent signals, he made another journey to the toilet and then hurried towards the school foyer so that he might get there ahead of Karen and have a chance of striking up a conversation with her when she did arrive. He grabbed some items from his pigeonhole and then took up a position just outside the main entrance, leaning negligently on the rail of the ramp that led from ground level up to the doors. Hearing footsteps which were unmistakably female clicking across the floor of the school building, he assumed an attitude of studied grace and began to carelessly flick through the items of post which he had grabbed.

As the footsteps approached, his stomach sucked itself involuntarily in and whether it was this action that caused the sudden loss his balance or whether it was down to the lager, before he knew it his arms were wind milling violently and a moment later, he found himself toppling slowly backwards over the rail and head first into the wheelie bin that lay behind it. Fortunately, the bin in question was filled with discarded cardboard rather than food waste, and having scrambled to his feet, O'Driscoll was debating whether to leap out and explain that he had been looking for material for the class recycling project when he heard Karen's footsteps approaching and a moment later she had passed by and was gone. After a suitable interval, a tousled head liberally decorated with wood shavings appeared over the rim of the bin and gazed forlornly in the direction of the receding figure. A moment later the rest of John O'Driscoll joined it and, a cursory examination of his beige chinos having revealed that at least the urine stains were gone, he headed disconsolately in the direction of The North Star, cursing yet another missed opportunity.

Saturday

The pub near Cheltenham Racecourse was buzzing with anticipation and animated discussions were taking place in every corner, except for the one which Rocky, who had been attending a works do the previous evening, was occupying. He sat with his head in his hands, refusing all nourishment and occasionally muttering "Fucking Bushmills", but if he expected his plight to elicit any sympathy from his companions, he was disappointed. Micky Quinn did offer to buy his friend a packet of pork scratchings to settle his stomach and recommended a local brand whose manufacturing process was said to be so organic so many of the pork rinds still had hairs attached to them when taken out of the bag.

This was enough to tip Rocky over the edge and he ran towards the toilets clutching his stomach and making convulsive retching noises. Upon making a shaky return to his seat, he found that a case conference had been convened and he had been prescribed a tonic consisting of a pint of strong lager topped up with double shot of neat vodka. When the glass was delivered to his table along with a firm injunction to "Drink your medicine," he steeled himself and took a long shuddering draught before retiring once more to his corner.

By one o'clock, the party was feeling sufficiently bullish about the afternoon ahead to move across to the racecourse proper. Cheltenham was O'Driscoll's favourite course and the prospect of standing there on a cold winter's day listening to the myriad accents of old Ireland competing with the soft Cotswold burr of the locals never failed to lift the spirits. For O'Driscoll and Duffy, however, the great festival in March was off-limits because it never, NEVER, coincided with the school holidays. It was, in their eyes, a genuine infringement of their human rights, and the plight of those forever denied the opportunity to stand in the packed grandstand listening to the famous "Cheltenham roar" - a unique sound which seemed to O'Driscoll to be comprised in more or less equal parts of Guinness, greed and fear - was one they felt Amnesty International should direct its attention to instead of piddling round with massacres and torture and all that kind of stuff.

The first couple of races on the card were novice hurdles but the next two were competitive handicaps and there was much scurrying between bookmakers' pitches in an effort to get the most advantageous prices, O'Driscoll being particularly proud afterwards of the 8-1 he got against Addington Boy when the starting price was 6-1. He was relaying this information to his friends with quiet pride when Faith interrupted him by saying, "But John, it lost, didn't it?"

"I still got 8-1, though," he replied.

Faith considered this for a moment. "Sorry, I may be incredibly stupid here, but if it lost, it doesn't actually matter what price you got."

"Yes, but I got 8-1," answered O'Driscoll, determined that his perspicacity should not go unrecognized. "Micky backed it as well but he only got 13-2, and that lightweight of a boyfriend of yours actually came back with a docket showing 5-1. I honestly don't know how he dared show his face!"

"So let me get this straight," said Faith, warming to her theme. "Every time you lot go to the races, you hand over all your money to some git in a check suit, but as long as you've managed to get some completely pointless and notional advantage over your mates, that's fine and you can all go home with your heads held high."

"You don't understand," interjected Duffy.

"The only thing I understand is that the whole lot of you are even more bloody stupid than I thought you were, if that was possible," replied Faith. "And now," she said, turning to Sweeney and smiling sweetly, "having got that of my chest, I think it's your shout."

"Where my next pint," said Duffy a couple of minutes later. Sweeney, who was by nature one of life's gentlemen, was still on the periphery of the mass of bodies that was crowded at least four deep around the serving area so, with a snort, Duffy entered the fray and somehow burrowed his way through and under the mass of bodies to emerge at the centre of the scrum right in front of a barmaid. Even more remarkably, he contrived to make the reverse journey with at least six glasses in his hands and he then waited until Sweeney arrived, laden with drinks and apologizing for his tardiness, before delivering the immortal put down, "What do you expect when you send a boy to do a man's job?"

Betting notes were compared at the end of proceedings and sad reading they made - no winners, nothing placed, "not even a shout!" except for Rocky, who by one of those perverse quirks of fate, had made a remarkable recovery and backed three winners at decent prices. He was in one of those deeply annoying states of drunken self-satisfaction that his friends knew well, and they were good-natured enough not to kill him on the spot when he softly intoned the words, "Sixteen to one!" for the tenth or eleventh time. By the end of the evening, the remainder of the party had attained that same state of happy incoherence, after which O'Driscoll and Quinn somehow found themselves back at the O'Driscoll residence in the company of an Indian takeaway.

Sunday

After a hearty breakfast consisting of the previous night's left-over meat vindaloo, O'Driscoll and Quinn made their way to Osterley Park to play Sunday morning football. To say that the quality of play in the Chiswick and District Sunday League (Division 3) fell short of the highest level would be to understate its ineptness. The matches took place on fields that were bumpy in the summer and muddy in the winter and the players who shambled about on their unkempt surfaces were the flotsam and jetsam of the West London football world - obese, uncoordinated, unfit, or a combination of all three.

Their pre-match ritual consisted of sixteen pints and a large doner kebab, they breakfasted on thousand calorie fry-ups, or, in the case of O'Driscoll and Quinn, worse, and their immediate pre-match warm-up consisted of a couple of fags and a communal bout of coughing. The only way in which they emulated their professional counterparts was in the renunciation of sexual activity the night before a match, but they observed this "love ban" not in a spirit of denial, but because for the most part, they were too unattractive to find a partner for such an act. Players of all shapes and sizes dotted the playing area before kick-off, flopping about like stranded aquatic creatures, and once the game was underway, great gobbets of vomit would line the edge of the pitch as the players evacuated the previous night's beer, that morning's breakfast, or both. It was, in short, a scene as quintessentially English as the fabled summer village cricket scene, just a bit less poetic.

O'Driscoll and Quinn arrived with just a few minutes to spare and before them, an eclectic collection of figures could be seen lumbering towards the field of play, nylon kits straining at the seams. The opposing team was already on the pitch, engaged in a warm-up routine which appeared to involve several players huddling around a single cigarette and after a perfunctory kick about, the match started only fifteen minutes late, which was, for Division 3 of the Chiswick and District Sunday League, something of an achievement.

Within a couple of minutes of play starting, there was a crashing collision involving Quinn and a rotund skinhead with tattoos and this set up nicely the bruising and over-physical encounter that was to follow. Towards the end of the first half, Sweeney, who was playing in goal, came out to punch a cross and landed a devastating right on his own full back, knocking him out cold, with the ball fortunately sailing past everyone and behind for a goal kick. The application of large quantities of freezing cold water from a dirty bucket had the desired effect, with the left back deciding that unconsciousness was, on balance, an overrated condition.

As he munched a scotch egg at half-time, Quinn identified the opposing number eight as the player whose pace and movement in midfield was in danger of turning the match against them and the manager looked meaningfully at Rocky, who was known, not without reason, as the hard man of the team. O'Driscoll, squatting on his haunches and sucking air into lungs that years of smoking had rendered unfit for purpose, wondered why it was that grown men indulged in such a cold, wet and generally unpleasant pastime. It was partly the fact that on the rare occasion when one played a blinder, or scored a cracking goal, the resultant high made all the cold, wet and unpleasant times worthwhile, but equally it was the feel-good factor in the bar afterwards whatever the result, the beer flying down and the satisfied feeling of a body stretched to the limits of its endurance.

Within five minutes of the second half starting, the opposing number eight received the ball in the centre circle and pivoted in preparation to releasing a through ball. At precisely this moment, coming in from the left, Rocky hit him with a tackle whose concussion could be felt on the next pitch. To call it a tackle didn't do it justice – it was really three tackles in one, involving the simultaneous use of the shoulder, the hip and the foot. The number eight's frame slid slowly and silently down the length of Rocky's body and into a crumpled heap on the floor as Rocky raised his arms in mock innocence, directing a "Sorry ref, couldn't stop, ref!" at the middle-aged official as he approached. The hapless number eight was carried off and the referee awarded the other team a free kick and Rocky, a finger wagging admonition to be more careful - this was, after all in the 1990s, when football was still understood to be a contact sport.

The foul and its aftermath were the only incidents of note in the second half, and the game meandered to a 1-1 draw, both goals being the result of defensive incompetence rather than attacking verve. As they sat in the cold draughty dressing room afterwards, Rocky lit up a cigarette with the satisfied air of a craftsman who has successfully carried out a particularly challenging piece of work. "Bloody hell, that tackle was dead late, Rock," said one of the lads, to which Rocky replied with a shake of the head, "I know, I should have done it in the first half."

A couple of hours later, fortified by an after match drink in The North Star, O'Driscoll found himself back at the church helping parents deposit their offspring in that area where the confessional boxes, two permanent and four which had been erected temporarily to cope with the extra demand, had been set up. As the pews filled with serious childish faces and bored adult ones, O'Driscoll saw Karen moving towards the confessional area and his heart lurched. He gave her a thumbs-up to signal that everything was going well and she smiled back at him before sitting several pews ahead of him and to his right. He took his own seat, shuddering at the memory of the preceding Sunday's fiasco and resolving that this week nothing similar would occur.

Shortly afterwards, Father Kennedy made his entrance at the front of the church, followed by five other figures wearing vestments who then seated themselves on one side of the altar. Introducing them as priests from a nearby order who had given up their free time to help manage the large numbers expected, Kennedy explained how the service would work. "Thank ye all for coming. We want to make this experience as positive as we can for the little ones." He smiled in the direction of the children and some of the more nervous began to whimper. "We will therefore be allowing parents to support their children in any way they like, although of course they will not be able to enter the confessional with their young ones. Members of staff will also be on hand to help the children, and as part of that process, they will partake of the sacrament themselves."

It was only then that O'Driscoll remembered he himself would have to make an act of confession and he mouthed a not inappropriate, "Jesus Christ!" and wondered whether he would be able to remember the correct form of words. At that moment the phrase, "Bless me father, for I have sinned...." swam into his mind and he heaved a sigh of relief. At least he would be able to begin, and after that it didn't really matter what he confessed to because the priests didn't know him and would never meet him again.

Then he remembered that one of the priests certainly did know him and would be meeting him again and it dawned on him he might be about to enter a place of confession and confide his innermost thoughts to the Ayatollah of Saint Catherine's, a man he had recently observed hoovering up great quantities of white pudding while flirting (if that's what it was) with his septuagenarian housekeeper. Fuck that for a game of soldiers, was his initial thought, and he crossed himself at having used profanity in the house of God, whilst wondering whether the church differentiated in its sliding scale of penances between the sin of saying "fuck" in church, and only thinking it. It was an interesting theological point, and one worth discussing if he could only get out of this bloody madhouse.

He took some deep breaths and forced himself to calm down. The idea of making a confession to Father Kennedy was clearly preposterous, but there were six priests, which made the probability of drawing Kennedy five to one against, excellent odds. Moreover, he could observe which cubicle the cantankerous cleric went into and avoid that one to make even those odds redundant. Breathing a sigh of relief, O'Driscoll sat back to await developments. There might even be an opportunity to indulge in a brief, although of course decorous, bearing in mind where he was, fantasy about Karen, whose delicious rear view he could observe ahead of him.

The first intimation that his relief had been premature was when he heard sounds indicating the priests were entering the confessional boxes from behind, rendering them invisible to the congregation. O'Driscoll consoled himself with the thought that it was still five to one against. It was as if the roles had been reversed at Cheltenham yesterday and he was now in the role of a bookie, with six runners in the race and only one that would cause him damage. It was easy money really, he reassured himself, but his pulse still quickened as he moved along the pew and by the time he was next in line, he observed the six confessional boxes in the way that someone playing Russian roulette might look at the chambers of a revolver. The sight of a small figure exiting one of the temporary boxes signaled that it was his turn, and as he stood up, O'Driscoll took this as a good omen. Kennedy would surely have claimed home advantage and gone into a permanent box rather than one of the flimsy contraptions hastily assembled from balsa wood screens.

The moment he stepped into the small dark space, however, he recognized with a sinking feeling the same combined aroma of bacon and beeswax his olfactory nerve had picked up in the sacristy the previous week. Mrs. O'Reilly's devotion to the cleaning agent was so complete that she regularly applied it to shoes, vestments and any other items of clothing which presented themselves before her during her rounds. O'Driscoll's nerves frayed even further as he recognized the well-known growl, although it was evidently intended to reassure as it intoned the words "Come in my child," and as he knelt before the wire grill, he struggled to retain his composure.

"Bless me Father, for I have sinned," he began, trying to disguise his voice, and then ground to a halt. The next line of the incantation was supposed to inform the priest how long it had been since one had received the sacrament, but O'Driscoll quailed at the thought of saying, "It is twelve years since my last confession". The alternative would be to lie in the confessional, and enough latent Catholicism remained from his childhood to make this a distinctly unattractive proposition. He struggled to find a way through this theological minefield, but just when he was in danger of becoming completely unmanned, O'Driscoll suddenly saw the light. "Bless me Father, for I have sinned," he repeated, but he now spoke in a voice that was assured and confident, "It is one week since my last confession."

The moment he heard the words, "And do you have anything to confess?" O'Driscoll replied with lightning speed, "I have lied, Father," and then sank back with a sigh of relief. He had cancelled out the lie by confessing to it, and what's more, by confessing to it within seconds of telling it, so surely it hardly counted? There was, reflected O'Driscoll at this point as childhood memories came flooding back, much to be said for the Catholic Church's attitude towards the redemption of sin. You could, when it came down to it, do what you liked all week as long as you confessed it at the weekend, thereby entering into a state of grace and ensuring the salvation of your soul should you be unfortunate enough to get run over by a 207 on the way home. You could even plan a sin and have it expunged from your record by the simple expedient of saying, "I am sorry." O'Driscoll was far from being the first member of his faith to reflect that this was a most convenient arrangement. Staunch Catholics down the ages had used it as a guiding star to orientate their moral compasses and generations unborn would, no doubt, continue to do so.

Having admitted to his confessor that he had committed the sin of telling whoppers, O'Driscoll was conscious of a growing silence in the tiny dark space and realized he needed as a matter of urgency to fill it. And something else was troubling him – the need to somehow disguise his voice so Kennedy would not be able to identify him as the perpetrator of the crimes to which he was about to confess. Racking his brains for a regional accent to disguise his voice, he remembered an interview on Football Focus the previous day with the footballer Paul Gascoigne, and, his mind latching greedily onto that image, he plunged, without further thought, into a Geordie dialect, or the nearest approximation of it that he could provide.

"Well, Father," he began, and was rather pleased that he had contrived to pronounce "father" to rhyme with "blather", "the thing is, Father….," he went on, frantically racking his brains to think of a sin to confess and the vocabulary with which to confess it. "I…. I…. OOST!" he blurted out, and realizing that this was not a very promising start, took a deep breath and made a conscious effort to gather himself together. At that moment a thought – nonattendance at church – occurred to him and he once more latched greedily onto what seemed a nice, safe topic.

"Well, Father," he said again, wrestling with the syntax necessary to frame this concept appropriately, "the thing is, Father, I … er …I divven …er… I divven bin gannin doon to chorch, like."

The effect of these words on the other side of the grill was to produce a lengthy silence which was eventually broken by Kennedy saying slowly and clearly, "If English is not your first language my son, we can still help you…."

"Noo, noo, Father, man," said O'Driscoll desperately. "I'll taak a bit more sloo, like," he went on, adding, after a slight hesitation, "… though, but!"

He was beginning to realize Geordie may not have been the best dialect to choose – the only words he could think of were "bonny lad," and "pet," either of which, if spoken to the priest in the current setting, might lead to a misunderstanding. By now, it was too late to substitute another regional accent, he would just have to do the best he could with the one he had.

"Well, Father," he began again, feeling that at least with this form of address, he was on safe ground. Trying to make his voice sound less like Paul Gascoigne and more like Alan Shearer, he went on, "Well, I've bin neglectin' the missus and the bairns a bit, you naa, going oot on the toon drinking the broon."

He stopped at this point, aware that it now sounded as if he was delivering his confession in rhyming couplets, but as he opened his mouth to continue, he became aware that some kind of disturbance was taking place outside the cubicle. An adult voice could be heard speaking in tones both cross and imploring, "Now Michael, you promised you would and it'll only take a few minutes."

"Don't want to!" answered a childish voice loudly, "It's dark and smelly in there, and anyway I don't like that man, I'm scared of him."

"But it's only Father Kennedy?" responded the adult voice. "What is there to be scared of?"

"He's fat and hairy and ugly!" came the emphatic rejoinder. "And I'm not going in there!" It was evident that some physical pressure was being applied for there came the sound of a fierce struggle and a moment later, the walls of the flimsy confessional began to gyrate wildly. Within a couple of seconds, the seesawing motion had gained such a momentum that the whole contraption began to rock back and forth on its axis and, accompanied by a loud tearing sound, it suddenly collapsed around the priest and his confessor, leaving them sitting in splendid isolation less than a foot from one another. It was hard to say which of them was the more surprised, but as the priest cast his mind over the confessional conversation that he had just taken part in, and it dawned on him who his confessor had actually been, his face darkened with anger and his nasal hairs commenced a monstrous tango.

"O'Driscoll!" he breathed and he struggled to find words to express himself as the full weight of the transgression revealed itself to him. Eventually, he managed to spit out the words, "*You*, O'Driscoll! It was you all along!"

O'Driscoll's mind raced as it sought desperately to find a way out of the nightmare. For a moment, he considered claiming that he had just stumbled into the confessional box after colliding with a man in a black and white striped shirt carrying a bottle of brown ale, but even he realized that this would not wash.

Father Kennedy was working himself up into a fearful lather and his face grew purple with righteous anger as he hissed, "O'Driscoll, you have profaned the confessional!"

"No, you don't understand," protested O'Driscoll, but the tide of the priest's anger rolled over him.

"You have made mockery of a blessed sacrament with your... games," thundered Kennedy. Still frantically seeking an exit strategy that would allow him to escape with his life, O'Driscoll wondered whether, because his speech had obviously been so incomprehensible to the priest, he could claim he had been speaking in tongues. Perhaps if he lay down and rolled about on the floor shouting out random bits of Geordie, they might consider him "born again" and proclaim it a miracle. But even as the thought struck him, he remembered that the Catholic Church didn't really do speaking in tongues and born again and things like that, they left all that stuff to the Protestants. The only remaining device he could come up with was to faint on the spot, and hope when they eventually revived him, his indiscretion would, in the general confusion, be forgotten.

But it was too late. Kennedy was so incandescent with rage that although the resemblance to a pig was still apparent, he now looked like a porker who has been fed so much protein-enriched food that it is literally about to explode. "You will burn in hell for all eternity," he roared and there was a silence in the church as he gathered himself for his final sally. "O'Driscoll!" thundered the priest, his voice thick with rage as he delivered his coup de grace. "You are a tinker *and* a gypsy!"

Not for the first time, O'Driscoll wanted to ask the priest why he differentiated between two words that were to him interchangeable terms used to describe travelling minorities, but looking at the priest's face, he decided now would not be the time to make such a semantic enquiry, and anyway, there was no time for further conversation, for Kennedy swept away from the confessional area and was gone, his vestments rustling reprovingly in his wake.

As he bent down to play his part in repairing the chaos caused by the falling screens, O'Driscoll's heart sank. Word would spread like wildfire that he had blasphemed against the church and made a mockery of all it stood for by impersonating Paul Gascoigne in a confessional box. It was, put like that, a damning charge and one that would surely end once and for all any lingering hopes he might have had of getting that contract for the following year. He would thus face a bleak future, unable to continue worshipping the woman he loved from a distance without being able to summon the courage to actually do something about it and equally unable to fund the trips to The North Star that he considered so important to his emotional wellbeing. As he surveyed the carnage around him and reflected that they would probably blame him for the collapsing confessional box as well, John O'Driscoll felt a familiar sensation - it was the churning of his bowels as once again, they began the metamorphosis that would reduce them to liquid form.

Week Three

Monday

It was a grey and bleak prospect that met the eyes of John O'Driscoll as he gazed out of his window the following morning. Rats scurried forlornly amidst the detritus of the cash and carry and a dog nosing around across the road wore the same air of weary resignation. Upon arrival at school, O'Driscoll learned that Father Kennedy would be away on parish business for a couple of days, allowing him some respite before the dreaded moment when he would have to face his nemesis. His thoughts turned once more to the events of the day before and he wondered how on Earth he had allowed himself to get into such a ridiculous situation. After all, other people didn't feel the need to impersonate celebrities of stage and screen to disguise their voices from priests. If they did, Saturday mornings might present a strange aspect, with cries of "It's the way I tell 'em!" or, "Come here, there's more!" emanating from behind the confessional curtain.

Duffy had cried with laughter when details the disaster had been relayed to him and had forthwith bestowed on his friend the title, "Wor Johnny." And O'Driscoll hardly dared think what Karen would think of him when the reason for the disturbance was explained to her, which it surely would be. Now, as he stood at the back of the staff room, his usual Monday morning feelings of depression intensified a thousand fold, and he cursed the day he had ever entered a confessional box.

Mr. Barnet began briefing by reminding staff that the two exchange students would be beginning their first full day of lessons. "Mrs. Goodwin and her husband very kindly showed them some of the sights of London over the weekend and as we speak, the girls in the office are giving them tea and stickies, can't beat tea and stickies to set you up for the day! John, you're teaching them first, so could you pick them up at the end of tutor time and show them where to go? I'll pop in to the lesson for a bit and see how they're settling in."

The prospect of having the head in his classroom and looking on while he was teaching immediately set alarm bells ringing in O'Driscoll's mind. He had been told by a colleague who claimed to have heard it from "someone in the know" that, with redundancies from within the ranks of the temporary staff almost certain to be a necessity, the leadership of the school would be watching the staff concerned like hawks during the remainder of the term. A series of outstanding lessons or a notable extra-curricular accomplishment might be enough to tip the balance favourably in a close race, while on the other hand, a blunder might turn out to be the nail in the coffin of the unfortunate perpetrator's Saint Catherine's career. So the fact that within the next few minutes the Head would be in his classroom observing one of his lessons caused O'Driscoll's heart to drop into his boots as he frantically tried to recall what he had planned for the double period.

He collected the lads and introduced them to their new classmates before beginning the Citizenship lesson. By a miracle of scheduling, Prudence would be spending the whole day going through an induction process with one of the Assistant Heads, so at least he wouldn't have to worry about her. Mr. Barnett had already taken a position at the back of the class and O'Driscoll was horrified to see he was holding in his hand an object whose presence in the classroom had come to strike fear into the hearts of all but the most self-assured practitioners - a clipboard. Trying to keep his voice strong and quaver free and affecting an air of nonchalance that he had a feeling wasn't fooling the Head for a minute, O'Driscoll introduced the lesson by recapping what the class had covered so far. The week before, he had introduced the class to Karl Marx and, as often happens, the idea of collectivization and the eradication of private property, when explained in simple terms, appealed greatly to the minds of the young.

"So that means," said a boy called Mathew thoughtfully, "that if I wanted to borrow my brother's bike, he wouldn't be able to stop me because it wouldn't be his anymore, it would be shared property." It looked as if 6J were ready to embark on the road to a socialist utopia, until O'Driscoll gently reminded Mathew that his brother would likewise be able to freely access his collection of James Bond videos and as the implications of this became clear, there was a sudden braking of the ideological vehicle.

Until now, the exchange students had not contributed, so, aware of the twin threats posed by Mr. Barnett and his clipboard as they sat at the back of the room, O'Driscoll asked Brett what the views of American children were on communism. It was the first time the "c" word had been used and it produced a remarkable effect on Brett. "Is that what you've been talking about the whole time, communism?" he asked.

"Yes," answered O'Driscoll, kicking himself for not having made the link more explicit during his introduction. He risked a glance in the direction of his leader and saw to his horror that the Head was scribbling furiously. "Most of the governments that followed Marxist principles were communist," he said, trying to keep the desperation out of his voice, "we did cover that last week, didn't we, class?" but his appeal elicited no response and the class continued to gaze at their teacher with the blank, incurious expressions that a field of cows might wear as a tractor passed by in the lane.

Brett paused for a moment, presumably to marshal his thoughts. "My pop told me Europe was full of communists," he began. "He says it's bad enough at home with that douche bag Clinton in charge, but he said you guys had it even worse."

"Thank you, Brett" said O'Driscoll hastily and, feeling that he might be on safer ground with the French lad, asked Henri if he would like to make a contribution from his own country's perspective.

"My father, 'e follow philosophy of Leon Trotsky," came the reply. "'E believe in principles of syndicalism, worker council make decision for everyone and this produce society that is most fair and most egalitarian."

Taken aback somewhat by this answer, O'Driscoll debated whether to develop the point and show how effortlessly he could extend his teaching to cater for gifted and talented pupils, but he only had a vague idea what syndicalism actually was, so he decided to play safe by asking for any final thoughts on the main topic. At this point, an earnest boy called Francis put his hand up and said, "I think communism was a good idea, it just didn't quite work out." O'Driscoll had rarely heard the great social and political experiment summarized with such economy and recalling the huge tracts of analysis he himself had to plough through on the subject, he couldn't help thinking that if the message:

"Dear Karl,

It was a good idea, it just didn't quite work out.

Best wishes,

Francis Hernandez, aged 9½"

was chiseled onto a certain gravestone in Highgate, the lives of countless future undergraduates might be rendered a mite less tiresome.

He was about to embark on what he hoped would be an amusing but informative summing up of Marxism in the twentieth century when, with a smile, the Head bade him farewell and took his leave. Risking a glimpse at the clipboard as his leader passed, O'Driscoll was able to make out that a series of entries had been made on the page. "*Sausages, Lincolnshire, thick,*" said the first one and underneath it were two more that read, "*Bacon, middle, smoked,*" and "*Bathroom cleaner, lemon, scented.*" Mr. Barnett passed by before O'Driscoll could make out what the other inscriptions were and a moment later, the door had shut behind the departing Head and O'Driscoll breathed a sigh of relief as he found himself alone with the class once more.

It was a battle wearied John O'Driscoll who finally fought his way through to the end of that particular Monday. He had yet to face Father Kennedy and he was unable to decide whether to find the priest and try to explain his actions of the previous day or just leave it and hope that the incident would fade away. And then there was Karen – although she had not been in the vicinity when the incident had happened, surely word would have gotten back to her. Should he see her and try and explain or leave it and trust to luck? Putting both decisions off until later, he made his way to Monday's after school meeting, which Mr. Barnet had promised staff he would keep as short as possible.

The Head led off with some routine matters before reminding the group that Brett's father, together with a small delegation from the American school's governing body, would be visiting Saint Catherine's the following Thursday and staying over for the weekend. This would give them the opportunity to watch the staff revue which was to take place in the church hall the following Sunday afternoon. The revue was a Saint Catherine's tradition in which staff dressed up in costume to sing, dance, perform comedy routines and otherwise make fools of themselves and it was very popular with the pupils.

It was also the one occasion during the year when Father Kennedy came down from his ecclesiastical pedestal and showed his human side by dressing up in a clown's costume and performing in front of the children. The arrival on stage of a hideously made-up Father Kennedy had, on more than one occasion, prompted a spontaneous stampede from the ranks of the infant pews and every year, there was talk of a staff delegation approaching their spiritual leader and suggesting a modification of his appearance for future events. But Father Kennedy in a cassock exerted the same terrible mesmerism on the staff as Father Kennedy in a clown costume did on the pupils, so the idea never proceeded beyond that initial discussion.

"The event should give our American cousins a chance to observe the school in its wider pastoral role," finished Mr. Barnet. "And, as I said last week, if this pilot scheme is a success, there is an excellent prospect of the whole show being expanded in future years, with opportunities for our staff to cross the big pond and visit the school over there."

With a final reminder to his colleagues to "pull all the stops out when the brass hats arrive," Mr. Barnet called an end to the meeting and his colleagues drifted gratefully away. O'Driscoll and Duffy met on the way out to make arrangements for later that evening it was Faith's birthday and a gathering was planned in an Indian restaurant in South Ealing. As they left the building, the well-known façade of The North Star could be glimpsed tantalizingly in the distance and a keen observer might have noticed both of them casting surreptitious glances in its direction. A short period of silence was broken by Duffy's opening gambit of "Warm weather for the time of year."

"It certainly is!" answered O'Driscoll. "Did you manage to get a cup of tea before the meeting?"

"You must be joking, I'm parched!"

There was another longer pause while Duffy fingered his collar and swallowed extravagantly. "If we just had the one," he ventured finally, "we could still drive, and there'd be loads of time to get showered and changed before the meal."

"What time are we meeting them?"

"Eight o'clock."

"Eight o'clock! That's hours away, come on we've got loads of time, just one quick pint and no harm done."

And so it was that at the unusual hour of 4.15 on a Monday afternoon, Duffy and O'Driscoll came to be occupying their usual corner of The North Star with pints of Stella in front of them. The sense of having somehow subverted the normal order of things made the illicit lager taste even sweeter, and all too soon the two were looking regretfully at their empty glasses.

"Is it one pint or two you can have without being over the limit," asked Duffy, adding, "didn't they change it recently?"

"No, I don't think so, it's still eighty gills."

"It's not gills, you idiot, that's a measurement of spirits. If you had eighty gills in your system, you'd be dead from alcohol poisoning…" he paused for a moment, "… or I suppose you might be addressing a religious meeting in Ealing Town Hall."

"Ha, bloody ha."

"No, it's milligrams, eighty milligrams of something in your something."

There was a pause before O'Driscoll said, "Eighty is quite a high figure if you think of it, so I'm sure we'd be all right to have one more."

The third pint took even less discussion, for midway through the second, O'Driscoll remembered they were drinking Stella, which was a more powerful lager than the standard strength one they had been using to make their calculations. Seeking clarification from the landlord, they were both told they were definitely over the limit and if they wanted to go out on the piss on a Monday night, why didn't they just get on with it and leave him in peace. Retiring to the corner, they worked out a complicated arrangement in which a single cab would make multiple journeys between Southall and Hayes before decanting two squeaky clean teachers in Ealing well ahead of the eight o'clock deadline.

It was the sense of having problem solved so effectively that now allowed a fatal relaxation to occur, for when Duffy glanced at the hands of his watch he realized, with a thrill of horror, that they were pointing to a quarter to eight. Turning to O'Driscoll, he asked with some asperity whether it was because he (O'Driscoll) was such a fucking idiot that it was always left to him (Duffy) to organize everything? O'Driscoll replied with equal warmth that it had been he (O'Driscoll) who had worked out the taxi schedule while he (Duffy) had been busy making eyes at the barmaid with the nose stud, and that, anyway it was his Duffy's girlfriend's birthday do, so it wasn't his (O'Driscoll's) job to act as a nursemaid. This exchange resulted in both parties working all angst from their systems most satisfactorily, and it only remained to perform emergency ablutions in the pub toilet, put half a packet of O'Driscoll's extra strong mints sideways into their mouths and jump a taxi for the ten minute journey to the restaurant.

As he sat down near Rocky and Sweeney, O'Driscoll could hear Duffy explaining to Faith that because he hadn't wanted to embarrass her by giving her a birthday present in front of everyone, he had left it at home so he could present it to her in the much more intimate setting of the candlelit dinner he had booked for them on the following night. A moment later, Micky entered hand-in-hand with Maureen, and while Maureen commenced the round of air-kissing among the girls that would last at least five minutes, Micky spotted his friends and moved towards them. As he approached the table, however, a waft of scented air preceded him and O'Driscoll and Rocky exchanged

175

glances before Rocky cleared his throat with elaborate care and said, "I don't quite know how to say this, Mick, and please don't be offended, but are you by any chance wearing perfume?"

"It's not perfume, you cheeky bastard, it's aftershave!"

"Are you sure it's not perfume, it smells a lot like perfume to me?"

"It's not perfume. I keep telling you, it's aftershave!"

"What do they call it, this aftershave that smells like perfume?"

There was a short silence before Micky ventured, "Paco Rabanne?" He paused again and then repeated, this time with more confidence, "Paco Rabanne. Yes that's it, Maureen bought it for me."

Examining Quinn more closely, O'Driscoll noticed several other changes. Gone were the battered Wrangler jeans and tattered Ben Sherman shirt he usually wore, and in their place he was attired in a green linen shirt and trousers of a material not immediately identifiable.

"You're looking very smart, Michael." said Rocky. "I haven't seen you in that outfit before."

"Maureen gave it to me as an early birthday present."

"Very nice, but not your usual style, Mick," offered O'Driscoll.

"No," conceded Quinn. "Maureen said I looked as if I could do with a makeover, so she went out and got the whole lot from Paul Smith."

"What, she borrowed them?"

"Paul Smith's not a person, you twat, it's a shop, there's one in Covent Garden."

"Thank you for putting me straight on that," said Rocky. "And by the way, could I ask, if I'm not being too presumptuous, how long you have known Paul Smith was not a person but a shop in Covent Garden?"

"Since Maureen told me yesterday," answered Quinn with a grin. "I know it's not my usual get up," he continued, lowering his voice, "but it keeps her happy and costs me nothing, so what the hell."

"What material those trousers are made from?" asked Rocky, peering at the garments in question.

"Moleskin," answered Quinn.

"Moleskin!" exploded O'Driscoll, who had spent the last few days immersed in a sea of small furry animals. "Fucking moleskin! Quinny, it's bad enough turning up dressed like a character from *The Wind in the Willows*, but if you start twitching your nose and talking about messing about in boats, I won't be responsible for my actions! And I'm certainly not letting you crash at my place wearing trousers like that, there might be talk."

"Actually, I don't think I'll be crashing at your place for a while," said Quinn. "I'm going to be staying at Maureen's for a bit."

"Yeah, and we know which bit!"

"No, seriously," said Quinn, "I'm…. er…. moving in to Maureen's place…. that is…. I'm moving in with Maureen." Aware that his words had caused his friends to put their glasses down and exchange looks of amazement, he hurried on, "Just for a bit, like…. to see how things go."

"Sorry Michael, I must be a bit on the slow side, tonight," said Rocky, "but I could have sworn I just heard you say you were moving in with Maureen."

"Well, just for a bit, like," repeated Quinn, the note of forced joviality causing his voice to go up an octave, "just to see how things go. Her flat mate moved out a couple of weeks ago so she said why didn't I move in for a bit and see how things went. She said we'll see how things go and… and… she's not going to even charge me rent … and … we'll see how things go,

178

and … well, you can't say fairer than that." He began to pick his nose with an air of nonchalance that didn't fool his friends for a moment.

"I know she does a nice breakfast, Mick," said Sweeney, "but I was wondering whether you thought the whole thing might be a bit…. premature?"

"Premature!" repeated Quinn indignantly. "There's nothing wrong in that department, I can assure you…." His voice trailed off. "Oh, I see… premature…" His brow furrowed for a second and he gave his arse a ruminatory scratch. "Well, you could say that, I suppose, but as far as I can see it's a shot to nothing. I'm not paying any rent, so I can't lose out whatever happens." His brow cleared and a look of reminiscence overtook his face. "And after what she did to me last night…."

"And I assume we're not talking black and white pudding here."

"To be honest, it was more black and blue by the time she'd finished!"

"Well, good luck to you both, anyway," said Rocky and there was a chorus of agreement. "She's a brave girl, she must be if she's happy to share a toilet with your arse."

"Right, who wants a beer?" said Micky, clearly anxious to change the subject. "I'll go and see if I can drum up some service." Soon the food arrived and O'Driscoll found himself tucking into a lamb vindaloo, which he knew would play havoc with his constitution the next day. By the time he finished his curry and had another couple of beers, he was in the mood for mischief. Noticing Rock's mobile telephone lying on the table, he nudged Micky and whispered, "Come on, let's make a phone call."

Rocky, who worked in I.T., was the possessor of a mobile phone, a great big clunking thing which he took everywhere with him because it was a condition of his employment that he be on call to deal with any unexpected systems problems. Although hardworking and conscientious, Rocky resented taking calls when he was away from the workplace and his friends had become accustomed to the sudden ring of Rocky's phone triggering a convulsive start and a querulous response along the lines of, "What do the bastards want now and why can't they leave a hardworking man to have a quiet evening with his mates?!"

It was not long before one of his friends (no one was sure who it was, although many claimed credit for it) had a brainwave and soon no night out was complete without a small delegation creeping off and calling Rocky's mobile from the nearest payphone. Tonight was no different and on at least four occasions, the large clunking phone began to ring, causing its owner to leap into the air and swear violently. Those watching made mental notes, like judges at a talent contest, of the scores they would later award his reaction, while behind Rocky in the foyer area, O'Driscoll and Quinn could be observed holding up the restaurant payphone and representing the action of laughter in an elaborate mime.

What time the party broke up it would have been difficult for O'Driscoll to say. All he knew was it was an inauspicious start to a week in which he had only that morning promised himself he was going to reduce his alcohol intake drastically, take up running and clean up his act. Never mind, he reflected to himself as he arrived home, he had got the devil out of his system early this week, and it would be easier to ignore his seductive whisperings in the days to come. Pouring himself a final nightcap, he offered a silent toast to his friend for accomplishing the not inconsiderable feat of turning up to his own girlfriend's birthday party late, pissed, unwashed and presentless and somehow managing to get away with it. A few minutes later the glass slipped from his fingers and red wine began to trickle gently down into the body of the sofa, and on that note John O'Driscoll drifted into sleep and into another day.

Tuesday

The moment he woke up, O'Driscoll's insides told him that he was in for a challenging day. His bowels had turned to water, but the combination of vindaloo and lager in industrial quantities had produced a more sinister liquidity than the common or garden one typically triggered by the prospect of facing Father Kennedy and his morning ablutions were of a protracted and painful nature.

Upon arrival at school, he decided to skip briefing and spend the time in his classroom preparing for the day ahead, but as he entered the corridor a familiar figure rolled into view and bade him good morning. Prudence, for it was she, asked whether he had had a pleasant Monday and upon receiving an affirmative grunt in reply, went on to say that she herself had had a most interesting day learning all about the business of the school and wasn't there a lot to remember but she supposed that everyone found it confusing at the beginning and it probably all became easier once one gained a little experience and she was so looking forward to seeing the little ones again and did he think that they had missed her, she had certainly missed them, and she didn't want to be premature but she thought that she had made just a little impression on them and did he think she had made an impression on them and she couldn't wait to get started because today was the day she was finally going to teach them and she had spent the whole weekend preparing a themed cross curricular multi-cultural project involving the Beatrix Potter characters and didn't he think it was a much more, well, exciting way of bringing the curriculum to the youngsters and wasn't it a privilege to be able to have a part in developing those wonderful little minds and had he noticed that funny smell again, it was a bit like a mixture of garlic and petrol?

Making a mental note to double his normal dosage of extra strong mints, O'Driscoll looked at the small figure bouncing before him and considered his response. He knew that part of the mentoring role he had agreed to undertake involved Mr. Barnett doing a lesson observation on Prudence after the first week or two, to see how much of a positive effect O'Druscoll's input had on her practice. At the time, he thought little of it but now, in light of the scrutiny the temporary teachers themselves were said to be under, he was uncomfortably aware that Prudence's teaching might hold the key to his future at Saint Catherine's. It was not a comforting thought and, as he regarded the rotund figure capering about in front of him, his heart dropped into his boots.

"Er…. do you remember on Friday we talked about what we'd do this week," he began, speaking slowly and patiently, "and we agreed that during lesson three and four you would do some differentiated phonics work, followed by a writing task based on the family histories the children have been working on."

The two great orbs that were Prudence's eyes regarded him with something like reproach. "I know we said that's what I'd do but I couldn't help looking at the Peter Rabbit stories again over the weekend and I got so excited and I'm sure the children will enjoy it much more than silly old phonics and I've done lots of preparation and it will be the best thing they've ever done and they'll remember it for the rest of their lives." She began to jump up and down clapping her hands and making little squealing sounds. "Oh, please say yes, John. Please…"

"Prudence, I did make a promise to Mr. Barnet that I would help to make your placement a successful one," said O'Driscoll, trying to speak in slow and measured terms. "And I do think it would be…. unwise to try that particular approach with 5R until you've got to know them a little better." She gave him a crestfallen look and he went on, "There'll be plenty of time to try your project out in the future. Now, do you want to go through the lesson plan before the kids come in, there won't be time during lessons one and two, and I've got to see that ed. psych. at eleven o'clock?"

"So you won't actually be with me during lesson three and four?" asked Prudence and if O'Driscoll hadn't been suffering quite so much from the previous night's depredations, he might have detected a gleam in her eye as she spoke.

"I'll be there for the first ten minutes to see you safely started but then I'll have to go," he replied. "I don't know how long the meeting will last, but I'll be straight back. Don't worry, everything will be fine."

"I'm not worried now," answered Prudence, and a more observant watcher might have observed the same glint in her eye as she spoke.

At the duly appointed time, and having overseen Prudence as she set the class a phonics activity, O'Driscoll made his way to the conference room to discuss the challenging behaviour of a child in his class which had led to a referral to the learning support team. Having agreed with the educational psychologist a home/school programme to address the child's needs, he made his way back towards the Year Five and Six corridor, looking at his watch as he did so and registering that he had been out of class for no more than twenty minutes. As he turned into the corridor, he could hear voices coming from 5R's room, and he slowed down so he could get an idea of how the children were behaving now that Prudence was, for the first time, alone with them in the classroom.

The first thing he heard was a female voice declaiming, "I'm Jemima Puddlefuck, I'm Jemima Puddlefuck!" to the sound of laughter and exaggerated intakes of breath.

"Oo-er!" There was a long drawn out exclamation of mock horror from another female voice. "Miss Poo, Miss Poo, did you hear what she said?"

"Yes darling, I did, but I'm sure it was just a slip of the tongue," cooed the voice of Prudence.

"If she's Jemima Puddlefuck, then I'm Peter Shaggit," said a deeper male voice which O'Driscoll recognized as belonging to Joe Cahill, and this generated another chorus of loud and ribald laughter.

Upon opening the door and entering the room, the first sight that met his eyes was the figure of Prudence, her face half-covered by a cardboard mask, bouncing along one of the aisles in a series of exaggerated hops. She was surrounded by a crowd of raucous, laughing children, some of whom were egging her on with whoops and shouts. His arrival was the signal for a magical transformation, with serried rows of little faces instantaneously replacing what had earlier been a scene of chaos.

186

"Oh, hello, John.... er .... Mr. O'Driscoll," said Prudence, smiling sweetly. "After you left, we had a discussion and the class decided to vote on whether to keep doing boring old phonics or try something different." She smiled proudly. "Do you know there wasn't one child who didn't vote against boring old phonics, that's what we've agreed to call them, by the way, and, well, I'm sure you can see how much we were all enjoying ourselves." Manfully resisting the temptation to tear his colleague limb from limb, O'Driscoll gently but firmly reminded her of the requirements of the National Curriculum and the remainder of the lesson passed off without incident.

Walking towards the staff room, O'Driscoll suddenly caught sight of the figure of Father Kennedy in the distance. He was still a long way off and deep in conversation with Sister Bernadette, but there was no doubt that if he continued on his present course, he would pass O'Driscoll in the corridor. It would be the first time they had met since the confessional calamity of the previous Sunday and O'Driscoll had spent the days since wondering if he should try to broach the subject with the priest. The trouble was he could think of no set of circumstances that would explain why anyone would feel the need to masquerade as Paul Gascoigne while partaking of a holy sacrament.

As his nemesis approached, still deep in conversation with Sister Bernadette, O'Driscoll looked wildly around, but seeing no obvious escape route, deciding he would just have to try and brazen it out. He began strolling casually down the corridor but the nearer he got to Kennedy, the more conscious he became that his body seemed to have taken on a life of its own, for he was progressing in a series of elongated loping strides that John Cleese himself might have struggled to emulate, while his arms had begun to swing like great hairy pendulums. Taking a deep breath, he stopped and, taking the plastic wallet containing his afternoon's lesson plans out of his pocket, began to examine the pages with studied concentration.

As the two approached, he decided to give the pose just the right note of relaxed unconcern by leaning negligently against the wall, but unfortunately he had chosen to execute the manoeuvre outside an open classroom with the result that he shot sideways through the door and crashed into a set of lockers in the entrance lobby. By the time he had extricated himself from the jumble of student possessions, Sister Bernadette and Father Kennedy were almost upon him. He snatched a look at them as they passed, and caught sight of Sister Bernadette's face wearing its usual benign but sober expression. Kennedy, on the other hand, gave him a glare that would have sent a whole cathedral full of first communicants running for their lives, and his nostril hairs danced a manic fandango of disapproval, but other than that, he said nothing and passed on his way, leaving O'Driscoll clinging weakly to the wall and reflecting that at least the meeting he had been so dreading had passed.

He spent an uneventful afternoon teaching, and as he killed time doing some marking ahead of five-a-side football, he reflected that he hadn't had an opportunity to speak to Karen since the confessional catastrophe, and worse than that, it had been at least two days since he'd had a chance to indulge in a daydream or fantasy. Did this mean his infatuation was diminishing, he wondered, wishing there was some database that provided such information and making a mental note to put some proper daydreaming space into his future planning.

His marking completed, O'Driscoll made a detour to his flat to pick up his kit and then headed off to five-a-side football. It happened that on that particular night, the pitch was available only between the hours of six and seven o'clock, leaving the players showered, changed and on the streets at the dangerously early hour of seven-thirty. They repaired to the nearest pub and an unknown number of rounds later and with closing time approaching, a consensus emerged that the Indian food of the previous evening had lit a gastronomic torch that would benefit from the oxygen of further indulgence. That was why at just after midnight, O'Driscoll found himself sitting down to his second consecutive late night lamb vindaloo, and by the time he arrived home, his system was experiencing the warm glow of today that precedes the hot fires of tomorrow.

Wednesday

It was a considerably chastened John O'Driscoll who finally appeared in the staff room at eight-thirty, his body having suffered another painful and protracted introduction to the day. The head began morning briefing by reading an extract from the current edition of *The Catholic Herald*.

Staff and governors from St. Catherine's primary school shared details of the community work they do in the parish during a recent public meeting at Ealing Town Hall. Parish Priest Father Kennedy led the meeting and was supported by Sister Bernadette Mahon, and there were also eloquent contributions from younger members of staff including Sophia Gillespie, John Driscoll and Caron Black.

O'Driscoll caught Karen's eye across the room and mimed the action of slamming a glass down and then drinking from it and she put a hand in front of her face as she stifled a laugh. He took her smile as an indication that she had either not observed the fiasco in the church on Sunday or did not hold him responsible for it. Either way, her manner was a positive sign and he took it as a good omen for the future.

Briefing was fairly uneventful apart from the news that there had been an outbreak of hostilities between Brett and his Year Six classmates during afternoon school. "Bit of argey-bargy between young Michael O'Brien and the American sprog," said the Head. "By all accounts, it involved some rather… colourful language and Miss Gillespie had them sent down to me. I put 'em both on a fizzer which means they'll be kept in at break, but other than that, I don't want to make a big thing of it, not with Brett's father and the other Americans coming in a few day. After all, we don't want to jeopardize the special relationship after so many years." With a chuckle at his own wit and a tweak of his left moustache, the Head brought the meeting to an end.

As O'Driscoll headed for his classroom, his insides fizzing with tiny, vindaloo infused eruptions, he contemplated the day ahead without enthusiasm. Approaching the door, his heart sank as he realized that, for the second day running, Prudence had deprived him of the few minutes' grace that he would normally enjoy before the arrival of his tutor group. Her great owlish eyes blinked rapidly as he entered and she immediately launched into a new monologue or to be more accurate, a continuation of the last one. Wasn't it a lovely day, she said, and she couldn't wait to get started and she didn't want to spoil their friendship but she was a little cross with him for making her return to boring old phonics the day before when it had all been going so well and the children had been expressing themselves naturally and creatively and that was the way children learnt best when they said what came from the heart and not parroting what came out of stuffy textbooks and now she had gained some experience in the classroom, surely he wouldn't mind if she introduced a little bit more of Beatrix Potter when she took 5R after break that morning and did he think he was sickening for something as he was looking a little bit peaky and had he noticed that funny smell in the air again?

Grinding his teeth with the effort of trying not to kill her there and then, O'Driscoll reminded her that as part of the history syllabus, she was committed to teaching 5R about the Nordic invaders who had terrorized the English countryside more than a thousand years before. He was beginning to understand how the English villagers must have felt if the Norsemen's invasion was anything like the one Prudence had perpetrated on him. Having gently but firmly ejected her from his room by sending her to the library to find the relevant set of textbooks (they were actually in his cupboard, but he was worried for his sanity and her life expectancy if she remained in his classroom a minute longer) he headed back to the staff room to grab a much-needed coffee. As he passed Sister Bernadette's office, he heard his name being called and when he entered, found the nun sitting with the telephone in one hand and a piece of paper in the other. "Ah, John," she said, "I wonder if you could give me some elucidation on a word I don't recognize?"

"Of course, Sister, if I can," he replied.

"Could you tell me," she said referring to the piece of paper in her hand, "what a douche bag is?"

There was a pause while O'Driscoll cursed with all his heart the fates that had sent him past the Deputy Head's office at that precise moment. His mouth opened and closed like a goldfish in a bag while his face contorted itself into a succession of its most manic masks.

"A parent has telephoned to say Brett Donnelly used the word as a term of abuse addressed at her child," went on Sister Bernadette, who, concentrating on the piece of paper in her hand, was oblivious to O'Driscoll's frantic gurning. "It is not a word that I am familiar with, but when I asked the parent if she knew what it meant, she would only tell me that it is something that American women use." Raising her eyes from the paper in front of her, she asked, "Are you able to enlighten me, John?"

O'Driscoll had been frantically wondering whether one of the strategies he had considered in the confessional box, that of fainting, might serve muster in the present situation and had already started the process of swaying that would precede a graceful descent to the floor, when he suddenly had a

194

brainwave. Screwing his features up into an expression suggestive of deep thought, he replied, "A douche bag is, I believe, somewhere where American women keep lipstick and rouge and…. er…. things like that."

Sister Bernadette brightened. "So, it is what we in Britain would call a make-up bag?" she said.

"Absolutely, Sister!" replied a relieved O'Driscoll. "You've hit the nail on the head!"

"So if the word is used as a term of abuse to a boy," went on Sister Bernadette, "it is rather as if in the old days, one called someone a sissy. Would you agree, John?"

"Absolutely, Sister!" replied O'Driscoll, who was prepared to agree with anything if it would only get him out of the room.

"In that case, I think, even in these times of political correctness, we can treat it fairly leniently. Do you agree?"

"Absolutely, Sister!"

Making good his escape, O'Driscoll again cursed the fates that had conspired against him. After all, how many times did Duffy find himself having to define an intimate item of female accoutrement to an elderly member of a religious order?

Brett's use of the term "douche bag" had had the same effect on his Year Six classmates as it had on Sister Bernadette and, not wishing to appear ignorant of what was clearly a choice term of abuse, a delegation hurried to the school library in search of a definition. But the dictionary they consulted offered little other than a rather mystifying reference to "intimate irrigation" and the boys returned to the playground none the wiser, where they were met by a triumphant Brett.

"You don't even know what a douche bag is," he taunted them. "Fancy not knowing what a douche bag is, ya bunch of limey douche bags!"

Backed thus into a corner, they were left with little choice other than to have a stab at a definition. "We do know what a douche bag is," announced Michael O'Brien, putting as much authority into his voice as possible. "It's … er…," he suddenly remembered the words in the dictionary and had an inspiration, "it's something to do with geography!" As he finished speaking, though, he knew this shot in the dark had been well wide of the mark and it was a long time before he was able to forget the howls of derisive laughter that followed him around for the remainder of the day.

With Prudence primed to begin 5R's double history lesson about the Vikings on her own, O'Driscoll had agreed join her towards the end of lesson four. The class had been underway for only a few minutes when he was driven from the adjoining room where he was teaching by the sounds of pandemonium emanating from 5R's classroom. On opening the door, the first thing that he saw was a boy in a cardboard rabbit mask wringing the neck of a boy in a cardboard duck mask, while all around the room, small children dressed as small animals were engaged in similar life or death struggles. In one corner, a label with the printed inscription, "Rabbits' Social Area," had been Blu-tack'd to the wall and under it three boys in rabbit masks had mounted three girls in rabbit masks and were simulating the act of sexual union with a realism that belied their years.

Behind them, O'Driscoll could see a boy in a Jeremy Rabbit mask swinging his bag around his head like a modern-day Eric Bloodaxe, while in another corner, Johnny Town-Mouse was operating a policy of slash and burn that would have satisfied the most demonic pillager. In the eye of this Hogarthian hurricane stood Prudence Pugh with a serene, almost seraphic expression on her face. It took a little longer to restore order this time, and it was lunchtime before an uneasy silence finally descended on the battlefield. As the dismissed 5R moved towards the door, Joe Cahill stopped in front of Prudence and, wearing an expression of beguiling innocence, said, "We were just saying, er…. Prue, how we haven't enjoyed a lesson so much for ages."

Putting her hand on Joe's head and smiling indulgently, Prudence answered, "Thank you, little man." The action caused a dangerous gleam to appear in Joe's eye, but it was extinguished in an instant and he filed dutifully out after the other children.

Prudence turned to O'Driscoll as the last pupils left. "You see, John," she said, "how their little minds soak up knowledge when they have the opportunity to express themselves naturally, rather than just regurgitating boring old history, that's what we've agreed to call it, by the way. I feel that my teaching methods, if applied across the curriculum, could benefit the school and I'm a little disappointed that you haven't been as supportive as you could have been." At that moment, perhaps fortuitously, Mrs. Goodwin arrived to say Prudence was wanted on the telephone and, firing off a final volley of reproachful blinks from behind her spectacles, she trundled off.

It was at the end of the day that O'Driscoll was able to sit Prudence down and try to explain the concept of the National Curriculum and the statutory requirement to follow it in the classroom. "So you see," he finished, "all of us have to stick to what the curriculum says when we deliver lessons because that's what will be assessed at the end of the year." He concluded by saying that in order for that class not to fall behind, she would have to re-teach the lesson the following day, only this time sticking to the themes in the Key Stage Two programme of study, "Invaders and Settlers", and not those suggested by the works of Mrs. Potter. He offered to sit down with her and jointly plan what she would teach, and with some reluctance, she agreed, although she did express disapproval over the acts of violence meted out by the Vikings, particularly their lack of respect towards women.

O'Driscoll had another problem and it revolved around whether to introduce the class to an English king from the Viking period who rejoiced in the name, "Cnut the Great." He couldn't help feeling that asking Prudence to introduce this name to the children offered too many hostages to fortune. It would be a simple matter for the fertile minds of Joe Cahill and his colleagues to rearrange the letter and word order to produce an alternative version of the name and apply it to their new teacher. After what had gone before, O'Driscoll counseled Prudence in the gravest terms not to use the name, "Cnut the Great," and she agreed, asking whether she could leaven the diet of "boring old kings," with just a little element of roleplay. O'Driscoll was now so worn out that, other than wearily reminding her it was easier to exercise authority when classroom activities were more tightly controlled, he did not protest.

There was a drink on at The North Star that evening to say goodbye to one of Faith's friends who was going abroad, and in the same scenario that had been played out a couple of nights prior, Micky and Maureen made their individual ways to fraternize with their nearest and dearest. Micky was tonight wearing a pair of linen trousers, topped by a paisley shirt, while an expensive-looking pair of brogues adorned his feet.

"You been borrowing clothes off that Smith bloke again, Michael?" asked O'Driscoll but Quinn failed to reply and his friends couldn't help noticing that there was a restive air about the great man.

"What's up, Mick?" asked Sweeney.

"I'm hungry," replied Quinn.

"Well, get something from the bar."

"I can't, I've just come from having dinner at Maureen's."

"It's not Maureen's anymore, remember – you live there," said Rocky.

"Whatever," replied Quinn and there was a plaintive note to his voice.

"Anyway, how come you're hungry?" asked O'Driscoll. "Didn't she feed you?"

"She fed me all right," answered Quinn. "It was what she fed me on!"

"What was it?" asked his friends, interest now thoroughly aroused.

Wearing the air of a barrister bringing forward a damning piece of evidence, Quinn enunciated one word, "Couscous!"

"Couscous?"

"Couscous!" There was a pause while his friends looked at one another before Rocky asked, "What is couscous, exactly?"

Micky gave this question consideration and scratched around in his unruly red hair before answering, "It's hard to say, really. I know lots of things it's not, but it's harder to say what it actually is."

"Semolina!" announced Sweeney. "I read somewhere that it's a bit like semolina."

Micky farted thoughtfully and then, clearly unwilling to take the irrevocable step of ruling out semolina, replied, "It could be something like that, I suppose." As he spoke, he hitched his trousers up, but tonight the action was carried out with the air of resignation with which an ancient mariner, trapped at sea for days without sustenance, might have hiked up his canvas slops. "Couscous!" he said once more and it was clear that first, magnificent post-coital fry-up was but a distant memory.

Someone suggested they should drink Guinness in honour of Faith's friend and in the twinkling of an eye, several congenial hours had passed and O'Driscoll was looking at a watch that said ten o'clock. He would definitely not end up in that bloody Indian tonight, he promised himself, and if he left after the next drink, he could be home by ten-thirty at the latest with a quiet and alcohol-free evening stretching ahead of him. It will come as no surprise to relate that two hours later, he found himself sitting in a room decorated with flock wallpaper, with a pint of Guinness in front of him, contemplating for the third time in as many days the large, laminated menu of the South Ealing Tandoori.

Thursday

The moment John O'Driscoll's eyes opened he realized that, after three days of extreme overindulgence, his system was in a bad way. Having ignored the siren call of the vindaloo in favour of a marginally milder Madras the previous night, he had hoped that all would be well when he awoke but in fact the addition of Guinness to the usual *pot pourri* of vile ingredients sloshing around his insides had produced truly awful consequences within his digestive tract. Three days of alcohol had done nothing for O'Driscoll's emotional wellbeing either, and the scorpions and spiders of the preceding week had been joined by other sinister visitors. Bats, locusts, weevils, stag beetles, even earwigs scurried or flew into the darkest recesses of his being, leaving his mind at the mercy of fluttery, insubstantial, random half-thoughts.

He considered giving morning briefing a miss but as this would mean facing Prudence Pugh in his classroom, he settled on Mr. Barnett as the lesser of two evils. Briefing was a desultory affair, containing nothing of note other than the introduction of two new temporary teachers, who would be on supply cover until Easter. One of them was a prim-looking lady of uncertain years, the other a dark-haired young man who acknowledged the greetings of the staff with a languid smile.

O'Driscoll left Prudence to finish the Invaders and Settlers lesson in period one, and settled down to work quietly in an empty classroom in the Key Stage Two corridor. No more than twenty minutes passed before what sounded like a stampede of BSE-infected cattle caused him to put his books down, swear softly and go outside to investigate. What met his eyes was the sight of one-half of 5R charging down the corridor in enthusiastic pursuit of the other half, the performance accompanied by a cacophony of whoops and shouts that had doors opening and angry members of staff appearing along the passageway.

It emerged, when the subsequent inquest took place, that Miss Pugh and 5R had decided to present an alternative version of history in which the Viking invaders would be met by a delegation of Anglo-Saxons carrying garlands who would explain that rape and pillage were rather anti-social practices as well as being particularly disrespectful towards women. This part of the roleplay apparently passed off successfully, but it was during the next stage, which was to have Vikings and Anglo-Saxons returning to the village and setting up a Dark Age collective where every individual would be respected regardless of gender, ethnicity and sexual orientation, that things started to go wrong. The Vikings had decided to revert to their traditional ways and, led by Joe Cahill, had set about raping and pillaging with gusto.

The Anglo-Saxons had responded with a war-like spirit that their historical counterparts would have done well to emulate and the resulting carnage was what had caused so much commotion in the Key Stage Two corridor. The disturbance had gone down badly with the teachers whose lessons had been interrupted, and one or two had even threatened to take the matter to Mr. Barnet. As a lesson, it could hardly have gone more awry, the one merciful crumb of comfort being that Prudence had resisted the temptation to introduce the pupils to the name, Cnut the Great.

It was after lunch that O'Driscoll got the message calling him to Mr. Barnet's office and in truth, it was one that he had been expecting. Passing through the outer office, he was met with a breezy, "Come in, young O'Driscoll, and take a pew," and dutifully entered into the inner sanctum where the Head was waiting.

"Well, well, here we are. And how are you, young John?" asked Mr Barnett, tweaking his right moustache as he opened proceedings.

"Fine, thank you," lied O'Driscoll, who was physically and psychologically far from well, and hoping Mr. Barnet would get to the point before he started to feel even worse.

"Capital, capital! And how are things in Years Five and Six?"

"Well, as far as I know," answered O'Driscoll, hedging his bets until he knew where the conversation was heading. It was becoming apparent that under the breezy demeanor, Mr. Barnet was not sure how to proceed, but until he knew what his leader wanted, O'Driscoll was at a loss to help.

"And how is young Prudence's teaching going?" went on the Head, giving his right handlebar another twirl. "Is it up there in the clouds doing figures of eight and victory rolls, or is it the kind of ground wallah that skulks around at the back of the mess looking for free drinks?" O'Driscoll now realized Mr. Barnet was asking him to comment on Prudence's teaching, and a truthful answer would have been that far from being a "ground wallah," it was more of a demented kamikaze attack, hell-bent on annihilating itself and everything in its vicinity. Realizing, however, that it wouldn't do to share this analogy with the head, he said, "Prudence is a hardworking and dedicated young lady," and Barnett nodded approvingly as he went on, "and she brings incredible enthusiasm to everything she does."

"Well said, young O'Driscoll," replied the head, "but I sense a 'but' coming. Is there a 'but' coming, young John?"

Every fibre of O'Driscoll was screaming to reply, "She's barking!" but he knew this would not do, so he tried to think of a form of words that would express his reservations more diplomatically. "It's just that she is attempting some very ambitious lessons from a limited experience in the classroom," he said, "and she is reluctant to take advice. We all agree that the courage of one's convictions is a positive attribute, but," he went on, rather pleased with the words that were rolling so fluently from his lips, "it should also be tempered with the wisdom to listen."

"Wise words, young John, wise words," said the head. "I want my teachers up in the cockpit flying their kites, not skulking around at the back like tail-end Charlies. But," he went on with a jowly wobble, "they must also be wise enough to take evasive action when a squadron of Messerschmitts comes at them out of nowhere." O'Driscoll couldn't help feeling that the comparison between 5R and a Messerschmitt squadron an apt one, considering the blitzkrieg they had inflicted on the Key Stage Two corridor that morning, but forbore to share this thought with his Head and instead, simply nodded.

"Tell you what I'm going to do," said the Head, lowering his voice. "It's Thursday now. I'll let young Prudence have some time off, give the girl a couple of days to get her head straight. Don't want to dent her confidence, but it does seem as if she might be a bit.… vulnerable to some of our more lively sprogs." He paused to disentangle a small piece of gravy-encrusted matter from his right moustache, it had been cottage pie for lunch. "Then the three of us can sit down on Monday morning and work out a plan to get her teaching back topside. What do you say?"

O'Driscoll's first instinct was to grab Mr. Barnet and dance a waltz of joy with him, but realizing this might be misinterpreted, he confined himself to agreeing emphatically with the Head's decision. No Prudence for two whole days! If you included the weekend, that made four days! He left the Head's office with a song in his heart, reflecting that perhaps there was a God after all and resolving that in future he would communicate with Him in a more respectful dialect than the one he had employed in the confessional.

His joy was tempered when he remembered tonight was the night of the bring-and-buy sale, which was due to start at eight o'clock, and his heart sank at the prospect of an evening spent shifting videos and books from trestle tables to other trestle tables in an endless loop. Upon leaving the building, he met Duffy, who had agreed to help with the event and between them, they decided one way to compensate for the loss of their

Thursday evening - the traditional start of the weekend, really, and a night when they had always gone for a pint - would be to move their usual pub session forward a few hours. This was how they came to be occupying their usual corner of the pub, pints in hand, as the clock struck four.

"No whiskeys," warned O'Driscoll, remembering the last time they had visited the establishment before a school event, "or Sister Bernadette might end up with another bag of braille."

They made strenuous, but only partially successful efforts to moderate their alcohol intake but O'Driscoll found the beer actually had a settling effect on a stomach still fizzing from the malevolent combination of Guinness and fiery Indian food. With a quick freshen up in The North Star toilets - an oxymoronic activity if ever there was one - they contrived to time their arrival at school to coincide with the eight o'clock starting time.

The hall was busy with staff and other helpers and the two spent the next half an hour diligently carrying items in and out of the room. During one of his entrances, O'Driscoll bumped into Karen who was coming towards him looking radiant in a dark-fitted top. She smiled and his heart did its familiar somersault but there was no chance to say anything because they were moving in opposite directions. After half an hour of activity, O'Driscoll's bladder was close to bursting, so he made his way into the Gents only to find that Duffy had got there before him. Greeting his friend, he leaned against the wall of the urinal and sighed with relief as the merciful release of liquid began to empty his bladder. At the same time, he shifted his weight slightly and farted, but instead of the expected discharge of wind, a jet of hot liquid exploded out of his arse and into the folds of his boxer shorts.

He stood rooted to the spot, hoping against hope he had imagined the damp emissions but an exploratory wriggle soon confirmed that his initial impression had been accurate. At the thought of what he had done, his blood ran cold, and a further wriggle confirmed the same lowering of temperature was happening to the emissions in his boxers, producing a most unpleasant sensation. Three days of lager, Guinness and formidably spice-laden Indian food had, perhaps inevitably, resulted in O'Driscoll's digestive system emitting a howl of existential pain.

Sensing a change in his friend's demeanour, Duffy quickly ascertained what had happened and sprang into action. Explaining that a similar thing had happened to him a few years before, he suggested that, as the excretions in O'Driscoll's boxers were liquid and relatively untainted by odour, the best way to deal with them would be for him to sit down and let his body heat dry them away.

"You're telling me to sit down?" said O'Driscoll, aghast.

"Yes."

"Just so we're clear, you're asking me to sit in my own shit!"

"Yes.... well.... put like that, I can see why you might not fancy the idea."

"I should bloody well think not!"

Duffy was insistent that his plan would work, but did warn his friend that after a time, he might find his boxers had become literally stuck to him. On the night it had happened to him, he said, he had returned home full of warmth and bonhomie and forgetful of the earlier accident, had attempted an act of physical intimacy with his then girlfriend, as a result of which it had been weeks before she had spoken to him or allowed him to come anywhere near her.

Meanwhile in the adjacent hall, Sister Bernadette was scanning the room, looking for an additional trestle table to cope with the unexpectedly high volume of books that had come in when she noticed John O'Driscoll enter the room and cross it with a curious stiff-legged gait. Remembering he had recently broke up a fight on the playground, she wondered whether he might have hurt himself and watched as he crossed the room and lowered himself gingerly into a chair, an expression of deep distress appearing on his face as he established contact with the plastic seat. Karen came in at this point carrying a handful of books and Sister Bernadette called to her.

"There don't seem to be any tables free, Karen, but you could take those books and the others into that little storeroom over there. John," she went on, "would you be able to give Karen a hand and take the books into the storeroom and put them into some sort of order?"

O'Driscoll rose with alacrity from his seat, stopped abruptly halfway up and then receded slowly into a sitting position.

"Er... sorry Sister, sorry Karen," he mumbled, a strange expression appearing on his face, "I think I might be feeling a bit.... er.... faint."

"Better stay there for a few minutes, then," said Sister Bernadette.

O'Driscoll's own feelings, as he sat, literally glued to the surface of the chair, were too deep for words. Here he was, offered the chance to spend time alone with the most beautiful girl in the world, quietly sifting and cataloguing books in an atmosphere of seclusion and intimacy that might have led to who knows what. And why had he had to decline the invitation? Because he had shat himself - that was why! As he gazed disconsolately at the "Toilet" sign on the door, it seemed to offer a final damning verdict, for O'Driscoll worked in an environment whose practitioners habitually used the term as a verb. He was a man of nearly thirty who couldn't even toilet himself properly.

Friday

With Duffy's advice having proved well-founded, O'Driscoll avoided further embarrassment and was finally able to make his way home to a much-needed hot soak in the bath. The following morning when he arrived at school, Sister Bernadette made a point of finding him and asking him in a most solicitous way whether he thought he was all right to be at work. He couldn't help think that the nun was a decent old stick, though of course he would much rather have had such concern expressed by Karen, and when it was announced at briefing that the leaving do scheduled for Saturday evening was definitely on, O'Driscoll's interest quickened and he wondered whether she was planning to attend.

The only other point of note at briefing was the introduction of the visiting delegation from America, who had arrived the previous evening. There were six of them, school governors of both sexes and they looked a nondescript lot except for Brett's father, who turned out, like his son, to answer to the name "Brett T. Donnelly". Mr. Donnelly wore a loud suit and tie, when he introduced the delegation it was with a loud voice, and when he wiped his brow afterwards, it was with a loud handkerchief. As is often the case when teachers observe parents in action, it was easy to see Brett T Donnelly III in the voice and mannerisms of Brett T Donnelly II and staff could be seen exchanging amused glances.

Later in the staff room, O'Driscoll found himself in earshot of Mrs. Goodwin as she brought her audience up to speed with the latest doings of the exchange students. "Reg had great fun with Henri last night. First he showed him Lord Nelson's statue on the map and made a point of saying it was in Trafalgar Square, then he made a joke about going to Waterloo Station to see another place where we'd given the French a good hiding. "Funny, I'd always thought it was abroad somewhere." A sound somewhere between a gurgle and a cough from the corner made her pause for a moment. "Then Reg told him that we've hated the French even longer than we have the Germans. He even made a joke that if it hadn't have been for the English, Henri would have been born in Greater Germany and called Heinrich."

She gave another little laugh. "The American boy was taken with that. As for Henri, he was a real wet blanket and spent the whole evening mooning around looking bored. The only time he showed any interest was when Reg showed him a picture of Oliver Cromwell and told him Cromwell and his friends had cut Charles the First's head off. He sat up and took notice then, did Henri, said he didn't know the English did that sort of thing and wanted to know why we'd kept quiet about it. Reg put him straight and told him that, actually, it was only one king and that, anyway the English weren't the kind of people to boast about such things. No, when we had to execute our king, we did it with a bit of respect – a simple, dignified, beheading – not like a certain nation you could mention, turning the whole thing into a performance!"

As he sat reading, trying to filter out the sound of Mrs. Goodwin's voice, O'Driscoll heard Karen's name being mentioned and his pulse immediately quickened.

"Karen? Yeah, she's definitely coming tomorrow, she said she could do with a night out after the break up."

"The break up?"

"Yeah, she split up with Darren a couple of weeks ago, didn't you know?"

"No, I didn't even know they were having problems."

"Apparently things haven't been good for a while, but it came to a head a couple of weeks ago and she gave him the boot – that's why she didn't go to the Shakespeare thing or come out on Tracey's birthday."

"Poor Karen."

"She's well rid, if you ask me."

As he listened, O'Driscoll's eyes focused on the copy of History Today that was resting in his hands, but inside his heart was racing. He had always known in a vague kind of a way Karen was in a relationship, but his mind had shied away from thinking about it on the basis that ignorance, while not being exactly blissful, was some kind of protective shield against the misery that would engulf him if he did consider it. However, it appeared she was footloose and fancy free and while the idea of him registering on her romantic radar was clearly preposterous, at least his fantasies could take place in a world that was a tiny iota nearer to the real one. With the words he had heard giving him much food for thought, he applied himself willingly to the grindstone that was Friday afternoon and managed to make it to the end of the day without further incident.

Saturday

By early evening, John O'Driscoll was in an unusually ebullient mood. Having found out that, due to the illness of an elderly relative, Karen would not be able to coordinate Sunday's concert, but she would still be attending tonight's leaving do, he felt that the fates were for once looking kindly on him. Against all odds and in the face of all the evidence from previous events that indicated only embarrassment and tongue-tied failure lay ahead, somehow he had the feeling that tonight just might be the night he got off with Karen Black.

His preparations for the evening were unusually comprehensive. Having bathed, showered and deodorised himself, he brushed his teeth repeatedly and rinsed his mouth out with enough mouthwash to take the top layer off his soft palate. He dressed himself in his best "going out" clothes and, having subjected himself to judicious scrutiny in the mirror, turned to the vexatious question of aftershave. There were those in his group who looked on the use of aftershave in the way of those eighteenth century Scottish Presbyterians who believed dancing in the village square was the first step on a road that led inexorably to sexual degeneracy.

Micky Quinn, for one, was of the opinion that any man who chose to wear the product was by that act alone "suspect." His own recent flirtation with Paco Rabanne he excused on the grounds that it was worn to please another, rather than flaunted provocatively as a lifestyle choice. So it was not without trepidation that, having sniffed experimentally at a dusty bottle of *Blue Stratos* and decided its contents probably hadn't gone off, he wasn't sure whether aftershave did go off, or whether, like a good malt whiskey, it actually matured with age. O'Driscoll took the plunge and applied a liberal splash to each jowl.

With the aftershave dilemma thus resolved, he considered his next move. The others had arranged to meet in a pub at six-thirty, but with the function proper not due to start in the church hall until eight, O'Driscoll was determined that for one night at least, the cupid dart of love would not be skewered by the Strongbow arrow of drunkenness. Arranging his beige chinos in a way that would best preserve their knife-like crease, he sat down to wait, and it says much for his strength of purpose that it was nearly seven o'clock before his nerve cracked. Crack it finally did, and shortly afterwards, he was taking up his usual position in The North Star, seating himself and his Blue Stratos so as to keep them firmly upwind of Micky Quinn's nose.

His delayed arrival at the pub meant when O'Driscoll did reach the church hall, he was relatively sober, and the moment he clapped eyes on Karen, he was glad he had kept all his senses about him. She was wearing a pair of dark green jeans and above it a checked shirt from French Connection which had been left open to the third or fourth buttonhole and, whether it was a natural phenomenon or the product of some artfully-constructed scaffolding, tonight her cleavage seemed to have more definition than usual.

The whole arrangement was framed tantalizingly and deliciously by the cloth of the unbuttoned shirt and as he gazed, transfixed, at the garment in question, some distant part of O'Driscoll's brain began to send signals to his eyes, telling them to stop counting the buttonholes. After all, he didn't want to give the impression that he had been staring at Karen Black's tits, although, of course, that was exactly what he, and probably every other man in the room had been doing. Karen's hair shone with health and vitality and tonight she had tied it up at the back, allowing a curled ringlet to fall on either side and frame her face. It was a style that O'Driscoll had seen her wearing before and tonight, it left him as numb with desire as it had on the previous occasions. Divining something of this, Duffy observed, "Hey up, John. Karen's got her Hasidic hair on again," but when O'Driscoll gave no sign of having heard, Duffy moved his hand up and down in front of his friend's face and looked at the others.

"What's up with O'Driscoll?" asked Sweeney.

"He hasn't had enough to drink, that's what's up with him, the shirking git," growled Micky. He opened his mouth to continue but stopped suddenly and like some vast Celtic Hannibal Lecter, raised a quivering nose to the air, nostrils flaring as he scented the atmosphere around him. Satisfied that the suspect fragrance that was polluting the air around him had not come from his friends, he made his way to the bar.

An hour later, O'Driscoll felt like pinching himself to make sure he wasn't dreaming as he looked into the eyes of Karen Black, who was dancing with sinuous grace a couple of feet away from him. In fairness, it should be pointed out the two of them were actually part of a larger group that was dancing, with varying levels of coordination, to Jeff Beck's 'Hi Ho Silver Lining', but what could not be denied was that Karen Black was occupying a space on the dance floor not two feet away from him, dancing with him and doing her best to have a conversation with him against the ear-shattering backdrop of the music.

"Your hair looks nice tonight," he said, his heart thumping in his chest as he spoke.

"What?" she mouthed, with a quizzical expression on her face.

"I said your hair looks nice," he shouted, desperately trying to keep his eyes from travelling southwards towards that shirt and those buttons. She smiled and moved towards him so that her mouth was inches from his ear. "Do you think so? I'm sure I heard your friend Micky saying it looked a bit … Jewish."

When O'Driscoll indicated that he hadn't heard what she said, it was done partly to buy himself time but also so that he might once more experience the gossamer touch of her breath on his ear as she spoke. She repeated the question and he leaned back and subjected her face to a solemn and judicious scrutiny. "No," he said in answer to her question, "there might be a hint of Afghan and those earrings do look a bit gypsy – better keep out of Father Kennedy's way or he'll chuck you out – but it's definitely not Jewish."

There a pause in the music so she was able to hear what he said and laughed, shaking her earrings as she did so in a way that O'Driscoll found most disturbing. Feeling things were developing along most interesting lines, he wondered whether inveigling Karen towards the more secluded setting of the bar might be a good move. "Fancy a drink?" he said, just as another guitar riff drowned out his words but she shook her head and said, "Let's stay out here a bit longer, this is fun." As she floated effortlessly across the dance floor and O'Driscoll clumped after her, straining to keep his dancing just the right side of embarrassing, she smiled again. Gazing into her eyes, O'Driscoll couldn't see what was reflected in them. Was it interest? If so, was it simply friendly interest or something more? For the life of him, he couldn't be sure.

At that precise moment, the DJ did what all good DJ's do, which is switch without pause and without warning from a fast record to a slow one, thereby denying the girls who are happy enough to dance in the vicinity of the males near them but wouldn't be seen dead in their arms the opportunity to retreat to the seating area. O'Driscoll found that at the precise moment the first soft chords of 10CC's 'I'm Not In Love' replaced the more energetic ones of 'Hi Ho Silver Lining', he was staring straight into Karen Black's eyes. He saw them change, but try as he might, her couldn't interpret the new expression.

Was it embarrassment or was it something more? Bollocks, he thought, there's only one way to find out, so screwing his courage to the sticking place, he started to cross the space between them and at that precise moment the music stopped, the lights went up and Father Kennedy's gruff tones could be heard announcing, "I'm sorry to spoil ye're enjoyment but as chair of governors, I want to take this opportunity to make a small presentation..."

Immediately, the crowd took on a new definition and those in front began to shuffle dutifully towards the stage. O'Driscoll looked round but Karen was gone, leaving a tantalizing memory of that final expression her eyes had worn as the lights had gone up. Was it regret.... or relief.... or something else? O'Driscoll couldn't be sure and, not for the first time, he was forced to concede that, although he had a relatively wide knowledge of books and literature, when it came to reading the eyes of women, he was functionally illiterate.

He was later unable to say what the catalyst was for the unfortunate incident that then occurred. Perhaps it was the emotional trauma caused by his near miss with Karen as he saw her leaving the hall a few minutes later, or perhaps it was the truly colossal volume of strong lager that he then took on board to moderate that disappointment, but a scant two hours after he had gazed longingly into the eyes of Karen Black, John O'Driscoll found himself occupying exactly the same spot on the dance floor, only this time with a very different figure dancing opposite him.

Some thought the four girls who joined the party at nine-thirty in a whirl of noise and laughter were friends of Sue in the kitchen, while others believed they were connected in some way to Tracey Reeves, but it turned out that they were known to no one and had actually been heading towards a different venue when they mistakenly entered a likely-looking doorway. The largest of the girls wore her hair in a style known as the "Rachel" haircut from by the TV series *Friends*, and she wore it with confidence and élan, but even her best friend would have had to admit any resemblance between her and Rachel ended there. The second girl was wearing a top that consisted of a Madonna-style coned bra and little else, while the third was clad in garishly-coloured knee socks and clogs. The fourth, distinguished only by a curly perm at one end and platform shoes at the other, seemed tame by comparison to her friends. Within moments, the four girls made their way to the bar and were demanding to be served by Mr. D'Souza, the middle-aged church deacon acting as barman for the evening.

"Oi, four Diamond Whites over 'ere, Gunga Din, jeldi, jeldi!" shouted the one in the knee socks and clogs as the four took up position at the bar. At that moment, Father Kennedy passed by wearing his usual forbidding expression and the one with the Rachel hair said, "Fuck me, Tray, I didn't know it was a vicar and tarts do."

"I'm not going down on me knees to that ugly old bugger for no one," said the one with the knee socks and there were screams of laughter from her friends.

"Might put a smile on his face if you did, miserable-looking old sod," said the one with the curly perm. "I bet his crucifix hasn't seen any action for years."

O'Driscoll could not later recall the precise sequence of events that culminated in him and the one with the curly perm gyrating and cavorting madly on the dance floor while a cheering crowd egged them on. He could only remember a mad, frenetic hour in which beer had followed beer and whiskey had followed whiskey as he determined to put the disappointment of the near miss with Karen behind him. It was when Chuck Berry's 'C'est La Vie' song, the one John Travolta and Uma Thurman had danced to in Tarantino's *Pulp Fiction*, began to play that O'Driscoll leapt to his feet and started imitating the Travolta half of the dance.

The one with the curly perm jumped up and within moments the two were out on the dance floor, doing their best to imitate the sinuous, sexy moves that the two stars had acted out in the film. When O'Driscoll kicked off his shoes, a la Travolta, a large white toe could be seen protruding from the end of not one but both of his black socks, and one of the socks also contained a second hole so large that Duffy's subsequent description of the garment as being "more hole than sock" could not be disputed. Concentrating all his attention on mirroring the movements of his partner, O'Driscoll followed as, Uma

Thurman-style, the one with the curly perm drew her nicotine-stained fingers backwards and forwards across her face.

The performance moved into territories that would have confirmed the worst fears of any watching Scottish Presbyterian as both dancers began to gyrate and make thrusting movements with their groins. A future generation would invent a word "twerking" to represent these actions, but in 1995 there was no language to describe them other than some variation on the generic term "making a cunt of yourself", which Micky Quinn employed to cover a multitude of sins.

"C'mon, Tray, hitch your skirt up a bit higher!" called out the one with the Rachel hair.

"Any higher and they'll be able to see me kebab!"

Abandoning himself to the moment, O'Driscoll began to fondle his own genitalia in an ostentatious manner, whilst grinding his backside into the receptive lap of his partner. He had just thrust his groin for the third or fourth time in the direction of the crowd when it parted as if by magic and he suddenly saw Karen, standing a few feet away and taking in the whole scene. In another second, the gap had closed and she was lost to view but O'Driscoll would recall forever that frozen moment, when he had looked into Karen Black's eyes and seen.... Afterwards, he couldn't be sure what he had seen but for this once, he was glad of his inability to read meaning in women's eyes. A moment later, the music stopped and O'Driscoll was swept away as part of the drunken scrum that moved towards the bar area and, although he looked around for Karen, she was nowhere to be seen and seemed to have left as suddenly as she had arrived.

Before long, the lights were going up and few moments later, still with the four girls in tow, the lads assembled outside on Ealing Broadway. The one in the curly perm was being sick to a noisy accompaniment of "Hoick it up, Tray!" and "Better out than in, babes!" while a trickling sound from further down the alley suggested the one with the Rachel hair was evacuating another part of her anatomy.

At that moment, while no one was looking, O'Driscoll took the opportunity to slip away – he wouldn't be missed in all the confusion and anyway, he wanted to be alone with his shame.

Sunday

It was a much-chastened John O'Driscoll who awoke the next morning and as he contemplated the hours ahead, he cursed his past Catholic upbringing and current Catholic employment for ruining yet another Sunday. The staff concert was to take place at four o'clock and with Father Kennedy expected to be busy getting made up and into costume, a few members of staff, among them O'Driscoll and Duffy, had been nominated to entertain the American delegation and generally keep an eye on things. Upon arrival at the sacristy they knocked on the well-remembered oaken door, and a few moments later, dragging footsteps signaled the approach of Mrs. O'Reilly, Father Kennedy's elderly and irascible housekeeper. She studied O'Driscoll's face with a look in which disfavour and dementia were represented in roughly equal parts, until memory triumphed and she recognized him as the young man who had been behaving strangely in the hall a couple of weeks before.

"Afternoon, Mrs. O'Reilly," he said brightly, before adding sotto voce, for it was well-known that the old lady was three-parts deaf, "you mad old biddy."

Mrs. O'Reilly looked at him suspiciously. "What did you say?" she asked sharply, twiddling the dial on what was evidently a new hearing aid, for its surface was as yet uncontaminated by dust or furniture polish.

"Er... I said those flowers look pretty," answered O'Driscoll, pointing to a vase of tired-looking daffodils. "I've come to help with the concert," he went on, speaking slowly and with exaggerated care.

"You don't have to shout, I'm not deaf," she snapped and opened the door to let them in. "Father Kennedy is preparing his performance," she continued, enunciating the last word with the reverence which Laurence Olivier's dresser might have referred to his *Hamlet*, "but I'll take you into the dining room." They entered the room to find that the visiting delegation had already arrived and Duffy, and asked if there was anything with which they could help.

"Thank you, young man," answered Mr. Donnelly, who had clearly taken upon himself the role of spokesman for the group. There followed a few minutes of desultory conversation before one of the group noticed a large map of Ireland on the wall and Mr. Donnelly asked whether one of their hosts would like to give them an interpretation of The Troubles from a UK perspective. O'Driscoll took up a position in front of the wall and indicated the large expanse of green which comprised the greater part of the map.

"This is free Ireland," he began, and was rewarded with several nods of recognition from his audience.

"And these," he continued, pointing to the area coloured red, "are the occupied territories...."

He was about to continue when he noticed Sister Bernadette had entered and was directing a warning look at him. The nun was looking a little flustered and, knowing how important it was to her that the visit was a success, O'Driscoll resolved to desist from further pissing about in front of the Americans. Sister Bernadette greeted the visitors warmly, enquired as to whether they had been given everything they needed and informed them that Father Kennedy would join them for a few minutes before completing his preparations for the performance. The visitors would then be escorted to the school hall where they could watch final preparations for the show and then the performance itself. The nun also informed the delegation that if anyone wanted to have a drink or use the toilet facilities, they would have to get the key from Father Kennedy, since the kitchen was kept locked after it had been broken into during a recent function.

At this point, Father Kennedy entered the room, and it was immediately evident that he had begun the process of preparing

231

for the performance because, although he was still wearing a cassock, his face bore evidence of the application of stage make-up, and he carried with him the small pencil case in which he kept his face paints. His entrance created something of a stir among the American delegation for though Father Kennedy scrubbed and polished and at his best was no oil painting, with the application of layers of heavily-tinted make-up, his face had assumed an aspect that almost defied description.

O'Driscoll could hardly blame the Americans for their reaction. As a child, the filmed version of *The Hunchback of Notre Dame* starring Charles Laughton had caused him to have recurring nightmares and as he looked at the priest, it was as if the faces of Laughton's Quasimodo and John Hurt's Quentin Crisp in *The Naked Civil Servant* had morphed together in some terrible act of transmutation. As Kennedy moved towards the centre of the room, one of the delegates took an involuntary step backwards, and from the rear of the group, there came something that sounded like a gasp. There was a discernible air of relief among the visitors when the priest left, reminding Sister Bernadette as he did so that the key to the kitchen would remain in the bag containing his face paints. Sister Bernadette too departed almost immediately on some unknown mission, leaving O'Driscoll and Duffy with the visitors.

There was a short, charged silence before a visibly nervous delegate asked, "Does Father Kennedy often wear…. er…. make-up?" The obvious response would have been for O'Driscoll or Duffy to explain Father Kennedy's role in the concert but some mischievous instinct prevented either of them from taking this step, with each discerning the same thought process in the other by some unholy act of osmosis.

"Make-up?" replied O'Driscoll while at the same moment Duffy said with feigned embarrassment, "Er… I didn't really notice."

There was no chance to explore the matter further, for Sister Bernadette re-entered the room and asked the delegates if they had everything they wanted, at which point Duffy and O'Driscoll took the opportunity to slip out. As they did so, one of the female delegates professed herself to be feeling faint and asked if she could have a hot drink.

"Certainly," replied Sister Bernadette, "I'll arrange that for you right away. We'll just put the kettle on in the kitchen." Noticing an air of unease among the Americans, she thought she might diffuse the tension with an act of cultural exchange by using a piece of their vocabulary, and she trawled her memory for one of the new transatlantic expressions that she had recently learned. Eventually, her face cleared and with a tiny smile of triumph, she said, "I'm afraid it will take a couple of minutes because we need to get the key from Father Kennedy. He keeps it in his douche bag."

Into the silence which greeted this remark, the dropping of a single pin would have sounded like the thunder of a hundred cannons. After what seemed like a lifetime, a tiny, trembling voice broke the silence. "I'm sorry but did you say Father Kennedy has a… douche bag?"

"Yes," answered Sister Bernadette brightly. "Although," she went on quickly, after all, she didn't want the Americans to think there was anything "sissy" about Father Kennedy, "of course he doesn't use it all the time, only when he's going on stage."

The silence which greeted this remark was, if possible, longer and more charged than the previous one as the delegates struggled to make sense of what they had been told. A child entered carrying the key and there was another interminable pause before a figure who was evidently the most junior of the delegates shuffled forward and gingerly accepted it, returning to his place with the offending instrument hanging precariously between thumb and forefinger.

Having performed her errand of mercy, Sister Bernadette hurried off on another of her mysterious errands, leaving behind a stunned silence which rapidly turned into a seething cauldron of debate. Mr. Donnelly appointed himself chief inquisitor and was not slow to express his disapproval of Father Kennedy's conduct. For the priest to flaunt oneself like a painted jezebel was bad enough, but the possession of the article which Sister Bernadette had identified by name hinted at physiological manifestations of the priest's wickedness so horrible that they didn't bear thinking of.

One of the delegates suggested rather diffidently that what went on in a man's private life was surely his own business but Mr. Donnelly swatted this argument away with disdain. He didn't know what form of Catholicism they practiced here, he said, but he hadn't come all this way to see men of the cloth disporting themselves like... a Vietnamese lady boy, and the whole thing didn't sit with any of the tenets of the Catholic Church that he knew.

There was mild unease among Saint Catherine's staff when the American delegation failed to arrive at the school hall for the performance, and it soon became apparent that something had happened to disturb the carefully cultivated atmosphere of harmony. Mrs. Goodwin appointed herself chief investigator and bustled backwards and forwards between the two delegations. Returning from one such visit and finding a group of Saint Catherine's staff chatting in the corridor, she approached them and in a loud voice said, "Could someone tell me what a douche bag is?"

There was a brief pause before Tracey Reeves, one of the young teaching assistants began tentatively, "It's something that they use in America…"

"Yes, go on!" demanded Mrs. Goodwin impatiently. Tracey moved towards her, lowered her voice and whispered in her ear. An expression of incredulity dawned on Mrs. Goodwin's face and she said, "What do they want to do that for?" In the end, it had taken several hours for the confusion to be resolved, with recrimination eventually giving way to reconciliation as the narrative of the misunderstanding had unfolded.

Duffy and O'Driscoll, engaged in the tidying away of scenery and stacking of chairs, were blissfully unaware that there was a problem and even when word finally did reach them, they listened at first with only half an ear, their minds focusing on the icy globules surrounding the first, well-deserved pint awaiting them in The North Star. Slowly, however, an antenna in O'Driscoll's mind began to oscillate, at first mildly but then with increasing urgency and he sent Duffy ahead so he could find out what had happened.

It was Mrs. Goodwin, of course, who brought him up to speed. A major incident had been resolved, she said, thanks in no small part to her own diplomatic activity, but the authorities had laid the blame for the misunderstanding squarely at the door of John O'Driscoll, who according to Father Kennedy, had played a really shabby trick on Sister Bernadette. When asked by a mystified O'Driscoll to furnish him with details of this trick, the school secretary said, with a toss of the head that he (John O'Driscoll) had deliberately misled her (Sister Bernadette) as to the function of an item which she (Mrs. Goodwin) would not dignify with a name.

With another toss of the head, she retired, leaving O'Driscoll alone in the sacristy with only Parnell, the church cat, for company. "They're going to blame me again," he said wildly as Parnell fixed an insolent eye on him from his vantage point on the arm of the sofa. "They're going to bloody well blame me again!" Parnell gave him a look of infinite contempt, spat silently and then, sticking his tail in the air, wandered haughtily off in the direction of the kitchen. It was for O'Driscoll, the final confirmation that his hopes for the future lay in ruins around him - even the cat despised him! He heard a voice saying, "Father Kennedy's coming this way and he doesn't look very happy," and O'Driscoll felt that unmistakable and familiar sensation as, for the third consecutive Sunday, his bowels began the boiling and churning process that would shortly reduce them to liquid form.

Week Four

Monday

Duffy had found the whole thing highly amusing, and O'Driscoll was forced to concede that, however well-intentioned his motives had been, he *had* misled Sister Bernadette about the nature of the item in question and in that respect, had been the architect of his own downfall. The next morning, he resolved to go and see the nun to offer his apologies, and when he found her in her office, she received him kindly and listened attentively as he explained that, while he hadn't been sure of the precise nature of the article that had caused all the confusion, he had genuinely believed the definition he had given had been an accurate one.

"It was an honest misunderstanding, John," she answered, "and one that was quickly resolved, so do not concern yourself unduly."

"I heard someone saying that Father Kennedy was angry," ventured O'Driscoll.

"Father Kennedy is a man of… fixed resolve" answered the nun, appearing to choose her words carefully, "and this great sense of purpose causes him to react with… passion, when unexpected events occur. For all that, he is a good man straining every sinew to do God's work. Give him time," she concluded with a smile, "and he'll forget the whole thing."

Considerably mollified by these words, O'Driscoll headed towards morning briefing, where any residual worries he may have had about the preceding day were swept away by the news of what had happened overnight in the Goodwin house. It was alleged that in the dead of night, Brett had, with malice aforethought, crept into Henri's bedroom and deposited into the *en suite* bidet that was the Goodwin's pride and joy, a turd of such formidable dimensions as to render even Reg speechless. While it was unclear whether the action had been a deliberate comment on the depths to which U.S.-Franco relations had sunk (the Goodwin's belief) or an accidental product of the low voltage night time lighting, (Brett's assertion) what could not be disputed owing to the physical evidence that was there for all to see, was that Brett. T. Donnelly had shat in the Goodwin's bidet.

Duffy had already christened Brett's act of rebellion a "dirty protest" inspired by events in the north of Ireland and was wondering whether the boy would be repatriated before he went fully "on the blanket." As it was, Brett was now in Sister Bernadette's office awaiting an interview with his father, while poor Henri, who had been the unfortunate discoverer of the offending stool, was considered too traumatized by the experience to attend lessons and was in Mr. Barnet's office awaiting developments. Mrs. Goodwin had been asked to make a statement about the incident at briefing and although clearly distressed, she moved to the front of the room with a stoicism that St. Joan, approaching the pyre at Rouen, might have envied.

"I do not wish to speak of the unspeakable events of last night," she began tautologically, gripping the lectern in front of her and struggling to control her emotions. "Suffice to say Reg and I have been inundated with support from our friends and colleagues. And the support from all those people who have given us their support will support us in the difficult days ahead. That is all I wish to say at this time." She spent a moment or two accepting condolences and then, flanked on either side by secretaries from the school office, processed slowly and with dignity from the room.

After a suitable period of silence, the Head reminded staff that Father Kennedy was organizing another service at the church to say goodbye to the delegation from America and was looking for volunteers. O'Driscoll received this news with mixed feelings, conscious of the fact that his performance over the course of the previous three services had not been an unqualified success. After all, he had embossed a hundred hymn books with the name of an intimate female part during the first, caused his parish priest to be suspected of transvestism during the third and in-between, made an act of confession masquerading as Paul Gascoigne.

Not even his best friend would be able to say he had enhanced his reputation over the past three weeks but aware that one good performance might yet yank his career out of the fire, he duly volunteered his services. The head rounded-off proceedings by asking staff to check the wet break rota and the new supply teacher, whose name was apparently Clive and who, in O'Driscoll's opinion, looked far too full of himself, announced that he had commandeered the school T.V. set for the morning.

Upon arriving at Mr. Barnet's office to find out when the Head wished to see him about the Prudence situation, O'Driscoll found the anteroom occupied by Henri and Mrs. Wagstaffe, one of the secretaries.

"You just wait there, dearie," Mrs. Wagstaffe was saying, "and Mr. Barnet will be along in a minute."

"But I can go to the class now, I am ready for the lessons," protested the French boy.

"No, you've had a nasty experience," replied the secretary, "and Mr. Barnet said you needed something for the shock. He said he'll be along in a minute to give you some tea and a sticky."

Henri considered this prospect without relish. The proclivities of middle-aged Englishmen were a well-established fact in his own country – indeed in an effort to provide him with a tool kit for survival, his parents had briefed him in what some might have considered lurid detail on what they called *Le Vice Anglais* – and the more he analyzed the words he had just heard, the more they filled him with anxiety. He did not like tea – nasty horrible drink – and could not understand why any civilized people should choose to drink it, but it was the final part of the message that disturbed him most, for while he had no idea what a "sticky" was, the prospect of Mr. Barnet giving him one conjured up images so uncomfortable that he leapt from his chair and took off down the corridor like a startled hare. Mrs. Wagstaffe and O'Driscoll looked at each other in surprise for a moment, after which the teacher enquired as to the Head's whereabouts and finding him otherwise engaged, returned to his own classroom.

At lunchtime, he nipped out to the nearby shopping precinct and returned with a pair of air-cushioned training shoes, two packets of organic muesli and several cartons of prune juice. He was determined to start a new chapter in his life and had resolved that henceforth each day would commence with an invigorating run followed by a hearty breakfast of muesli and prune juice, with perhaps some additional segments of fresh fruit on special occasions. In addition, he would cut out alcohol altogether, well not actually cut it out completely, but he would reduce it considerably to weekends and, of course, Thursday, because Thursday had always been the start of the weekend, so didn't actually count as midweek, and then there was Sunday, and, of course, it went without saying that Sunday counted as the weekend. But apart from Thursday, Sunday and the weekend, he would cut alcohol ruthlessly and irrevocably out of his system and he would stop eating the kind of meals dispensed by fast food outlets in the small hours of the morning. He couldn't reduce his smoking, because he had already given that up, but he promised himself he would never, absolutely never consider taking it up again.

In the state of self-righteous piety which often accompanies such endeavours, he made his way back to school for an afternoon that turned out to be as uneventful as the morning had been. Upon passing the office at the end of the day, he was handed a message from the Head cancelling their meeting, but indicating that he and Prudence could meet O'Driscoll in the lounge bar of The George at five o'clock, if that was convenient. Noticing his mystified expression, Mrs. Wagstaffe explained that the school site manager was leaving early that afternoon and the building would be locked up immediately after school. Mentally shrugging his shoulders, O'Driscoll reflected that if the Head wanted to hold a meeting in the pub, so be it as long as the old bastard put his hand into his pocket.

He took his place at the bar of The George at the appointed hour and bought himself an orange juice and lemonade, an unusual experience but one that in the present circumstances seemed wise. Warily sipping the concoction, he wondered how on Earth he was going to extricate himself from the job of being Prudence Pugh's keeper, for that, in view of the behaviour she had exhibited during her time at Saint Catherine's, was how he now saw his role. He was also hoping he might be able to glean some information from the Head about the leadership's plans for the future so he could assess his own chances of being part of them. He had wanted to sound out Sister Bernadette about next year when he spoke to her earlier in the day, but something in her expression made him draw back from enquiring. A moment later, Mr. Barnet entered and two things were immediately apparent; firstly that he was alone, and secondly that he had, as O'Driscoll's mother would have expressed it, "drink taken."

"Ah, young O'Driscoll," the Head said as he approached. "No, don't stand up, no ceremony here old chap. Sorry I'm a little late. Have you got a drink?" He looked at O'Driscoll's glass in horror. "Orange juice! By the Lord Harry, we'll soon put that right!" Turning to the barman, he said, "Large gin and tonic please, whatever my young friend would like, and one for yourself." When they were seated at a table, Barnet with his gin and O'Driscoll with a pint of lager, the Head sat back, wrapped his whiskers round his glass, gave a sigh of satisfaction and started to speak. "You'll have noticed I'm on my own," he began and immediately stopped to refresh himself further. "Yes, thought you'd notice, didn't think something like that would get past young O'Driscoll."

He attempted to tap his nose knowingly, missed, gathered himself and continued. "Fact is, went to see Prudence's father. You remember me telling you about my chum Douglas, fathers flew Spitfires in the war, thick and thin, unbreakable bond handed down to children, lifelong friendship resulting." He took another long pull from his glass. "Fact is, Douglas asked me to come and see him because he's a bit worried about the gel, head packed full of new-fangled ideas, he said. Talking a lot of rot about women's cooperatives apparently, and then there was something about Peter Rabbit, couldn't follow a word of it myself so no wonder he was confused.

Anyway, cut a long story short, when I got there I decided the best thing to do was for the three of us to go to lunch. Took 'em to a nice little French place in Barnes and gave 'em a rather a superior lunch, if I say so, m'self. Trouble is," he lowered his voice confidentially, "not sure how much experience young Prudence has with taking a glass of wine with her lunch. She was all right with the sherry she had before we went in, then I gave her some Pinot Noir with the starter and a rather fine Shiraz with the guinea fowl. By the time we'd had a *digestif* and got back to Douglas's, she was feeling a bit faint - took herself off to bed and we couldn't raise her for love nor money.

"That's the long and short of it, young O'Driscoll," he concluded with an expansive shrug. "She's not here. And because she's not here," he continued, having slaked his thirst with another draught from his glass, "can't have the meeting. Can't have a meeting to discuss someone's teaching," he went on, wagging an admonishing finger at O'Driscoll, "when the person whose teaching is to be discussed isn't here. Simply can't! Wouldn't be right! Rotten show!" He raised his left hand with care, focusing with difficulty on a large Rolex, and O'Driscoll risked a swift glance at his own watch, wondering how on Earth he was going to extricate himself from the situation.

"Tell you what, O'Driscoll, let's have one for the road. My shout. I'm in the chair." He began to fumble in his pocket but O'Driscoll, feeling he couldn't let the old soak get another round in so quickly after the last one, jumped up and went to the bar for replacements.

"Capital! Cheers! Bottoms up!" said the Head when O'Driscoll returned with the drinks and immediately took another lengthy swig from his glass. "Fact is," he said, "haven't any particular need to get home tonight." He leaned towards O'Driscoll and lowered his voice. "Wife's gone into hospital for a minor op. Undercarriage job!"

He took another pull from the rapidly diminishing glass of gin and, burping softly, went on, "….so no need to get back to base to face the music." O'Driscoll, feeling that he had heard too much already, made for the toilets, and having washed his hands several times, returned to the lounge to find that Mr. Barnet had been to the bar again and got them both large gin and tonics. "Yes," the Head was repeating as O'Driscoll sat down, "undercarriage job. They're taking out the whole kit and caboodle. Dear wife's a bit upset about the whole business, you know what the ladies are like for worrying. Not," he went on, lowering his voice, "that there's been any action of that kind for some time, so can't think why she's so agitated. No," he continued, lowering his voice even further, "I have an address in Ladbroke Grove for all that gubbins. Very discreet!" He made another attempt to tap his nose knowingly, this time successfully making contact. "I'll let you have it if you'd like to, you know, avail yourself of the…." he started to search through his pockets as O'Driscoll shook his head wildly and wondered again how on Earth he was going to uncouple himself from his inebriated leader.

Twice he tried to begin the process of leave taking, only to find, on each occasion, Mr. Barnet headed him off at the pass by producing fresh rounds of gin. It was by now six-thirty and the Head had passed through the expansive phase and was entering the maudlin one. "How did I end up in education?" he asked rhetorically as O'Driscoll, who hadn't been listening to a word, reluctantly re-engaged his attention and tried to appear as if he knew what the old fool was talking about. "Fact is, should have joined the R.A.F. Father wanted me to, would have been proudest day of his life to see me wearing those wings on my shoulder. Trouble was," he went on, leaning across the table and nearly overbalancing, "went up once in a Hercules transport as a cadet and found whole thing bloody terrifying. Got back to terra firma, promised self would never go topside again, and never have.

Had to say something to the mater and pater at home, couldn't tell truth, my guv'nor would have died of shame, so made up story about having vocation for teaching." Mr. Barnet's eyes were growing moist and rheumy. "Ironic really, isn't it?" he said, "Boko Barnet's son afraid of flying!" A large tear began to form in his right eye as he went on. "Boko Barnet's son frowsting in a funkhole on the ground! Not even a tail-end Charlie, skulking about at the back of the kite, that would have been bad enough! But a ground wallah! Boko Barnet's son a ground wallah!"

His hand moved towards his right handlebar in that familiar gesture but this time bypassed it and absorbed the large teardrop that was running slowly down the side of his face. Terrified at what disclosures might result from the continuation for even a minute of this conversation, O'Driscoll suddenly remembered a sick relative that required visiting, and with an efficiency and sense of purpose that would have surprised his friends, contrived to get himself out of the pub and a confused but compliant Mr. Barnet into a taxi, all within a matter of minutes. He had hoped the meeting might provide him with some hard information about staffing plans for the following year, or at least offer him an insight into the thinking of the leadership team, but with the interview having left him none the wiser as to future plans, he made a weary journey home by bus, leaving his Cortina to face yet another lonely night in the school car park.

Finding he still had the bag containing his lunchtime purchases, he unpacked the items when he arrived home and put them away. The trainers went into the bottom of the wardrobe in his bedroom and took their place next to a metal-framed tennis racquet, a gift wrapped water bottle and sweatband, and a pair of cycling shorts. During the next few days, in the first flush of the healthy new fitness regime, a few portions of the muesli were consumed, but the prune juice sat alone and unlamented in the kitchen cupboard for several months until it was finally called

250

into action as a mixer, with rum, when all other non-alcoholic beverages had run out.

Tuesday

O'Driscoll's first thought upon awaking the next morning was that for once, he didn't seem to be suffering from alcoholic poisoning, something he doubted his leader would be able to claim. That Mr. Barnett, who revered the memory of his father and lived and breathed in a world dedicated to the celebration of all things celestial, should turn out to be a sufferer from vertigo was richly ironic and a timely reminder that those who appeared to be navigating their way through life's waters without a care in the world could sometimes be struggling against its treacherous currents.

The Head was present at briefing though, looking none the worse for the previous evening's experience. "Morning, young O'Driscoll," he said as they passed, and it was apparent from his demeanour that he either had no memory of the previous night's ramblings, or had chosen to forget them. Of Prudence, there was no sign at briefing, and later, when O'Driscoll made his way to his classroom offering silent prayers that he would find the room empty, she was again conspicuous by her absence.

After an uneventful morning, he found himself sitting in the staff room listening to Mrs. Goodwin holding forth on the subject of the new supply teacher. "Clive, his name is - nice name, don't you think. Anyway, he came to the office to get some photocopier paper and I said to myself if I was twenty years younger, and didn't have Reg's infection to dress, you could end up doing something you might regret, Mavis Goodwin!" She ran her fingers through her hair. "Smouldering! That's the word they used in the Mills and Boon Medical Romance I was reading to describe this doctor who ends up winning the heroine's heart. That Clive can take my temperature any time he likes." There was some half-hearted laughter as she went on, "In fact, I don't mind saying that I'd be prepared to faint on the spot if there was half a chance of him resuscitating me."

"How is Reg's…er… infection," asked Duffy innocently.

"It's funny you should ask that, because he's been having a difficult time of it *down there*." She lowered her voice. "It wasn't so bad until he got a touch of the old Farmer Giles, but once that lot got established, things got more complicated, and now… to be honest, sometimes it's hard to know where the piles end and the fungal infection begins. I'll be standing there with the pile ointment in one hand and the Canisten in the other and by the time I've finished, it's like a pepperoni pizza down there."

She lowered her voice even further. "Reg actually likes me rubbing on the oils and ointments, he says it's quite.... arousing, if you know what I mean." She gave a small grimace. "Once he was enjoying it so much, he started to get... you know! I didn't know where to look, reminded me a bit of that film *Alien,* you know, the first time we see..." There was a sound somewhere between a gasp and a moan from the other side of the room and Mrs. Goodwin smiled. "Yes, I can see *you* know the bit I mean!"

Leaving Mrs. Goodwin to talk to a rapidly dwindling audience, O'Driscoll made his way to the Year Six classroom. As he reached the door, the first thing he heard was Brett's voice forth in its usual direct and forceful manner. "Goddam Brits, can't even swear properly."

"What are you talking about?" said a bored-sounding voice.

"Take a nice, simple word like *"fuck"*. You limeys say it every which way and you still can't get it right."

"What do you mean?"

"When we were in London last weekend, there was this big fat guy in a kinda shiny tracksuit selling tickets for some soccer match. Anyway, he said it so it sounded exactly like *'fack.'*" Brett assumed a wide-legged pose and, waving imaginary tickets in the air, shouted, *"Twenty-five quid for two! Yer 'avin' a faarcking laarf, yer faarcking caarnt!"* He paused for breath and O'Driscoll couldn't help thinking that his grasp of London lowlife vernacular was rather impressive.

"That's the way we speak in London, yer faarcking caarnt!" said another voice and there was a chorus of laughter.

"OK, what about guy who delivers the Goodwin's milk, then? I heard him tell Mr. Goodwin about some office where he delivers milk. *'Boonch of fooking soothern poofters',"* said Brett in an accent that George Formby might have employed on the front at Blackpool.

Then, there was an intervention from a surprising quarter. "I agree this is strange," came the sound of Henri's voice, "but there is not alone these two ways to say this word, there is a third also. Yesterday, Father Kennedy, he drop his book on the ground and I hear him say, *'Ah, feck!'"*

At last, thought O'Driscoll as he heard the class trying out various versions amidst much laughter, the two exchange students had found something to agree about, even if it was only out of a shared sense of mystification at the myriad ways in which the British pronounced their most famous linguistic export.

"Hey, teacher man," called out Brett as O'Driscoll entered the room. "Can you help us out, we want to know whether it's *"fack," "fook,"* or *"feck?"*

"It's actually f...." began O'Driscoll before he remembered himself, hastily cleared his throat and silenced the tittering class with what he hoped was one of his most withering looks.

He managed to avoid the necessity of dipping further into the world of Anglo-Saxon invective and Tuesday afternoon wended its way to an unremarkable conclusion. He was then faced with the dilemma of whether to head for The North Star, where the lads had arranged to meet for a drink, or go home and continue his new life of abstinence and self-denial. But had he not already broken his self-imposed curfew the night before by issuing forth on an errand of mercy to help a colleague in need? And then there was the leaving do on Wednesday, which would lead into Thursday, and everyone knew Thursday was the start of the weekend and didn't count as a weekday, not really. On reflection, he decided to keep things administratively tidy by simply putting off the start of his new life until the following week and, resolving to check that the prune juice would still be in date, he did some marking and headed off to The North Star ahead of the designated meeting time of six-thirty.

He bumped into Micky on the Uxbridge Road and as they fell into step, Quinn asked for enlightenment on a question that he said had been bothering him. Was it true all male staff at St Catherine's owned douche bags or was it only those called to holy orders? Choosing not to dignify these words with a reply, O'Driscoll instead laid about his friend with a rolled up copy of the *Evening Standard* and the two arrived at the pub considerably cheered by the exchange. As they entered, they saw Duffy deep in conversation with the new supply teacher, Clive, and having got themselves pints, they arrived at the table to find that Clive was speaking. He flicked them a glance before turning his head to Duffy and continuing his conversation, and although the glance had been brief, it told him that as they were neither alpha males nor female, they were unworthy of further consideration.

"I took that little blond piece out over the weekend - Tracey, I think its name is," he was saying.

"Tracey Reeves?" said Duffy. "You're a fast mover." (Tracey was one of the teaching assistants who worked with the infants and was considered something of a beauty).

"Anyway, I took it over Richmond way, fed it, gave it a bit of a dance, and then back to my place." He flicked his hand through his hair and shook his head as he went on. "Well, it showed her gratitude in the traditional way. I hardly had the strength to stagger out of bed the next morning. And I tell you what, I don't know where it was educated, but it knew a few things that would impress any teacher." He lowered his voice slightly. "Shall I just say that during the course of the night, every orifice saw some action." He took a swig from his drink and flicked a hand through his hair again. "All three."

O'Driscoll and Quinn looked at each other and Micky said, "Well, he can count then."

"Course he can, that's why they gave him Maths to teach," answered O'Driscoll. "Nothing stupid about the management at Saint Catherine's!"

Clive gave no indication of having heard any of this but continued to talk to Duffy, who gazed inscrutably back at him.

"What about earholes, don't they count?" said Quinn to O'Driscoll. "As orifices, I mean."

"Good point," answered his friend, "and then there's nostrils, as well. I mean if ears count, you'd have to include nostrils as well."

"*And* they count as two each, don't they?" said Micky, receiving an affirmative nod from his friend. "Altogether that comes to…. er…. well, it's a lot more than three, anyway."

"Which makes Mr. Duffy's friend here a bit of a lightweight," finished O'Driscoll, and they turned their attention back to the conversation going on next to them.

"Keep me informed of any gossip that might be useful," Clive was saying. "You know the type of thing I mean." He gave Duffy a slow wink, drained his glass and, completely ignoring the other two, stood up and strolled casually towards the door, his head moving almost imperceptibly from side-to-side as he walked.

"Seems a nice bloke, your friend," observed Micky as they watched the retreating figure moving towards the exit with those tiny lateral movements of the head that proclaim, "I am a cool person."

Duffy smiled slightly and it was evident that he shared their misgivings about the new teacher. "A bit too much information, to be honest," he said referring to Clive's disclosures, and in truth, it did compare unfavorably with his own conduct, for Duffy never felt the need to boast about his conquests, even though he could probably have kept the room amused for several hours had he wished.

"Anyway," he went on, changing the subject, "how's it going with the lovely Maureen, Mick?" A shadow passed over Quinn's face and as he stirred restlessly in his chair, hints of Pacco Rabanne scented the air around him.

"I'm starving, that's how it's going," he answered and there was a plaintive note to his voice. "I've come straight over here from dinner. She did ask me to go on with her to some aerobics class afterwards but I managed to get out of it, thank God, or I'd have collapsed with exhaustion after what she gave me."

"What did you have?" asked O'Driscoll.

Quinn gathered himself together and made an obvious effort to control his emotions. "Tofu." He spat the word out. "Fucking Tofu. That's what I had."

There was a short pause before Rocky, who had arrived in the middle of the conversation asked, "What?"

"Tofu!"

"What's tofu?"

There was another, longer pause as if Micky was considering his next words carefully. He started to hitch his trousers, gave up halfway, and eventually replied, "I don't know what it is exactly, to be honest."

"What does it look like?"

"Lots of little grey cubes, but they sort of collapse when you try to pick them up."

"What does it taste like?" asked Rocky.

Micky picked his nose thoughtfully as he gave the question his full attention and there followed another lengthy period of contemplation. "It's hard to say what it tastes like, exactly," he replied.

"You're not giving us a lot here, Michael," said Duffy. "Have you got anything else at all to say on the subject of tofu?"

"Not really, except to say that I never thought anything would make me nostalgic for couscous, but fucking tofu managed it."

"Apart from the food, is everything else OK?" asked Duffy.

"It's all very well for you to say, 'Apart from the food,'" replied his friend. "Apart from the food's easy to say for someone who's getting a proper meal every once in a while." He rubbed his great paunch and there was a quaver in his voice as he went on. "There's an aching void where my stomach should be. An aching void! Do you know how long it's been," he said in a voice that would have melted the heart of a graven image, "since I had a pie?"

"So apart from the food, everything else is OK?" repeated Duffy, wearing the same inscrutable expression.

"Up to a point," replied his friend. "She's got me reading this," he said, shaking his head and pulling out a paperback from his pocket. O'Driscoll picked it up and read the title: *The House of the Spirits*, by Isabel Allende.

"What's it about?" asked Sweeney, who, pint in hand, had joined them.

"Dunno really," answered Micky, "can't get my head around it. I mean it starts off in some South American country and there's all these people shagging one and other. I haven't got any problem with that," he added hastily, clearly anxious to show that he was as broad-minded as the next man, "but next thing you know they start flying around the place."

Rocky, who as a boy had been a keen collector of the *Top Trumps* cards, looked up with interest. "Flying what?" he asked.

"Not flying anything, you idiot, just flying around."

"Just flying around on their own?" Rocky considered this crime against the laws of physical science and shook his head. "Well, that's just bloody stupid."

"You don't have to tell me it's bloody stupid!" replied his friend. "And the other thing that really pisses me off is the way it keeps jumping around in time. At least I think it keeps jumping around in time? It's hard to say, to be honest. Doesn't it annoy you when books do that?"

"Have you discussed it with Maureen?"

"Have I discussed what with Maureen?"

"The book, you twat!"

"Well," answered Quinn, "it's more of a case of her discussing it with me. I tried to say I didn't understand it and leave it at that, but she wanted to know what bits I didn't understand and she started explaining them to me. Have you ever had someone explaining to you in great detail something you didn't want to know in the first place?" He paused and sighed. "It's bloody annoying, I can tell you."

"If she explained it, you must know what it's about," said Duffy.

Quinn snorted. "You obviously haven't heard Maureen explaining stuff. She said it was all to do with something called…. er…. 'magical realism.' He paused, and after a moment's thought, went on, "or it might have been 'realistic magic.' Made my head spin, it did, the whole thing, but it's apparently a way of writing that allows you to put any old bollocks into a story, and no one can say it's bollocks because of this 'magical realism' thing."

"Just to get back to these people flying about," interjected Rocky, who was of a literal bent. "Was that to do with the magical thing?"

Micky screwed his face up with the effort of remembering. "I did ask her about that and she said that the flying was… allegorical."

"Ally who?" asked Rocky.

"He used to play for Dundee United," said Duffy, who was tiring of the discussion. "Look, it's dead simple – women's brains are wired differently from ours and that's why they can read books where people fly about without getting pissed off. It could have been worse, it could have been one of those stories where they spend all their time getting emotional and crying and talking about how they *feel*. Just tell her you've finished it, Mick, and that you liked it."

"I did! I tried to pretend I'd finished it but she started making up questions to try and catch me out." Quinn's great shoulders sagged. "She did catch me out, as it happens, several times." He cast a dolorous look at his friends. "She said she was disappointed in me!"

A keen observer might have detected suppressed amusement in the looks that were exchanged around the table. "So where does that leave you?" asked O'Driscoll with studied gravity.

"I've got to finish it, that's where it bloody leaves me!" answered his friend. "The other day I was pretending to read it and I had a Tom Clancy inside the pages and she caught me." He winced at the memory. "I've got to finish it. Just for a quiet life. I've got to finish a book that I don't understand with loads of characters whose names I can't remember flying about the place like fucking bats, and then I've got to answer questions on it. I wouldn't mind," he went on gloomily, "if there was any *sense* to it." He sighed, shook his head and muttered, "No terrorists, no guerillas, no SWAT teams, no nothing. Five hundred and sixty-two pages and the word *Kalashnikov* doesn't appear once!"

By now, it was approaching the time when a decision needed to be made about whether to call it quits when the pubs shut at eleven, or move on somewhere else. Fortunately, Rocky knew of the launch of a new IT product that was taking place at a hotel in Acton and though it turned out to be a disappointingly tame event, there was enough free wine to provide some consolation for the lack of sparkle among the delegates. And so it was that, having made his weary way home via the Chinese takeaway and a portion of sweet and sour pork balls that contained enough cholesterol to clog up the Blackwall tunnel, John O'Driscoll finally drifted into sleep and into another day.

Wednesday

On arriving at school the next morning, two thoughts were uppermost in O'Driscoll's mind. The first concerned Prudence and her nonappearance the previous day. The effort of trying to maintain a positive attitude when working with her was turning him into a nervous wreck and the fact that she was, in spite of her foibles, a decent person with decent instincts made him feel all the more guilty for his intolerance. He promised himself he would make a special effort to be nicer to her. After all, she was dedicated and hardworking and actually seemed to like the kids, something that couldn't be said say for many of her colleagues. So summoning up what Christian spirit he had left after a Catholic upbringing (not much), he stiffened his sinews and prepared to spend a day doing good work with the needy.

The other thought concerned the rearranged leaving do taking place later that day. Unlike many functions to which he reluctantly dragged himself, this one promised to be a good night, because the teacher who was leaving was gregarious and well-liked and, of course, the event had the additional incentive that Karen would be there. He hadn't seen her since Saturday and his stomach lurched as he wondered which Karen would reveal herself to him later that night – the one who had flashed her eyes at him and whispered in his ear on the dance floor or the one who looked on in horror as he frolicked lasciviously on the same spot an hour later.

Mr. Barnet commenced briefing by wishing everyone a breezy good morning and reminding them that on Friday, the school would be closed to the children while staff took part in a training day on the subject of multicultural awareness. He also reminded staff of the special service Father Kennedy had organized for the following Sunday to say goodbye to the delegation from America.

The first person O'Driscoll saw after the meeting had finished was Prudence, and she immediately fell into step beside him, her great owlish eyes blinking furiously as she began to speak. She was sorry she hadn't seen him for a few days, she said but an unexpected family matter had called her away and it was *such* a shame just when she felt her teaching had *really* started to open up those little minds and she had missed the children, they were *so* wonderful in their innocence and of course she had missed him because he had been *so* helpful but he would understand she missed the children a bit more and did he think that the children might have missed her just a *little* bit and had any of them said anything about her?

It was true that 5R had found the classroom a strangely tame place without Prudence and O'Driscoll contrived to give that impression in his reply but it was more difficult to put a positive spin on her final question, for O'Driscoll had heard Joe Cahill and his gang referring to her in terms which suggested that his worries over the name Cnut the Great had been well-founded. He confined himself to replying it was clear she had made a significant impression on the 5R pupils, and he was mercifully spared the need to comment further when Prudence was called away for a meeting with Mr. Barnet.

O'Driscoll's day passed off in a desultory fashion, with Prudence shadowing him in the morning and then disappearing on a mission to prepare literacy resources for another Key Stage. By seven o'clock, he was showered, changed and having a quick pint in The North Star with Duffy and Rocky ahead of the leaving do in Hanwell.

"Did Micky say he was coming here first?" asked O'Driscoll.

"Dunno," answered Duffy absently, his attention focused on the barmaid with the nose stud.

Rocky, who had overheard this exchange on the way back from the bar, said, "No, I spoke to him a bit earlier and he said he'd meet us there. He called me on this," he went on, holding up a great unwieldy mobile phone. "Surprised me, really, because I don't know if you've noticed but whenever it rings, it nearly always turns out to be the office. Pisses me off sometimes, it does." His companions carefully avoided meeting each other's eyes as Rocky went on, "Anyway, he was in a right state, kept moaning about being starved to death."

"Sounds like they've finished dinner, then," said O'Driscoll with a smile.

"I wonder what they had tonight?" asked Duffy.

"It was a dodgy line so I couldn't hear what he was saying half the time," went on Rocky, "but he kept on repeating the same thing. *'Hummus - fucking hummus – fucking twatting hummus'*. And there was something about three bean salad, that got him going again, *'Salad - fucking salad - fucking twatting salad.'* He's obviously got a right downer on salad. He said he hadn't moved in with Maureen so they could *eat* like rabbits."

"Was that all he phoned up for, to have a moan about Maureen's dinners?" asked Duffy.

"No, he wants someone to get him something to eat from the Seven Eleven, and slip it to him at the do."

"Bloody hell, he must be desperate. There's bound to be some kind of food there," said O'Driscoll.

"That's what I told him," answered Rocky, "but he said he couldn't take the risk – a man's life was at stake."

The others looked at each other. "We'd better get him something then," said O'Driscoll. "After all, he's begged us for help and you can't let a friend down in his hour of need, can you?" His friends nodded their heads gravely and O'Driscoll asked, "So does anyone know where the nearest tofu shop is?"

Upon arriving at the pub in Hanwell several rounds later, the first person they saw was Micky Quinn, but he was unrecognizable from the ebullient figure that usually met their eyes. He was attired in the elegant costume that Maureen's accomplished eye had put together with the help of Paul Smith, but the clothes seemed to hang from his body with a forlorn, defeated air, and even the elaborate coiffure which Maureen had constructed with industrial quantities of styling mousse lay flat and lifeless on his head. As soon as he saw them, he hurried over, his face working silently but frantically.

"Have you got it?" he muttered through clenched teeth. His face wore a hunted look and as he spoke, he glanced behind him.

"Have I got what?" replied Duffy, who being closest to Quinn, was first in the firing line.

"The food, you cunt!" replied Micky, and it was evident from the terseness of his reply that the intervening hours had not improved his temper. Of course, it transpired they had forgotten the food, and Duffy's attempt to explain that the warmth and conviviality of The North Star had driven the matter from their minds was abruptly terminated as Quinn grabbed the lapels of his jacket and began to shake them violently. "Is anyone going to get me something to fucking eat!" he gibbered madly, his eyes rolling and his face and hands shaking and twitching.

"Can't you nip out yourself?" asked Rocky.

"I can't! She watches me! Look, she's watching me now." Quinn suddenly disengaged himself from the group and headed back towards Maureen, but not before turning on his friends the kind of look worn by a spaniel that hasn't been down to the paper shop for a week.

In the face of such suffering, it was impossible to do nothing, and Rocky was nominated to nip down to the adjoining convenience store and get some food. While this was going on, O'Driscoll's eyes had begun a surreptitious search of the bar area and his stomach gave a familiar lurch as he spotted Karen in the middle of the room. He had spoken to her that afternoon and it was clear she had either not noticed or chosen to ignore his embarrassing performance on the dance floor the previous weekend, for there had been no constraint in her manner when they had chatted. He began the process of trying to edge closer to where she was standing, but by this time Rocky had returned from the Seven Eleven and O'Driscoll found himself dispatched on a mission to divert Maureen's attention for a few minutes.

A little later, a close observer might have thought he had wandered into the pages of *The Dandy* for under a trestle table, devouring a family steak pie with scant regard for etiquette, crouched a figure that, except for its flaming red hair and a hint of Paco Rabanne, could have passed for Desperate Dan. Rocky had bought a hummus wrap to supplement the offer but his friend had rebuffed this offer in words that were, perhaps fortunately, rendered indistinct by pie.

The next half hour passed in the desultory way of an event in its early stages, with people arriving and ordering drinks and finding their friends. Duffy relieved the monotony by slipping off to make a couple of phone calls to Rocky's mobile, while O'Driscoll remained on hand so that he could subsequently report back on the reactions to the calls, a disappointing four followed by a spectacular ten. By nine o'clock, the venue was starting to fill up and the lads were ensconced comfortably in a corner, close to the bar to call for replenishments should the need arise (it would).

At one point, Clive the supply teacher strolled in their direction, again walking with those almost imperceptible sideways motions of the head that screamed, "I am the dog's bollocks," and as he passed them, he nodded at Duffy, while ignoring the others. His journey took him past Tracey Reeves, who could be observed looking at him with red-rimmed eyes and a tear-stained countenance. Gracing her with a lop-sided smile, but otherwise paying her no attention, he passed languidly by, and into the area where the main body of revelers were gathered in the centre of the room.

By this stage, the pie had revived Michael Quinn to the point where, if still somewhat terse, his mood was at least was an improvement on the famine-induced fury of half an hour before. The offer of the hummus wrap had been repeated and had been again declined, but without the curtness which had earlier been displayed.

"So you're not a fan of this hummus then, Mick?" asked Rocky. "What exactly is it anyway?"

Quinn hitched his trousers up in a way that Sherlock Holmes, puzzling over a two-pipe problem, might have hoicked up his cavalry twills. His brow furrowed and he scratched his arse thoughtfully while his other hand began to wrestle with the undergarments at the front if his trousers.

"Sludge!" he finally pronounced with the air of a difficult problem satisfactorily solved.

"Sorry?" said Duffy.

"Sludge!" repeated Quinn. "Hummus! Sludge! That's the nearest I can get. It's like a sort of grey sludge." He paused and thought for a moment. "And it tastes like sludge as well."

"How are things with Maureen, then, Mick?" asked Duffy and the others suppressed smiles as Quinn looked at them with a face that wore an expression of almost comical melancholia. "I don't mind her trying to improve my mind and I don't mind her making me wear different clothes and I don't mind her giving me poncey shampoo and hair mousse and all that stuff...." he paused for breath, "....if only she wouldn't try and starve me!"

In a hollow voice, he enumerated the gastronomic crimes which she had visited on him. "I've had hummus, I've had tofu, I've had couscous, I've had Mexican bean stew. Last week, she gave me something so bad I can't even remember what it was called. I must have blanked it out. Bloody hell!" he went on as a new thought appeared to strike him. "Maybe I'm starting to have memory loss. They say that people who are starving start to experience memory loss and hallucinations." His hand continued to work away to untangle whatever was amiss within his trousers and the resulting pelvic gyrations caused some of the people standing near him to wonder whether the dancing had started early.

By now, the group had moved towards the centre of the room and O'Driscoll noticed that Karen was only a few feet away, talking to June Taylor, the English coordinator, and a couple of others. He was working out how best to move closer to her when he noticed Clive had insinuated himself into the group and was making good headway, if the smiling faces around him were anything to go by. There seemed to be a lot of laughter and he noticed Clive directing a significant number of looks in Karen's direction. To his consternation, amidst the babble of voices and the sounds of laughter coming from the group, she appeared to be reciprocating the eye contact. To his horror, he noticed Karen had started to play with the strands of hair on the side of her head, threading them through her fingers as she looked at Clive. "Don't play with your hair! Don't play with your bloody hair!" his inner voice silently screamed and, in desperation, he did what he always did in a crisis, which was to down three-quarters of his pint in one convulsive draught, and head off to the bar to get another round in. On his return he once more took up position where he could hear what was going on in the adjoining group and his ears picked up June Taylor's voice extolling the virtues of George Eliot.

"Have you read her, Clive?" asked someone.

"George Eliot? Yeah, I've read her stuff," said Clive.

"And what did you think of it?"

"Early chicklit," he replied laconically and there was a burst of laughter. . Someone could be heard saying, "Ooh, Clive, you are a one," and O'Driscoll noted with mounting horror that Karen's mouth was half-open in laughter and her eyes appeared to be dancing with delight. Grinding his teeth in impotent fury, he resolved that he was not going to be outdone by that sleazy bastard Clive. If it was witty literary banter they wanted, he would bloody well give them witty literary banter!

He heard Duffy's voice asking him if he wanted another beer, and he drained the glass in his hand and called for whiskeys to be added to the next round. Right, his inner voice said as he squared his metaphorical shoulders, he would show them there was more than one person in the room who could talk about English literary classics in a witty and erudite way. A few moments later the drinks arrived and he grabbed two glasses from the tray and, beer in one hand and whiskey in the other, prepared to go into battle.

Thursday

Flight Lieutenant John "Dizzy" O'Driscoll leaned negligently against the sleek, sinister-looking fuselage of the Mosquito fighter bomber that was his pride and joy. It was 1943 and the scene was an RAF airfield somewhere on the East Anglian coast of wartime England. As he looked across the flat airfield, and as dusk began to fall, he could see lights beginning to appear here and there among the rows of Nissen huts. Two figures could be observed standing together, their silhouettes sharply defined by the rows of lamps behind them. As they moved into the gloom, their outlines became less distinct, the backlighting effect of the lamps enveloping them in an ethereal, romantic glow. One of the figures was Group Captain Clive "Corky" Corcoran, and even at a distance, his peaked hat could be observed making those minute lateral motions that proclaim to the world, "I am an awfully accomplished pilot."

As the other figure, slim and lithe in form, detached itself from him and made its way towards O'Driscoll, it revealed itself to be Karen Black, senior WAAF officer attached to the planning corps at the station. She was not in uniform, but the printed floral dress she wore accentuated the graceful curves of

277

her body, and her hair, tied up behind in the prevailing fashion, provided a fitting frame for her lovely face. She slowed down as she neared the aircraft, and there was an air of hesitation about her, unusual in one normally so confident.

"John. I just wanted to… wish you luck before you took off," she ventured and there was a tremor in her voice as she spoke.

O'Driscoll looked back at her, a crooked half-smile playing on his lips, but the smile did not extend beyond his mouth and if one looked into his eyes they had a dead quality to them that was frightening. They were the eyes of a man who has looked too often into the face of death, (a bit like that bloke played by Richard Attenborough in The Great Escape, to be exact) and seemed out of place on the face of one so young. Other than repeating the half-smile, O'Driscoll said nothing, and it was Karen who was finally forced to break the silence.

"Which mission are you going on?" she asked in the clipped tones of the 1940s. "I know you're not supposed to share that kind of information," she went on with a wan smile and with the same hesitant, imploring look she had worn before, "'careless talk costs lives' and all that, but if I knew which one you were going on, I could perhaps…. think of you."

There were three top secret missions leaving the base in the next few hours, one to attack the German heavy water plant near Stavanger in Norway, the second to drop a group of partisans into an impenetrable mountainous region in central Yugoslavia, and the third to carry out a perilous reconnaissance mission on the heavily fortified dam system of the Rhur Valley in northern Germany. O'Driscoll tapped a Players Number One on the back of his hand and prepared to light it, the same half-smile playing around the corner of his eyes. "I thought I'd have a crack at all three," he said casually.

Karen's hand shot up in front of her face. "All three," she repeated in a dazed tone. "But the Wing Co said that each one alone is as hazardous a mission as we've ever undertaken. John, you can't go on all three, it would be…. suicide." O'Driscoll gave a microscopic shrug which appeared to signal his indifference to the danger that lay ahead.

"John…." she began again and then hesitated. "I wish things could have been different, but…." she faltered again and neither of them needed to voice their unspoken thoughts or refer to the silhouetted figure that was framed against the evening sky, its peaked cap performing tiny self-satisfied oscillations. Suddenly, Karen gave a convulsive gulp and broke down in tears.

"It's this awful war," she said between sobs. "It's turned everything on its head and I somehow feel that things will never be the same again."

O'Driscoll moved towards her and there was a new tenderness in his voice as he said, "Come on, old thing, chin up, can't have beautiful WAAF's blubbing while on duty, bad for morale." She gave him a tentative smile through her tears as he went on, "Don't worry, we'll all be back tomorrow morning for beer and bacon and eggs in the mess, with old Squiffy tinkling the ivories in the corner."

Karen looked at him for a moment. "Didn't you hear?" she asked, and there was a quaver in her voice as she said, "Squiffy bought it, copped one over Cologne yesterday."

There was a pause while O'Driscoll digested this news and then, with a perceptible stiffening of the upper lip, he took two more cigarettes from his case, lit them with the same match, and handed one to Karen.

"What about Blister?" he asked.

"Flew into a barrage balloon over Berlin. It took a wing off his Spitfire and he went straight into a spin. They say he was still giving the thumbs-up through his canopy as he went down, but I'm afraid there's no hope."

O'Driscoll sighed heavily. "And The Caterpillar?"

"I'm afraid The Caterpillar bought it as well, ditched his kite in the channel on the way back from the Hamburg run."

"There's no hope he might have survived?"

"They sent a rescue boat to try and reach him, but it was too late. All they found was his pipe."

As the wind sent eddies scurrying across the flat East Anglian landscape, the two figures regarded each other for a moment, and the vanished hopes and dreams of a generation were implicit in that exchanged look. Then, slowly, the female figure retreated into the half-light, leaving O'Driscoll standing alone, his tall figure etched starkly against the bleak fenland skyline. At that moment, the figure of Wing Commander Barnet came into view, accompanied as he was everywhere by his jet black Labrador, Nig...., er.... Blackie. Known to everyone as the Old Man, the Wing Co. and was a familiar figure on the base and led his team with a relaxed affability that was said to conceal a formidable intellect.

"Well, well," he began breezily, twirling his moustache. "Young O'Driscoll. Capital! Capital! Looking forward to the big show, young John? Looking forward to giving Fritz a bloody nose?" He paused to apply a large spotted handkerchief to his own nose, and a moment later there was a trumpeting noise and his whiskers shook. "Love to be going with you, old chap," he went on, carefully avoiding O'Driscoll's eye. "Nothing I'd like better as I'm sure you know, but someone's got be a ground wallah, I'm afraid. Someone's got to stay behind and deal with all the bumf and the boring old red tape."

281

He gave his right moustache a flourish and, drawing O'Driscoll away so they could not be overheard, went on in a more confidential voice, "Glad I've caught you, young John, I've been meaning to have a quiet word with you. Fact is, there's this young WAAF, who's a kind of friend of the family and she's coming to the base next week. Won't bore you with the details, but she needs someone to take her under their wing and I was wondering if you could…."

At this point, O'Driscoll woke up drenched in sweat and screaming for mercy and as he reacquainted himself with the real world, he took comfort from the fact that at least it didn't contain a 1940s version of Prudence Pugh. She would probably have wanted to christen the planes with the names of characters from Winnie the Pooh, and send the pilots aloft garlanded with rings of posies.

As he shaved, he cast his mind back and recalled the gathering of friends in The North Star the previous evening and the subsequent errand of mercy that provided Micky with his pies. He also recalled having a sinking feeling that Karen was going to cop off with Clive the supply teacher, but after that, try as he might, he couldn't remember a thing. Realizing that it might have been a mistake to commence proceedings so early, he dragged himself wearily out to his car and made his way to work.

The six o'clock tolling of the town hall clock found O'Driscoll in the back bar of The North Star with his hand cradling a pint of Stella as the discussion turned to the events of the preceding evening.

"That bloody Tracey knows how to dance," said Micky, a smile of memory playing around his lips. "I thought she was going to take someone's eye out at one point."

"I didn't really notice," answered Rocky, "I was too busy listening to Melvyn Bragg here." He gestured towards O'Driscoll.

"Yes, your views on the nineteenth century novel certainly caused a stir, John," said Duffy. "Iconoclastic is probably the word that best describes them, wouldn't you agree, Michael?"

"I would if I knew what it meant," said Quinn. "If it means that he got right on that June Taylor's tits, then I agree one hundred percent."

"Refresh my memory on what exactly I said," enquired O'Driscoll, deliberately keeping his voice light. "When you're a brilliant iconoclast like what I am, it's hard to remember all the individual pieces of brilliance."

"Well," said Duffy, settling back in the manner of someone who has a story to tell, "as you know, they were talking about women writers, George Eliot and all that, and then they got on to Jane Austen."

"And that Taylor woman said she reckoned Jane Austen's books were shit hot," said Quinn.

"A vibrant but subtle depiction of the relationship between the sexes was what she actually said, but you have the general thrust of her argument, Michael," said Duffy gravely. "And that was where Melvyn here came in. What was it that he actually said?"

"He said that Jane Austen's works were overrated."

"Yes, although weren't the words 'a load of old bollocks' the ones he actually used?"

"Did I say those actual words?" asked O'Driscoll.

"Oh, yes," answered Duffy, with a chuckle, "and you said a lot more besides! As far as I can remember you said the novels of Miss Austen were stereotypical and formulaic and most of them had similar plots, and it all came down to the fact that her female heroines were sexually frustrated."

"Although the phrase you used was 'desperate for it!' said Rocky.

"Gagging for it!" corrected Quinn.

Duffy acknowledged this with a slight nod of the head. "As always, Michael, you have hit the nail on the head. 'Gagging for it' was indeed the phrase that was used."

O'Driscoll listened to this with growing apprehension. The words had a ring of truth about them and he did dimly remember resolving to "show them" that if witty banter about books was the order of the day, he could generate as much of it as the next person. But June Taylor was someone he hardly knew and who had only ever registered with him as one of those slightly forbidding middle-aged women who takes life very seriously and has no time for flippancy or frivolity of any kind. So the fact that he had used the phrase "gagging for it" to describe her favourite author's heroines did not auger well for future relations. However, if that was the worst he had said, then the evening had not been a complete disaster and he hoped that the conversation might now move on.

Yet, Duffy's next words killed that hope stone dead. "Anyway, you went on to recommend a form of therapy the girls might have benefitted from, isn't that right, Michael? What was the turn of phrase he used?"

"'A good seeing to,'" replied Quinn. "He said any woman who was getting a regular portion would be highly unlikely to worry about whether someone spoke to her in a haughty manner or snubbed her at a dance."

"Yes, he was quite eloquent on the subject," went on Duffy.

"He was," agreed Rocky. "He said Elizabeth Bennett could have put all her troubles behind by simply loosening her stays and heading down to the… what did he call it?"

"The tupping shed."

"For a good seeing to."

"With a strapping young farm labourer."

"Called Amos."

"Or Obadiah."

"And that went for the other Bennett girls as well."

"Apart from the youngest one."

"The one who was getting shafted by a squaddie."

O'Driscoll's heart dropped further into his boots as he heard this. "And how was my theory received?" he asked, trying to keep his voice as light as possible.

"To say June Taylor was not amused would be putting it mildly," answered Duffy. "But she got even more pissed off at your next suggestion?"

"Which was?"

"You said that as the Jane Austen stories took place at a time when slavery still existed, it would have made sense to put the whole thing on a proper business footing by sending to Liverpool for a virile and well-endowed young slave to deliver the service the ladies were missing out on."

"Only you didn't use the words, 'virile and well-endowed,'" said Rocky. "What was it he actually said, Mick?"

"'Hung like a donkey.'"

O'Driscoll's horror was increasing incrementally with the unfolding of the story but he tried to keep his voice light as he asked, "And how was that received?"

"I've got to be honest with you, June Taylor didn't look happy," answered Duffy. "I'm not sure she trusted herself to speak."

"She did say that looking at you, she could see how you might know a lot about sexual frustration," remembered Rocky. "That got a laugh."

The conversation ran on in this vein for a few more minutes, but the words did not register with O'Driscoll. He remembered now his fears about Karen copping off with Clive and his resolution not to be outdone in any sophisticated verbal sparring that might take place and wondered glumly if there was any social group he had not offended in the course of what had clearly been an incoherent, drunken diatribe. He could only hope and pray Karen had not been at hand to witness his disgrace.

His mood was only marginally improved by the intelligence that Micky, restored to his old ebullience by the pie-induced protein hit, had offered to perform his renowned striptease act in front of the assembled guests, and had only been prevented from doing so by the swift intervention of Duffy and Rocky, who had wrestled him to the floor with his modesty just about preserved. O'Driscoll ruefully congratulated himself on having at least one friend who was nearly as much of a twat as he was. He had, as far as he was aware, managed the considerable achievement of getting to the end of a school function without releasing any of his bodily fluids into the environment, for he had not, as far as he was aware, puked into any one's bag and the only diarrhea he had generated had been verbal.

Friday

As O'Driscoll made his way to school the next morning, he consoled himself with the thought that, because it was a training day, at least there would be no kids around. The downside of this, however, was that staff would more than likely spend the day bored out of their skulls while an "expert" talked to them about curriculum planning. Or worse, they might be asked to get into small groups with a flipchart and "feed back" the results of their deliberations to the whole room. Or, horror of horrors, the course leaders might be creative types who would ask delegates to engage in roleplays designed to create an atmosphere of relaxed engagement, but which, because they involved people having to bark like dogs or walk like penguins, usually had the opposite effect.

Mr. Barnet opened proceedings by stating that decisions relating to the following year's staffing were still under review but would be resolved "very shortly", causing a wave of anxiety to ripple around the room. He went on to explain that the morning's training would be delivered by a team from Ealing Council's Inter Cultural Support Service who would be running a workshop entitled *Multi Culturalism for the Next Millennium.*

The initiative was aimed at increasing awareness about issues relating to ethnicity in view of the diverse make-up of the borough's population.

The Head went on to say that the subject matter dovetailed nicely with the nondenominational service Father Kennedy had organized for the following Sunday. The service would be the culmination of the visit by the party from the United States and would celebrate the life of Saint Catherine, giving the visitors the opportunity to increase their knowledge of the school's patron, whilst enabling the U.K. audience to learn more about the work of the American pastor and civil rights leader, Martin Luther King Jr. Dr. King had been chosen by Father Kennedy and Sister Bernadette to demonstrate their sensitivity to multiculturalism, and the U.S. delegation had been asked to prepare a short presentation on his life. Although the Americans had taken on this task with apparent willingness, the choice had not met with universal approval. Mr. Donnelly had been overheard referring to Dr. King as a "philandering commie bastard" when compared to church leaders like Jerry Falwell and Jim Bakker, and the suggestion that neither of these gentlemen could escape censure on the philandering front, he had dismissed as left-wing propaganda.

Unaware of any dissent amongst the American delegation, the Head invited all staff to take part in the service and told them the P.T.A. had organized another discounted staff Shakespeare trip, this time to see *Othello*. After that, people trooped to the hall with varying degrees of reluctance and took their seats around the tables that had been set out. The training had been considered of such importance that office staff, as well as a smattering of other support staff, had been asked to attend.

Governors had been invited, which was why Father Kennedy could be seen taking his place at a table on the far side of the room, his craggy face straining with the unaccustomed effort of being polite. O'Driscoll had just sat down on the opposite side of the room, when to his annoyance, it was announced that in order to ensure each table contained a healthy mix of teachers, support staff and governors, a seating plan had been worked out in advance. Hoping against hope he would not find himself seated anywhere near the turbulent priest, O'Driscoll found that for once his prayers had been answered, only to realize with a sinking heart that he had been placed next to Mrs. Goodwin.

The first part of the day passed off without undue incident and at 10.30, staff made their way in the direction of hot refreshment or outside the building for a smoke. In the second session, the groups were asked to discuss terms or labels whose use might be wittingly or unwittingly disrespectful when applied to minority groups. Having grown up in a London where the

Irish were routinely referred to as "thick paddies" or worse, O'Driscoll was aware of how language can be used to represent minorities in crude and insulting terms. No one of Irish extraction could fail to remember the "JAK" cartoons in the London Evening Standard, which represented Irish people of both sexes as simian figures in donkey jackets. It was racial stereotyping up there with anything Dr. Goebbels had produced and O'Driscoll, like many who shared his tradition, instinctively empathized with other minority groups living in the capital. It was, therefore, with a mixture of exasperation and amusement that, as he dragged his thoughts back to the present, he became aware of the familiar sound of Mrs. Goodwin cranking up her verbal weaponry as she prepared to launch another blitzkrieg on those around her.

"You see, what I can't understand is how things can be fine one minute and then the next they're offensive. When I was young, you never said *black*, the refined word to use was *coloured*. Then one day suddenly it was all turned on its head and *coloured* was out and *black* was in." She shrugged her shoulders. "It's the same when we talked about those poor little unfortunates who are neither one thing nor another. When I was a girl we called them *half-breeds*, which I suppose, in fairness, did sound a bit like something out of a western, so decently and fairly people started to use *half caste* instead so as not to cause offence. They got up in arms about that and now and we're supposed to say *mixed race*. I can't keep up with it all. The other day, to cap it all, I heard someone saying even *mixed race* was out and the new word was something called...." she frowned with the effort of trying to remember, "....I think it was *jewel heritage*. Don't ask me what that's supposed to mean, probably something to do with rubies from India!" She blew her nose with just the right amount of righteous indignation and, temporarily exhausted, sat back in her seat.

After a short pause, someone hesitantly suggested that they should look at the instructions which the course leaders had left on the table, and from there, the conversation turned to the task of finding words and phrases that describe ethnic minorities without causing offence. Mr. Li made the point that in China, all minorities were identified by an official title which referred to them and the autonomous region they inhabited, and that everyone got used to using this one designated title. One of the trainers visited their table at this point and suggested that they each try to write down suggestions for non-offensive ways of identifying minorities. The delegates worked in silence for a few minutes until Mrs. Goodwin, who was clearly working up yet another head of verbal steam, could contain herself no longer.

"I was talking about this with Reg last night," she said suddenly. "Now don't get me wrong. We're very tolerant me and my Reg, *very* tolerant. But he couldn't understand and neither can I, why we need training on what to call foreigners. I believe in calling a spade a...." she broke off hurriedly and cleared her throat before continuing, "....calling people the traditional names that everyone knows rather than mucking about with all this new language that confuses everyone. Now, take an expression like *wog* - nice friendly word that everyone used in the old days and nobody took offence. Reg says it's one of those words where each letter stand for something. What do they call one of those words - an acriflex, or something like that? Anyway, Reg says the 'g' in *wog* stands for gentleman, you know, *something, something, gentleman.* It stands to reason, how can something be offensive that's got *gentleman* in its title?"

She looked around the table and, taking the silence as confirmation her logic was unassailable, said, "Exactly! And, of course" she directed her final remark at a bewildered Mr. Li, "if I had thought for a minute that *wog* was an offensive term, I wouldn't have used it, not with you in the room." She smiled winningly at the elderly Chinaman and he, for want of anything else to do, smiled back.

There was hardly time after this to offer feedback on the vocabulary that delegates had come up with to describe minorities. O'Driscoll's table had suggested *non-European ethnic minorities,* but he was curious to see what Mrs. Goodwin had written on her own paper, for judging by the expression on her face, she had been giving the matter serious consideration. As the delegates headed off to lunch, he glanced at her sheet to see that in answer to the question, *Try to think of a positive collective term to describe people whose origins are in the developing world*, she had initially opted for the term, '*Darkies*' but had evidently had second thoughts for she had crossed that word out and replaced it with, '*Commonwealths*'.

It was with a profound sense of relief that O'Driscoll exited the hall at lunchtime, with the prospect of an hour mercifully free of the voice of Mavis Goodwin ahead of him. Upon returning after lunch, he found the groups had been mixed up again for the afternoon workshop. The delight with which he greeted the intelligence that he would not be at Mrs. Goodwin's table was only matched by the gloom which descended upon him when it became clear that he would be in the same group as Father Kennedy. O'Driscoll murmured a greeting to the company as he took his place and the priest raised his great craggy head and grunted something unintelligible at him. A moment later, a waft of scent disturbed the air and O'Driscoll looked around to see that Karen was slipping into the seat directly to his left. His stomach performed its customary impression of a spin dryer but he tried to keep his voice light as he greeted her. As they waited for the session to begin, she lowered her voice and said with a smile, "Sounds like you got on the wrong side of June Taylor the other night."

"Did I?"

"You could say that - she was *not* happy. I didn't hear it myself, but you apparently cast aspersions on the personalities of Jane Austen's female characters."

"I might have suggested some alternative plotlines," he answered.

She laughed. "That's one way of putting it. I suppose I should be scandalized like June, but the look on her face was so comical when she told me what you'd said, and to be honest I can't help finding all those Jane Austen books a bit earnest. Anyway, you're a brave man to knock June Taylor's heroine off her pedestal."

"She's a bit of a fan, then?"

"Didn't you know? She once spent a whole night in the pub telling us about how the main characters in *Sense and Sensibility* represented the dichotomy between the two faces of woman, constantly fighting for supremacy. It made me feel quite schizophrenic, to be honest, and we only got her off the subject when Tracey pretended her drink had been spiked and about six of us volunteered to take her to the ladies to help her recover. There was only Miss Gillespie left and when we got back, June had her pinned against the wall talking about Marianne Dashwood's passion for John Willoughby and how it represented female carnal desire in all its earthiness. I've never seen poor old Miss Gillespie so traumatized and the look of relief on her face when she saw us coming back from the bar...."

"You reckon I've blotted my copybook with June Taylor, then?"

"Big time! You're making a bit of a habit of this plain-speaking business, aren't you? Were tequila slammers involved, by any chance?"

He shook his head ruefully. "Whiskey, I think was the culprit this time. And lager. Oh, and there was that cider they had on special offer. In fact, I blame the cider for the more controversial of my comments - it's inclined to loosen the tongue."

"God knows what your insides must be like," she said, shaking her head. "Are you coming to the service on Sunday, they've asked me to do the teas and coffees and I've got no one to help me unpack the urn and all the crockery?" She said it with an air of resignation that melted his heart and before he knew it, he was volunteering his services as dishwasher, packer and general handyman.

"It's all right about the teas and coffees on Sunday, Father," Karen called across the table to Kennedy. "John's volunteered to help me." The priest favoured O'Driscoll with one of his more baleful glares and accompanied the look with an audible tut, but other than that, forbore to comment. There was no opportunity to talk further as the course leader was calling for order and the next two hours passed for O'Driscoll in a happy blur. The stretching of legs and gathering of possessions that signaled the end of the afternoon session was a welcome relief to most, although O'Driscoll would have happily sat through another two hours discussing the price of oranges if it meant Karen remaining at his side.

Amid the bustle and movement, Father Kennedy took a piece of paper out of his pocket. "Before ye go," he addressed himself to the table, "there are a few things I need for the parish newsletter. Could someone tell me the date of the summer fete?" Geoff Turnbull furnished him with the necessary information.

"And there's the next Shakespeare trip," said Kennedy. He looked at O'Driscoll. "You, what's the name of the next play ye're going to see? I can't remember if it's *Othello* or…. or…. *Caesar and Cleopatra*, but I'm sure an *intellectual* like yourself will be able to tell me."

John O'Driscoll was a man of such timidity that in normal circumstances, he would never have dreamed of bearding such a lion as Father Kennedy, but there was something about the sneer in the priest's voice that made him momentarily see red. "It's actually called *Antony and Othello*," he blurted out before he had time to think and then, feeling he might as well be hung for a sheep as for a lamb, went on, "Yes, *Antony and Othello*, the.... er.... story of two star-crossed lovers."

He registered the startled looks being exchanged around the table but plunged on recklessly. "It's a ground-breaking new interpretation of Shakespeare in its treatment of gender, race and sexuality, and... I'm told it's been recommended as essential viewing for members of the Catholic clergy."

As Father Kennedy grunted and reached for his pen, O'Driscoll became aware of the stunned silence around the table. Geoff Turnbull, Karen and the others were looking at him with odd expressions which he struggled to interpret. As he gazed at their faces, O'Driscoll began to wonder whether the look they all wore could possibly be, and here he could not be certain because it was an expression he received so rarely, could it possibly be a look of respect? At any rate, they remained frozen in immobility as Father Kennedy, unaware of any significance in the words other than as a reinforcement of his opinion that gypsy O'Driscoll talked too much, asked him to repeat the play's title. Having received confirmation of the name, the priest picked up his pencil stub and, tongue protruding, began to laboriously inscribe the words, *Anthony and a Fellow*.

Saturday

O'Driscoll, Duffy, Rocky and Sweeney were snugly ensconced in The North Star and about to attack their second pints when the door swung open and in walked Micky Quinn. It was immediately apparent that there was something different about him and as he approached, his friends were able to see that a pair of tattered Wrangler jeans once more covered his lower body and a battered Ben Sherman shirt adorned his upper area. Of the items purchased from the emporium of Mr. Paul Smith, there was no sign at all.

"What's up, Mick?" asked Rocky and the others added their greetings.

Micky stopped in front of them. "What's up?" he said dramatically. "I'll tell you what's up... Maureen's up, that's what's up. Or rather her time's up... I've left her!" He sighed and sat down heavily.

"You've left *her?"* asked Duffy after a short pause. "I was wondering, after your Gypsy Rose Lee act the other night, whether it might have been the other way round."

"Bollocks!" answered Quinn. "I'm not saying she wasn't cross about it. She made that clear enough - bloody hell, did she! In fact, it was the striptease that indirectly brought things to a head." He paused. "Let me get a round in and I'll tell you the rest. In fact, I think I'll get two rounds in."

When he returned, he confirmed that Maureen had indeed been upset, not just by the striptease, but by his conduct in general which she claimed had been so embarrassing as to call into question the future of their relationship. Micky had admitted his wrongdoing and put it down to the kind of youthful immaturity that had been all but eradicated from his character since he had come into Maureen's morally uplifting orbit. In this way, he had been hoping to smooth over what he considered to be a little, local difficulty and had thus been totally unprepared for the bombshell that Maureen had then delivered out of the blue.

She had, she said, been pleased at the way he had stuck to the diet she put together in conjunction with the health and beauty section of *Marie Claire*, but with his stomach stubbornly refusing to shrink, and alcohol clearly identified as the culprit, the problem could be solved by the simple expedient of Micky cutting it from his diet. After all, "hadn't he managed the transition to her new food regime without a care in the world and on that basis, it should be a straightforward process to

302

simply cut alcohol out of his diet." She apparently accompanied the final words with a snap of the fingers. Micky paused in his narrative and took a long, shuddering draught from his pint.

"She wanted you to give up the drink?" asked O'Driscoll and there was awe in his voice.

"What, *altogether*?" breathed Sweeney.

Quinn shook his head as if he could hardly believe the story he was telling. "She actually said," and there was a tremor in his voice, "that we could review the situation after the first six months. *The first sixth months*!" He repeated the words as if in a trance.

"What did you say, Mick?" asked Duffy and there was a hush as the others waited for his answer.

"Put it this way," answered Quinn. "I'm not a violent man but it was the final straw. I told her where to stick her couscous, I told her where to stick her tofu and I told her where to stick her hummus. And when I told her where to stick them, I'm afraid all orifices featured." He drained his pint and finished emphatically, "All three!"

"So it's definitely over, then, Mick?" asked Sweeney.

"Can't see any way back after that," answered Quinn and with the telling of the story and the passage of the second and third pints, some of the tension seemed to have left his body.

"Do you know what I had for tea tonight?" he went on when another drink had been placed before him. "A pie! A Tesco family steak and kidney pie with extra gravy. And do you know what I'm having tomorrow night? Another fucking pie, that's what I'm having. Come on," he said getting to his feet, let's tie one on and celebrate being young, free, single and beautiful." He headed off towards the bar and the way he hitched up his Wranglers as in days of yore almost brought a lump to the throats of his friends. Arriving at the counter, he paused for a moment and then said with authority, "Rum, I think!" at the same time delivering himself of a rich and exuberant fart, a million miles from the weak, timid efforts of the Maureen era. Even the way his red hair stuck up wildly from his head proclaimed to the world that the old Michael Aloysius Quinn was back.

Faith joined them at nine o'clock, by which time they were in a condition to make her question her wisdom in rejecting the alternative of a quiet evening at home with a Maeve Binchy and a box of chocolates. She made the best of it, however, and by the time they had moved on to a club, was offering to accompany Micky in the impromptu striptease he had decided to perform. The bouncers managed to restrain them in such a way as to keep relations on a positive footing, thus allowing the group to remain in the club until it closed at 4am.

Sunday

They must have repaired to his flat for a final nightcap, for when he opened his eyes an unknown number of hours later, O'Driscoll found himself occupying a hard corner of his own living room floor. Duffy and Faith had, of course, been offered the O'Driscoll bed, while Quinn had stretched his form out on the one decent armchair in the O'Driscoll living room. The snore emanating from its depths was sufficient proof that he was still in residence, but upon exploring further, O'Driscoll found that Rocky and Sweeney had left.

He showered and made himself a cup of coffee, hoping the caffeine hit would disperse the spiders, who were once again scuttling round his head on their mysterious spidery journeys. It was while he was drinking his second cup that he suddenly remembered his promise to meet Karen at the church and help her with the teas and coffees. A knock on his own bedroom door and the message that it was now twelve-thirty elicited an indistinct reply from Duffy that sounded like '...k off!' It was apparent that Duffy was unlikely to make his promised appearance at the church and Micky, who in his newly-restored state of bachelorhood had no plans for the day, kindly offered to stand in for him, something he had done once or twice before. At this point from the bedroom came sounds that suggested the inhabitants had woken up and were engaged in activities more temporal than spiritual, so Quinn and O'Driscoll hurriedly withdrew and made their way to the church.

Upon knocking once more on the well-remembered sacristy door, they heard a dragging sound and a moment later, Mrs. O'Reilly's wizened face was glaring at them suspiciously through a crack. She opened the door and allowed them through, then followed them down the hall. As they reached the dining room, she put on a sudden spurt and overtook them. Opening the door, she cleared her throat and announced, "It's Kitty O'Driscoll's boy, you know, the simple one, and the other one with him, I don't know his name but he looks a bit simple as well." As they looked around, it was clear their arrival had interrupted something of a feast, for there was evidence all around the room that a good lunch had been enjoyed. The party consisted of Father Kennedy, Sister Bernadette and other members of the order as well as assorted governors and the delegation from the United States.

What was apparent from the atmosphere of conviviality was that everyone in the room had had a good lunch and that some of them had dined, as the saying goes, not wisely but too well. Mr. Donnelly's tie was askew, while the network of tangled veins that ornamented Father Kennedy's terrible visage glowed with a variety of hues including violet, puce, purple and black. And the fact that Mrs. O'Reilly hiccoughed softly as she withdrew hinted that she too may have partaken of the feast.

It was clear that O'Driscoll and Quinn's arrival had interrupted Father Kennedy in full flow, for the first words they heard were the priest's. "…And when the wine ran out, the mother of Jesus said unto him, 'What shall they do?' And Jesus called the steward and pointed to six stone jars, each containing twenty to thirty gallons and asked that they be filled with water."

Kennedy paused to take a sip from in his own drink, which assuredly was not water, and it became apparent that, for whatever reason, the priest was telling the story of the Wedding Feast of Cana. It was a story that every young Catholic would hear a thousand times. In fact as a miracle, it was a familiar old friend, the kind of miracle that carried with it images of a comfortable chair and a wood fire crackling in the hearth at the end of a long day. Why Kennedy should be choosing to share this hoary old chestnut with the company was, thought O'Driscoll, something of a mystery but, with nothing better to do, he and Quinn settled back to enjoy the denouement.

"When the contents of the stone jars were tasted, they were found to contain….," Kennedy paused for artistic effect, then bellowed triumphantly, "….not water, but *wine!*" There were expressions of wonder and murmurs of surprise that were clearly simulated, for surely there can be nobody in the western world who is not familiar with the story.

"And they found to their surprise that the wine was of the highest quality, and when they looked in the other jars, they found that they *all* contained wine!" Pausing again to refresh himself, Kennedy gathered himself for his final peroration. "And do ye know," he declaimed in a voice softened by awe, "what was the greatest miracle of all? Everyone at that wedding drank their fill from the stone jars, and at the end of the evening, there wasn't one of them palatic!"

There was a silence before someone said hesitantly, "Palatic?"

"Yes," replied Kennedy. "Palatic! Drunk!" He took a swig from his glass and O'Driscoll reflected that if he went on like this, the maniacal minister was in danger of becoming 'palatic' himself. It was certainly an interesting interpretation of the parable, for if Kennedy's version was to be believed, Jesus had not only rescued a large gathering from embarrassment and disappointment, but had also managed to produce an early prototype of that popular 1990s beverage 'Shloer.'

Looking around, he noticed that Mr. Donnelly had his arm around the shoulder of one of the nuns and was telling her that

Martin Luther King Jr. wasn't such a bad sort, a bit of an old ram, certainly, but like any other man, entitled to his weaknesses, while various other American delegates were disported around the room in attitudes of extreme relaxation. O'Driscoll and Quinn judged this a good time to make a strategic withdrawal, O'Driscoll to find Karen and help her with the drinks, and Quinn to find out whatever it was that Duffy was supposed to be doing and take over that role.

They made their way into a church which had been made ready for the service with a board on one side of the altar displaying information about Martin Luther King Jr. and a similar one on the other side giving information about Saint Catherine. Between these and behind the altar was another board upon which had been attached huge plastic letters that fitted, Lego-like, onto the background. 'BY THE GRACE OF GOD' read the first giant message and under it was 'I HAVE A DREAM', a reference to the famous speech with which Doctor King had inspired a generation.

The Martin Luther King board also contained the final words of the speech:

When we let freedom ring from every village and every hamlet, from every state and every city, we will be able to speed up that day when all of God's children will be able to join hands and sing in the words of the old Negro spiritual:

Free at last! Free at last! Thank God Almighty, we're free at last!

Mrs. O'Reilly was skulking around at the back of the altar and behind her, O'Driscoll saw Karen pushing a trolley. The smile she bestowed on him sent the O'Driscoll stomach into a series of gyrations almost identical to the ones it had performed a month before near Sister Bernadette's bag, but fortunately, without producing the same results. Karen approached them and, still smiling said, "Thanks for agreeing to help me, John," at the same time leaning across and brushing his cheek lightly with her lips. Quinn said hello and explained why he was there, informing Karen that Duffy was unavoidably detained and explaining in his usual direct manner, the nature of the activity that was the cause of his nonappearance.

"Too much information, Mick!" interposed O'Driscoll lightly, but in truth he was in a condition of some confusion, following the soft but exquisite contact from the lips that had been, for so long, the subject of his fantasies. The kiss also set off a series of titanic convulsions in his trousers, but perhaps fortunately, Father Kennedy arrived, resulting in an immediate and merciful reverse of that process.

As the priest approached, the hearty lunch he had partaken of was evidenced both by the stains on the front of his soutane and in the slightly exaggerated care with which he walked. He bestowed a terrifying leer on Karen and nodded coldly to O'Driscoll before looking enquiringly at Quinn. When O'Driscoll explained that Duffy had been unavoidably detained and Micky had kindly stepped in to fill his boots, Kennedy frowned. "It's not like Mr. Duffy to miss a function as important as this," he said. "He is usually a most devout young man."

"We share your concern, Father," said O'Driscoll.

"I hope he is not struggling with his belief?" went on the priest.

O'Driscoll shook his head and said solemnly, "I fear that even as we speak, he may be wrestling with his Faith."

Quinn had been surreptitiously sampling the coffee from the urn and at this point, there was a violent explosion of liquid from his vicinity. At the same time, Karen appeared to have become intensely interested in the workings of the timer on the tea urn for she turned her back on the company so she could give it her undivided attention. While this was going on, Kennedy subjected O'Driscoll to a scrutiny which suggested that, rather than concerning himself with Duffy's spiritual welfare, he would do better to reflect on his own doomed condition. Accompanying this baleful look with a sniff, the priest turned to Micky and having informed him that Duffy had been due to help with sandwich preparation, offered to show him where this was taking place.

Karen's stiff-shouldered posture as the priest and Quinn moved out of earshot gave way to one of helpless laughter and it was several moments before she was able to compose herself. "Oh God, I hate it when you need to laugh and you know you can't so you have to bottle it up and it feels like you're going to burst," she said. "Bloody hell, John, you're a brave man, that's twice in days you've taken the piss out of the scariest priest in the Western world. A girl could get taken with that." As she looked at him, her eyes dancing with laugher, she looked so incredibly beautiful that before he knew it, he said, "How do you fancy being taken with that tomorrow night over a meal?"

"Tomorrow night?"

"Yes."

"With you?"

"Yes."

"John, are you asking me out?"

"Er, yes"

"On a date?"

"Yes."

"Yes."

"Yes, what?"

"Yes, I would like to go out on a date with you tomorrow."

It would be hard to do justice to the effect these words had on John O'Driscoll. The woman he had longed for with all his heart from the moment he first set eyes on her had just, unless his sensory organs were playing tricks with him, agreed to go out with him. He realized that he must try to retain some semblance of composure so, endeavouring to give the impression of a man to whom the arranging of liaisons with beautiful women was a daily occurrence, he put his hands in his pockets and leaned casually against the tea urn. Unfortunately, he forgot that the urn was still attached to a trolley, with the result that he, trolley and urn shot across the aisle and landed on the floor against the opposite wall in a tangle of arms, legs, lids and crockery.

"Remind me to make sure it's not a self-service restaurant we go to on that date," said Karen as she helped him up, "or I don't suppose either of us will last the night."

Having made hasty arrangements as to time and place of meeting, Karen hurried off to find some replacement crockery, but not before bestowing on him another kiss, this time magically on the lips. She left behind her a John O'Driscoll in something of a daze at the events of the preceding few minutes. Karen Black was going on a date with him, he was going on a date with Karen Black. Whichever way he said it and however many times he said it, the words had a magical quality to them. Now John O'Driscoll was something of a realist and he realized that on all past form, he would mess this opportunity up by booking the wrong restaurant, or using the wrong utensils, or falling head first into the soup, or by doing something so stupid it couldn't be foreseen. But in spite of all this, it couldn't be denied that he was actually going on a date with the beautiful Karen Black, and the surge of energy that he felt coursing through his body, if not quite an epiphany, gave him some hope that, for once, he might not cock the situation up.

In a spontaneous gesture of celebration, he ran down the corridor like a footballer and punched the air, but being John O'Driscoll, his punch missed its intended target and collided with the reverse of the board that was serving as the backdrop to the altar. The contact caused the board to rock gently backwards and forwards and resulted in one of the giant Lego letters dislodging itself from the surface and dropping forward into the folds of the purple cloth that lay on the floor. In the heat of the moment and in his eagerness to find his beloved, O'Driscoll did not notice this accident, but Mrs. O'Reilly, lurking malevolently in the shadows behind the altar, did.

Twenty minutes later, Father Kennedy rose in front of a packed congregation to commence the service of celebration. He stood for a moment, arms outstretched, his giant figure framed

314

by the board behind him and, rocking almost imperceptibly backwards and forwards, began to speak. As he enunciated each word with elaborate care, the messages that had been affixed so carefully earlier in the day were outlined starkly against the purple of the cloth behind him:

BY THE GRACE OF GOD

I HAVE A DR AM!

It took a few minutes for the congregation to connect the message with the figure standing in front of them, but slowly and incrementally, a frisson of laughter began to ripple its way across the church. It took a few minutes for the priest to discern something was amiss and to realize the cause of it was the board behind him.

Half an hour later, O'Driscoll, basking in the glow of his recent conquest, was standing at a sink in the church kitchen with his beloved next to him. They were engaged in washing several hundred dirty cups and saucers, a task which would normally have had no appeal to O'Driscoll, but now seemed charming and delightful in its simple domesticity. It was while he was thus engaged that an excited Mrs. Goodwin came bustling into the corridor and, nose twitching and eyes darting, informed him that yet another calamity had happened in the church and that, having had the blame for it laid squarely at his door by Mrs. O'Reilly, Father Kennedy was on the warpath.

Amplified by the church's acoustics, a strangled cry of "O'Driscoll!" echoed maniacally around the walls and along the corridors and a moment later, it was followed by a muffled bellow that sounded like "Fecking sabotage!" The volume of the second cry told O'Driscoll that, like a predator approaching its prey, the priest was getting closer to his victim, yet curiously as he waited for the arrival of his nemesis, he felt a strange sense of detachment. The waves of panic he should have been feeling were conspicuous by their absence and, as another muffled cry that sounded like "Interfering gypsy!" echoed down the hall, O'Driscoll realized something strange was happening to his bowels. The something strange that was happening was that nothing was happening. He checked again and yes, he could say with certainty that his insides were resolutely refusing to liquefy.

Having earlier ruled out the assertion that he himself might be having some kind of epiphany, O'Driscoll wondered whether his bowels might be undergoing one. Could a set of bowels experience an epiphany? It was yet another one of those interesting theological question that seemed to punctuate his life, but O'Driscoll reflected that now would not be a good time to raise it as a subject for debate with Father Kennedy.

At any rate, he suddenly realized that his bowels were free! And not just his bowels, for he himself was free. He knew not why but he no longer walked in fear of the maniacal minister and no longer cared what happened about his job or his future at Saint Catherine's because he now knew in some indefinable way that everything was going to be all right and that the future would take care of itself. At that moment Parnell strolled by and gave O'Driscoll a look very different to the one he had turned on him the last time they had met. It was a look that might have passed for a wink, the sort of look one elderly roué might have given another as they sat in their club, the sort of look Errol Flynn might have exchanged with David Niven after a hard day's shagging.

O'Driscoll looked at the display board upon which were displayed the final words of Martin Luther King Jr's "I Have a Dream" speech. Those uplifting final words had been used in a million situations but O'Driscoll was fairly sure that they had never before been applied to a collection of intestines. As he looked at them, he realized how perfectly they represented the momentous journey his own bowels had made in emancipating themselves from the tyranny of Father Kennedy:

Free at last! Free at last!

Thank God almighty we're free at last!

Made in the USA
Charleston, SC
13 March 2016